"Harper is to be commended for keeping to what we know about Tudor history . . . and for making the factions of Elizabeth's court clearer than many history books have done."

—*Chicago Tribune*

"A wonderful web of drama and deceit that would make Shakespeare envious . . . This is great stuff."

—*Toronto Globe and Mail*

THE QUEENE'S CURE

"A neatly plotted mystery with genuinely terrifying scenes."

—*Publishers Weekly*

"Fully rounded, sometimes baroque, but always engaging . . . The plot quickens to the very end."

—*Booklist*

"Superb . . . a winner."

—Amazon.com

"Based on historical fact, *The Queene's Cure* is an Elizabethan fan's delight . . . [with] several red herrings that will delight the hearts of mystery lovers."

—RomanticTimes.com

THE TWYLIGHT TOWER

"Harper's exquisite mastery of the period, lively dialogue, energetic plot, devious characters, and excellent rendition of the willful queen make this a pleasure for fans of historical mysteries."

—*Library Journal*

"The sleuthing is fun, but what makes *The Twylight Tower* comparable to the fine works of Allison Weir is the strong writing of the author."

—*Midwest Book Review*

"Exciting . . . and as cleverly crafted as only Karen Harper can be . . . A hugely appealing and fast-paced tale that keeps the reader satisfied and yearning for more."

—Romancereviewstoday.com

THE TIDAL POOLE

"A nice mix of historical and fictional characters, deft twists and a plucky, engaging young heroine enhances this welcome sequel."

—*Publishers Weekly*

"Harper delivers high drama and deadly intrigue . . . She masterfully captures the Elizabethan tone in both language and setting . . . Elizabethan history has never been this appealing."

—*Newsday*

THE POYSON GARDEN

"Impressively researched . . . The author has her poisons and her historical details down pat."

—*Los Angeles Times*

"Intoxicating . . . Whether you love history, romance, adventure, or mystery, you will be intrigued by this view of Elizabeth as queen and as a brilliant detective."

—*Romantic Times*

The *Queene's* *Christmas*

KAREN HARPER

St. Martin's Paperbacks

For my family, with whom I have shared many a happy Christmas,
especially my mother, Margaret Kurtz,
and husband, Don.

And to many more to come!

1533   Henry VIII marries Anne Boleyn, January 25. Elizabeth born at Greenwich Palace, September 7.

1536   Anne Boleyn executed in Tower of London. Elizabeth disinherited from crown. Henry marries Jane Seymour.

1537   Prince Edward born. Queen Jane dies of childbed fever.

1541   Unlawful Games Act bans sporting activities and some Yule customs at Christmas.

1544   Act of Succession and Henry VIII's will establish Mary and Elizabeth in line to throne.

1547   Henry VIII dies. Edward VI crowned.

1551   Holy Days and Fasting Days Act. Strict Sunday and worship laws passed.

1553   Queen Mary (Tudor) I crowned. Tries to force England back to Catholicism; gives Margaret Stewart, Tudor cousin, precedence over Elizabeth. Queen Mary weds Prince Philip of Spain by proxy.

1554   Protestant Wyatt Rebellion fails, but Elizabeth sent to Tower for two months, accompanied by Kat Ashley.

1558   Mary dies; Elizabeth succeeds to throne, November 17. Elizabeth appoints William Cecil Secretary of State; Robert Dudley made Master of the Queen's Horse.

1558   Elizabeth crowned in Westminster Abbey, January 15. Parliament urges queen to marry, but she resists. Mary, Queen of Scots becomes Queen of France at accession of her young husband, Francis II.

1560   Death of Francis II of France makes his young Catholic widow, Mary, Queen of Scots, a danger as Elizabeth's unwanted heir. Elizabeth names Earl of Sussex Lord Lieutenant of Ireland.

1561   Now widowed, Mary, Queen of Scots returns to Scotland. In London, St. Paul's Cathedral roof and spire burn.

1564   Earl of Sussex returns from Ireland to royal court in May.

HOUSE OF TUDOR

House of Lancaster		*House of York*	
Henry VII r.1485-1509	m.	Elizabeth of York	

Henry VII m. Elizabeth of York

Arthur
d. 1502
m. 1501

Henry VIII
r. 1509-1547

Margaret Tudor
d. 1541
m.
James IV of Scotland
d.1513

Mary Tudor
d. 1533
m.
Louis XII of France
d. 1514

Archibald Douglas
Earl of Angus
d. 1551
m.

James V of Scotland
m.
Mary of Guise

Margaret Douglas
m.
Matthew Stewart
Earl of Lennox

Mary
Queen of Scots

Henry Stewart
Lord Darnley

1509 Catherine of Aragon
ann. 1533
d. 1536

1533 Anne Boleyn
ex. 1536

1536 Jane Seymour
d. 1537

1540 Anne of Cleves
ann. 1540
d. 1557

1540 Catherine Howard
ex. 1542

1543 Katherine Parr
d. 1548
m.
Thomas Seymour of Sudeley
Lord High Admiral

Mary
r. 1553-1558
m.
Phillip of Spain

Elizabeth I
r. 1558-1603

Edward VI
r. 1547-1553

Mary Seymour

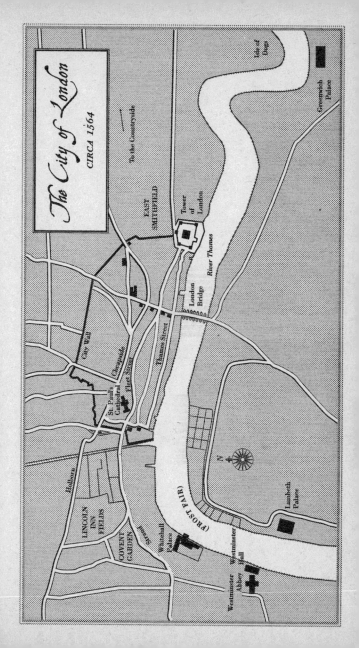

The Queene's Christmas

The Prologue

Cardamom Christmas Cake

Cream 1 cup country butter and blend in ⅔ cup brown sugar, beating with a spoon 'til frothy. Stir in 1 beaten egg. Stir ½ teaspoon grated lemon peel, ¾ teaspoon crushed cardamom (having been dearly imported from the Portuguese), ½ cup ground almonds, and 1 cup of currants into 2½ cups of fine white flour. Beat the dry ingredients into the sweetened butter. Pour into a greased cake pan or two layer pans and bake in a brick oven mayhap some three-quarters hour or until toothpick inserted in center comes out clean. Yon cake can be frosted with brown sugar icing. Dress cake with holly sprigs.

SEPTEMBER 29, 1564

ST. JAMES'S PALACE, LONDON

"I SWEAR, YOUR GRACE, THAT MAN WILL BE THE DEATH of you yet!"

"Robin Dudley, my Kat?" Elizabeth asked. She forced herself to stand still as the frail, elderly Kat Ashley, First Lady of the Bedchamber, and Rosie Radcliffe, her favorite maid of honor, pinned the ermine mantle to her shoulders over her russet velvet gown. If anyone but these two had spoken such impertinence to her, the thirty-one-year-old Tudor queen would have rounded on them soundly.

"Of course, that's who I mean," Kat pursued, fussing overlong with a jeweled pin. "Lord Robert Dudley, alias your dear Robin, about to become Earl of Leicester by your hand. I fear he'll think he's king in waiting."

"Or at least your main advisor, if not heir apparent," Rosie muttered as she fastened a diamond brooch.

"You too, Rosie?" Elizabeth asked of the pretty young brunette. "*Et tu, Brute*, and you with that sharp object in your hand?"

The queen kept her voice light, but her heart was heavy. Today she was creating Robert Dudley, her staunch ally and longtime court favorite, the Earl of Leicester despite the resentment of the court faction that detested him—led by Rosie's cousin, the Earl of Sussex.

"Your kith and kin had best not be saying I will name Robin my heir," Elizabeth warned.

"But you did name him Protector of the Kingdom when you were sore ill with the pox," Rosie replied.

"Those were desperate times. I've said I will not marry him nor name him, or anyone, my successor. If he weds my cousin Queen Mary of Scots, as I have counseled, he shall rule through her."

"But you've said you'll not name her heir, either," Rosie added, "though she's your nearest royal kin."

"They shall rule Scotland, not England. If I named an heir," Elizabeth said so sharply that both women stepped back, "disgruntled courtiers and conspirators for my crown would latch on to that heir like leeches, and my life could be more at risk than it already is. As for Robert Dudley, he is being created a peer not to make him worthy, for he already is.

"I'm ready," she announced with a toss of her red head that

rattled the pearls on her jeweled cap. "Let's brighten this dreary day outside with a fine old ceremony inside."

"It's still pouring cats and dogs," Kat observed as if they could not all hear the drumming of raindrops against the mullioned windows. "However wet the weather in the olden times, it never seemed so chilling. How I long for the good old days!"

"In the good old days, I was not queen but likely locked away in sundry country houses in tawdry gowns," Elizabeth reminded her. She took the old woman's mottled hands in hers. The skin felt as dry as parchment. "You said the other day, dear Kat, you longed for an old-fashioned Christmastide. Perhaps we shall have one."

Kat's flaccid features lifted a bit. Suddenly, she seemed younger, stronger. She had been withering like one of the brown chestnut leaves on the trees in the park, and Elizabeth had been deeply distressed at knowing no way to halt her slow slide toward a deathbed. Elizabeth's first governess and longtime companion, Katherine Ashley had been the only mother she had ever known, since her own had been beheaded when she was but three.

As the women left the privy chamber and her other attendants fell in behind them, Elizabeth glanced out the corridor windows. In sodden clumps, Londoners were gathering along the parkside lane, hoping for a glimpse of their queen. Once when she'd ridden into St. James's after hunting, a crowd of ten thousand had greeted her, shouting, "God save Elizabeth!" and throwing flowers.

That was one of few happy memories of the place, for St. James's had little to commend it to Elizabeth Tudor other than its being set in a fine hunt park on the edge of her capital city. It was an outmoded, small palace her half-sister, Queen Mary, had favored and died in. Here "Bloody Mary," as the people called her, had confined Elizabeth before having her hauled off to prison in the Tower; that hardly endeared this russet pile of bricks to her, either. She came only for particular ceremonies she did not want to seem overly grand and for respite from her favorite city palace, Whitehall, when the jakes needed to be cleaned. As soon as this investiture was over she would ride back there, muck and mire on city streets notwithstanding.

When the queen's crimson-liveried yeomen guards swept open the double doors to the presence chamber, her sharp eyes scanned the crowd. As handsome as ever, though he'd managed a humble demeanor today, Robin Dudley awaited amidst his little entourage of loyalists. He was attired sumptuously in blue and gold; for good reason had his rivals given him the sobriquet of "the peacock"—among other names.

Her dear, brilliant chief secretary, William Cecil, bearded and thin, looked hardly happy about this necessary charade. In truth, he was no friend of Robin's either, though the two tolerated each other for the sake of queen and kingdom. The clusters of courtiers included Rosie's cousin Thomas Radcliffe, Earl of Sussex, who would rather, no doubt, skewer and roast Robin than honor and toast him.

The queen's gaze settled on the two men she wanted most to impress today, so that they would report Robin's elevation to their Scottish queen. As diplomats, both spoke several languages including their native lowland Scots, but they were rapt in whispers now as they went down on their knees before her.

The queen wanted everyone, especially her too clever Catholic cousin, the Scottish Queen Mary Stuart, to know Robin was eligible to sue for Mary's hand. At least that is what Elizabeth and

Cecil had publicly promoted. Their actual plan was, of dire necessity, much darker and deeper.

"Ah, my lords, you must tell your queen, my dear cousin," Elizabeth announced so everyone could hear, "how greatly my court honors Lord Dudley, soon to be Earl of Leicester."

"Indeed, we shall tell her all," Simon MacNair spoke up.

"Of course you will," the queen countered quietly with nary a change of expression but a roll of her eyes toward the hovering Cecil.

MacNair was the younger and handsomer of these Scots, an aide to the seasoned Sir James Melville, who was Queen Mary's envoy to the English court. Melville was leaving for Edinburgh on the morrow, so Elizabeth would soon have only MacNair to keep an eye on. MacNair looked more the part of a braw Scot, auburn haired and big shouldered, while Melville seemed more polished and urbane. Elizabeth trusted them both in opposite proportion to how much Mary Stuart relied on them.

"Tell me, my lords," Elizabeth said, drawing herself up to her full height of five feet, six inches to peer down at them as they knelt, "whether your royal mistress is taller than I or not."

"Six feet tall, she is, higher by half a head," the black-bearded Melville said as she gestured for them to rise.

"Then she is too high," Elizabeth retorted with a set smile. "But not too high to take to herself as husband, consort, and king our illustrious Earl of Leicester. Come close and stand by me for this," she invited them and swept toward the throne awaiting on its dais under the crimson cloth of state.

As Robin knelt before her, the queen tapped his broad, fur-draped shoulders with the ceremonial sword and intoned in her clarion voice the traditional words creating him Earl of Leicester.

At her accession to the throne, she'd named him her Master of the Horse; she'd given him money, a wool monopoly, and Kenilworth Manor in Warwickshire—and her heart, though cursed if he would ever be sure of that while there was breath left in her body.

"And so, it is done," she whispered for Robin's ears alone and stroked his warm neck once with her left thumb. The ceremony was over. Her hand on the newly created earl's arm, Elizabeth preceded her entourage out of the crowded chamber. "I'll need my cloak," she requested as her women divested her of the ermine mantle. "With Ladies Ashley and Radcliffe and the Earl of Leicester, I am going in my carriage to Whitehall forthwith, and the rest of you shall come when you will."

The big, boxy city carriage was brought around from the mews. When Elizabeth was certain the rattle of its iron wheels on cobbles was not another deluge, she stepped outside. The rain had momentarily stopped. A roar went up from the hundreds of people who had waited outside the gatehouse.

"Come on then," she said to her courtiers, who she knew would soon be scrambling to follow her to Whitehall. "We shall walk a bit, as we've been closed in for days."

As ever, she glanced up under the arch of the stone and brick gatehouse at one of the few sets of the entwined initials, *H & A*, of her parents, which someone had failed to chisel away when her father wed his later queens. Ah, she did now recall a happy day here at St. James's during her father's reign; it must have been when Catherine Howard was briefly queen.

Elizabeth had been allowed to watch the Yuletide hanging of greens in the great hall, the decking out of the grand staircase, the bay and ivies being suspended in hoops from this gatehouse. At the banquet table that night, her father had smiled at her and shared with her a mammoth piece of his favorite Cardamom Christmas Cake. And Kat had been there, smiling, ever watchful and protective.

Elizabeth of England climbed the carved mounting block just outside the gatehouse, but she did not get into the carriage, which had followed her. She turned to her people and held up her hand. At first the crowd cheered and waved until someone realized she would speak. Slowly, the roar became chatter, murmur, then silence, while her guards held their halberds out to keep back the press of people.

Just when she was ready to speak, Robin, frowning, whispered up at her, "Your Most Gracious Majesty, it's going to rain again. Your coach is here, so—"

"So it will wait for the will of its queen even as the earls of her realm must," she told him. "My good people!" she called out. Men doffed their wet wool caps; children popped up, hoisted onto shoulders. "On this Michaelmas holiday honoring the archangel Michael, I wish to give to all an early gift for our next and grandest holiday, the Twelve Days of Christmas."

She glanced down at Kat. For once, she seemed avidly intent, excited, almost young again.

"This year, by order of your queen," she continued, "London shall have a Yuletide festival of old, even with mummings, setting aside the more recent strictures. And when these sodden skies turn to crisp, clear ones, we shall have a Frost Fair again, if, God willing, the Thames freezes over. Then all may frolic, wassail, give gifts, and cast off their common trials and woes for a few days, rejoicing in our Lord's coming to the earth to save our souls."

In the silence, she heard a man's mocking voice behind her, a courtier she could not name, hiss, "At least we'll have that, because we'll never frolic over Dudley's coming to the peerage, damn his soul." If anyone else heard or said aught, it was drowned in the shout of the crowd and patter of new rain.

Elizabeth saw how happy Kat looked, as if her queen had already given her an olden Yule with all its golden memories. She would simply hang the naysayers, the queen told herself, right along with the mistletoe and holly. Surely no one, in court or out, could argue with a good old-fashioned Christmas.

Chapter the First

To Make a Kissing Bunch

The size depends upon the span of the two hoops, one thrust through the other, which form the skeleton of the hanging. Wrap the hoops in ribbon, lace, or silk strips. Garland the hoops with holly, ivy, or sprigs of other greens, even apples or oranges. If at court, for a certain, string green and white paper Tudor roses from the hoops. Lastly, a sprig or two of mistletoe must needs be centered in the bunch for all to see. In the spirit of the season, hang the bunch where folks, high and low, may kiss beneath. Include enough mistletoe that men who kiss under its greenery and claim a berry for each kiss do not denude the bunch and ruin all the fine preparations.

DECEMBER 24, 1564

WHITEHALL PALACE, LONDON

"NOTHING BETTER THAN A YULETIDE HANGING," MEG Milligrew, Elizabeth's Strewing Herb Mistress and court herbalist, said as she came into the queen's privy chamber with a basket of white-berried mistletoe.

"The decking of halls is not to begin until the afternoon," the queen remarked, looking up from her reading. "I want to be there to see it, mayhap to help."

"It is to be later, but your maids were trying to snatch these to make a kissing bunch when I need them for Kat's new medicine."

In the slant of morning light, Elizabeth sat at the small table before a Thames-side window, frowning over documents Cecil had given her to read. She could hardly discipline herself to heed her duties, for the palace was already astir with plans and preparations. This evening began the special Twelve Days of Christmas celebration she had promised her people, Kat, and herself, though December 25 itself was always counted as the first day.

"Kat seems to do well with that mistletoe powder in her wine," the queen observed, sanding her signature. "Using it has been worth the risk, and heaven knows the royal physicians haven't come up with anything better."

"I'll never forget the look on your face, Your Grace, when I told you that taking too much of it is poison. But just enough has calmed the heat of Kat's heart's furnace and given her new life."

"I knew to trust your knowledge on it, and pray I will always know whom to trust," Elizabeth said as if to herself. She rose and turned to the window. Scratching the frost off a pane with her fingernails, she gazed out. Though a small stream of open water still flowed at the center, the broad Thames was freezing over from both banks. She took that for a fortuitous sign that a Frost Fair on that vast expanse was a good possibility.

As the queen returned to her work, the mistress of the herbs worked quietly away, and the mistress of the realm was content to have her here. Since before she was queen, Elizabeth had gathered about her several servants as well as courtiers she could trust. She and Meg Milligrew had been through tough times together, and Meg was a member of what the queen dubbed her Privy Plot Council. Should some sort of crime or plot threaten the queen's court or person, Her Majesty assembled her covert coterie to look into it and work directly with her to solve the problem.

Meg greatly resembled the slender, red-haired, pale queen and so could stand in for her, at least at a distance, if need be. Kat Ashley had been a valued member of the secret group before her faculties began to fade, and the brilliant, wily Cecil had ever served his queen as well privily as publicly. Stephen Jenks, Meg's betrothed and a fine horseman, had been the queen's personal bodyguard in her days of exile and now was in the Earl of Leicester's retinue, though ever at the royal beck and call.

The queen's cousin Henry Carey, Baron Hunsdon, a courtier she relied on, had served in her Privy Plot Council, too. Edward Thompson, alias Ned Topside, a former itinerant actor and her Master of Revels at court, was invaluable whether working overtly or covertly. Ned, the handsome rogue, was a man of many faces, voices, and personae and rather full of himself at times. But however witty and charming the blackguard could be, she would scold him roundly for being late this morning.

The queen had sent for Ned to hear of his preparations for the holiday traditions and tomfooleries. For the six years she had been queen, Ned had served as Lord of Misrule, the one who planned and oversaw all Yuletide entertainments, both decorous and raucous. She wondered if Meg had appeared because Ned was coming. Elizabeth knew well that the girl might be betrothed to the quiet, stalwart Jenks but had long yearned for the mercurial, alluring Ned.

"It's a good thing for you," the queen clipped out the moment Ned was admitted, "that the Lord of Misrule's whims can gainsay all rules and regulations in these coming days, for your presence here is long overdue, and I must leave soon."

Ned swept the queen a deep, graceful bow. "Your Most Gracious Majesty," he began with a grand flourish of both arms, "I will be brief."

"That will be a novelty. Instead, write out what merriments we shall see each night, for I want no surprises. As penance for my own frivolity, I must meet with the Bishop of London's aide, Vicar Martin Bane," she added with a dramatic sigh that would have done well in a scene from one of the fond romances or grand tragedies Ned staged for the court.

"That Puritan's presence here these next days will be enough to throw a pall over it all!" Ned protested.

"Keep your impertinence for the banquet tonight, or I will put a lighted taper in your mouth to keep you quiet," she retorted, but they exchanged smiles, and Meg giggled. Ned's eyes darted to the girl; it was evidently the first he had noted her here.

"Ah, but that's only for the roasted peacock," he recovered his aplomb, "and I intend to skewer with barbs and roast with jests everyone else. But there is one thing, Your Grace, a boon I would ask which will enhance, I vow, the entertainments for the court."

"Say on. Some new juggler or more plans for that mummers' morality play?" she asked, moving toward the door.

"To put it succinctly, my former troupe of actors is in town. Lord Hunsdon, patron of the arts that he is, tells me the Queen's Country Players are performing at the Rose and Crown on the Strand. I'm surprised they have not sought a family reunion yet. Of course, compared to my work here at court, theirs is rustic and provincial, but I thought," he went on, pursing his lips and shrugging, "if I went to see them, we could arrange a special surprise for Twelfth Night or some such—"

"A fine idea," she cut off his rambling. "Is your uncle still at their helm, and that other popinjay, ah . . ."

"Randall Greene, Your Grace. I know not, but will inform you as soon as I discover the current state of their affairs."

"But don't be gone long to fetch them. You're needed here, is he not, Meg?"

"Oh, yes, Your Grace," came from the coffer's depths where it seemed Meg hid her head as if to keep Ned from seeing her. "For all the responsibilities on his shoulders for the Twelve Days, that is," she added.

Elizabeth pointed to her writing table, and Ned hastened to take a piece of parchment. He dipped one of the quills in her ink pot, though he dared not plop himself in her chair, at least not until he began his reign as Lord of Misrule. That so-called King of Mockery could get by with anything, however much he was the butt of jokes in return for his own wit.

"At least you didn't say you'd stuff an apple in my mouth as if I were the roast boar," Ned mumbled without looking up as his pen scratched away. "I'd much prefer the lighted taper."

She had to laugh. However full of bombast, Ned always made her laugh.

Meg hoped Ned didn't realize she was watching every grand and graceful move he made.

"What are you doing in her coffer?" Ned asked her when the queen left the room. "You seem as busy as I truly am." He didn't even look up from his scribbling, although when the door closed behind the queen he scooted his paper before her chair and sat. The man, Meg fumed silently, was always busy at something or other, including chasing women, but never her. Yet there had always been something between them. Ninnyhammer that she was, Meg scolded herself, now that she was wedding Jenks just after the holidays, she'd never know what it was.

"Just hiding some mistletoe," she told him. "It's for Kat's potent medicine and not for the kissing bunches. Her Grace's ladies are making them now, and I've seen her Lady Rosie go through her coffers more than once."

"Fancy fripperies, kissing bunches. But, you know, one thing I remember about my mother," he said with a sigh, "is that she'd always hang little cloth figures of Mary, Joseph, and the Christ child in the hoops, so she'd never let my father kiss or pinch her under them, mistletoe or no. She'd have made a good Puritan, eh?"

"Unlike her son," Meg bantered, always striving with Ned to give as good as she got.

"Maybe you should make a kissing bunch just for Jenks."

She looked across the chamber at him when she had been trying not to, and, silent for once, Ned glanced up at that moment. Their gazes snagged. Silence reigned but for the crackle of hearth flames and the howl of river wind outside.

"I hope you're happy, my Meg, and make him happy."

"I intend to be and do so. And I'm not your Meg. Not now and never was."

"As prickly as holly, aren't you? Who taught you to read and walk and talk to emulate Her Grace, eh?"

"You did because she commanded it. And who used to chide me all the time that I was clumsy and slow?"

"God as my judge, not anymore. You've grown up in every way."

"But," she said, her voice tremulous, "I will make a kissing bunch for Jenks, a special one with sweet-smelling herbs like dried heartsease and forget-me-not, lovers' herbs."

"Alas and alack the day," he murmured, his heavily lashed green eyes still on her. He started to put his hand over his heart and hang his head most mockingly—she could tell that was what was coming—but he stopped himself. Instead, he gave one sharp sniff and went back to his writing.

"Always jesting, even when you're not the Lord of Misrule!" she scolded, surprised at her sharp tone after sounding so breathless a moment ago.

Ned had always been the Lord of Misrule in her life. He'd turned her emotions topside more than once, but she was certain, she told herself, that she was right to accept Jenks's suit. Now *there* was a man to be trusted.

"I've much to do and can't be wasting time with you," she added and threw a stray mistletoe berry at him as she slammed the coffer closed and hurried from the room.

The queen found Secretary Cecil and the Bishop of London's aide Vicar Martin Bane awaiting her in the presence chamber. At age forty-three, Cecil looked thin, pale, and careworn, but even compared to that, Ned was right: Bane could cool a room quicker than anyone else she knew.

"You requested a brief audience, Vicar Bane," she said when both men rose from their bows. "How does Bishop Grindal at this most important time of the Christian calendar?"

"It's of that I've been sent to speak, Your Most Gracious Majesty," Bane began, gripping his hawklike hands around what appeared to be a prayer book. Ordained in his own right, Bane served as liaison to her court from Lambeth Palace across the Thames, the traditional home of the Bishops of London, both in Catholic times and this Protestant era. Yet in the winter months, when Grindal was often in residence at his house on the grounds of St. Paul's Cathedral in the city itself, Bane spent even more time here at the palace.

Despite his somber black garb, the man was good-looking, with classical features and a full head of graying blond hair to match his neatly trimmed beard. But he was of stringy build and always seemed to be shrinking within his clothes. His cheeks were hollow, as if something inside his head sucked in his face and sank his icy blue eyes beneath his jutted brows.

"You see," he went on in a clear, clipped voice when she nodded he might continue, "there is some concern with all this coming merriment. The bishop and I did not realize at first you meant to flout your own family's statutes."

The queen felt her dander rise. "You refer, I assume," she clipped out, "to the Unlawful Games Act of 1541, banning sporting activity on the twenty-fifth day of December, and the Holy Days and Fasting Days Act of 1551, prohibiting transport and merriment, laws enacted in my father's and my brother's reigns."

At that rapid recitation, Bane's Adam's apple bobbed, perhaps in danger of also being sucked inside the dark void of the man. Did he not think she had a brain in her female head? She knew full well that both Bishop Edmund Grindal and his right arm, Vicar Martin Bane, favored the rising Puritan element in her country. They were men who saw the Catholic Church as nearly satanic but also viewed the Church of England, of which their queen was head, as dangerously liberal and in need of severe reform.

"I did not know you would be so . . ." he stumbled for a word, "current on those laws, especially seeing that your promise to your people on Michaelmas, in effect, Your Majesty, appears to have rescinded said laws—"

"Suspended them for this year alone, after which they will be assessed anew," she interrupted, her voice as commanding as his was cold. "The Tudor kings allowed such statutes to be enacted for specific reasons which are not pertinent now, in *my* reign, Vicar Bane."

"Yes, of course, I see," he said, his voice noticeably quailing as he shuffled a wary step back. He glanced askance at Cecil, only to find no help from that quarter. "Perhaps I was a bit wide of the mark," he added, "but we of the bishopric of the great city of London believe that even snowballing is a profane pastime, and if you encourage a Frost Fair on the Thames after all these years, London's citizens will be buying and selling on holy days, let alone running hither and yon on the ice."

"But we are leaving that all up to the Lord God, are we not?" Elizabeth inquired sweetly. "If the Thames freezes over by His will, when it has not in ages, I shall take it as His most gracious sign that my housebound and hardworking people may truly enjoy this holy season by holding a fair on the river. I myself recall earlier Frost Fairs with great fondness after not having seen one whit of profane behavior."

"But do you not live a rather sheltered life, Your Majesty? And we must consider your reinstituting of mummings. The earlier laws were partly passed because crime rose so severely when everyone was going about willy-nilly masked in playacting of sundry sorts."

"Yet my father himself, who cast off the excesses of the Catholic Church, loved masques and mummings at court and more than once played Lord of Misrule himself. I repeat, the decrees are for this one year, Vicar Bane, to see how things go. I assure you the precious, holy aspects of Christmas will be made dearer if they are not stifled by poor, plain rituals. We must have joy in this season of the year, for the Lord's gift to us and even for our gifts to each other. I am certain you will convey my words to Bishop Grindal and bid him come to court tomorrow to lead us all in prayer at the morning service. And you, of course, are welcome always to increase our happiness here."

When Bane saw he was beaten and bowed his way out, Cecil's stern face split in a grin. "The man doesn't know what hit him, but I warrant it feels like a jousting steed at full tilt," he told her, rubbing his hands in glee. For once those capable hands were not filled with writs or decrees, so perhaps even the diligent Cecil was ready to slacken up a bit at Christmas.

"He'll be back, lurking in corners," Elizabeth said, "but I refuse to let him or anyone else overthrow my hopes for these holidays. My most important tasks of the day are to present the new livery to my household staffs and to oversee the hanging of garlands and greens—and the Earl of Sussex has asked for some time, no doubt to warn me against listening to Leicester again."

A sharp knock on the door startled them both. At her nod, Cecil went to open it. Two yeomen guards blocked the way of the agitated-looking Scot Simon MacNair, brandishing a letter. Behind him, looking even more distressed, was Robin Dudley, whom everyone now, except the queen in private, addressed as Leicester.

"Your Gracious Majesty," MacNair clipped out, "forgive my intrusion, but I have a message of utmost import."

"What import, man?" Cecil demanded, plucking the letter from his hand as the guards let both men enter and they bowed.

"From Edinburgh, I see," Elizabeth said, noting well the familiar large, crimson wax seal the Queen of Scots employed.

"From your royal cousin to you, Your Grace," Cecil said. She saw him skim the letter even as he handed it over.

"Tell me what it says, Sir Simon," Elizabeth ordered MacNair. "Or, by the look on your face, Leicester, should you tell me?"

"Very well," Robin said. "The Scots queen has flat refused my suit for her royal hand."

"*Your* suit? *Mine* rather!" Elizabeth cried. She hoped that MacNair not only thought she was shocked and distressed but would report it forthwith to his royal mistress. Mary Stuart had taken the bait, though she was not yet hooked. If she rejected the Earl of Leicester, as Elizabeth had hoped, she might bite all the quicker and harder on the tasty Henry Stewart, Lord Darnley, whom Elizabeth intended to dangle before her.

Both royal Tudor and Stuart blood—for *Stewart* was the Scots' version of Queen Mary's Frenchified *Stuart*—ran in Darnley's veins. At the prompting of his parents and without Elizabeth's permission, the comely twenty-year-old Darnley had courted the newly widowed Queen Mary in France, before she returned to Edinburgh. Distantly related to Elizabeth, Darnley was a dissolute weakling. If he were king, he would sap the power Mary of Scots would need for any bid to seize her rival Elizabeth's crown and kingdom.

Elizabeth lowered her voice and tried to look morose. "I am deeply grieved the Scots queen, my dear cousin, does not think to take that which I have so lovingly offered and advised."

"How could she, Your Majesty," MacNair put in, "when the earl wrote privily to her he was not worthy of her?"

"What?" she demanded. "I have made him worthy of her, said he is worthy of her!" She felt her skin flush hot. Over anyone else, friend or foe, she could remain calm, but not over this freebooting blackguard she had long loved. Now Robin had defied her again when she had told him to keep clear of this business, that she and Cecil would handle it. But no, he had gainsayed her and jumped in with both feet as if he were bidden to make royal decisions here.

"You wrote her privily, in effect warding off her affections?" she cried, striding to Robin and hitting his shoulder with her balled fist. The wretch stood his ground.

"I was surprised, too, Your Grace," MacNair went smoothly on, "since it has long been noised about that the earl has a cur-tained painting of Mary Stuart he dotes on. I hear 'tis in his privy rooms at Kenilworth, near the corridor on which hangs a smaller one of Your Most Gracious Majesty."

Elizabeth was so furious her blood rang in her ears, thumping with the beat of her heart. She steadied herself as she had count-less times ere this and said in a well-modulated voice, "Thank you, Sir Simon, for delivering this letter and for your additional information. I assure you I shall read most carefully my cousin's thoughts and respond to her in kind. Farewell for now. Leicester, you may stay."

When the door closed on the Scot and the queen heard her yeomen guards move back into their positions outside, she said calmly to Cecil, "Please ask Ned Topside to join us for a moment, my lord." He nodded and complied instantly, going out the back way by which she had entered.

"Topside?" Robin said, fidgeting and moving toward the other door as if he would flee. "What has he to do with any of this?"

"I won't even ask you about the portrait of *her* you have hanging in your rooms while the smaller one of *me* is in the corridor. I am wearied to death with your caperings, to put it prettily, my lord. I give you an earldom, but you presume to play king."

"Hell's teeth, Your Grace," he exploded, "you've been using me as a pawn to be taken by a foreign and enemy queen, so I thought I'd at least ascertain what the woman looked like. It's a poor portrait of her, especially next to any of you, including this one!" he cried and yanked a locket on a chain out of his doublet. He tried to pry it open with some difficulty.

"Never mind trying to make amends," Elizabeth insisted. "It's probably rusted shut from disuse if it hides my likeness!"

"If it is rusted shut, it is from my tears. You no longer love me as you once did—at least said you did!"

"And now I want nothing but silence from you! You were to keep to the side in my dealings with Mary Stuart, not get your sticky, greedy fingers into the Christmas pie like Jack Horner in the corner," she told him, wagging her finger as Cecil knocked once and entered with Ned.

"You called for me, Your Grace?" Ned said. He and Cecil looked almost as nervous as Robin.

"Master Topside, I regret to inform you that there is someone else I must appoint as Lord of Misrule this year, one who believes he can go his own way, so he will be perfect for the part. And you shall be his aide."

Ned looked confused, hurt, then angry. "But I—things are already greatly planned, Your Grace, and I was just about to visit my former colleagues, the Queen's Country Players, at the Rose and Crown, as you said I might, to invite them to help me with a play."

"You may still do so, but you will be assisting the new Lord of Misrule, especially at the Feast of Fools, where he will rule indeed."

She glanced at Robin, then away. He had gone from deathly white to ruby red. And he had not yet learned when to keep his mouth shut.

"You first raise me to the earldom, then offer me to your cousin queen, then make a laughingstock of me?" he demanded.

"When people remark that I keep my friends so close, Cecil," she said, turning to him, "I merely smile and nod, but the unspoken truth is, of necessity, I keep my enemies even closer. Ned, you may fetch your players, but be certain, if you stage a play, that the Earl of Leicester as the new Lord of Misrule takes the part of buffoon—or villain!"

"Holly and ivy, box and bay, put in the house for Christmas day." The queen's maids of honor and ladies in waiting chanted the old rhyme as they decked the halls where kissing balls hung from rafters and lintels. *"Fa, la, la, la, las"* echoed in the vast public rooms of the palace. But the queen's mood was still soured as she watched all the frivolity. Truth be told, she'd like to feed both Martin Bane and Robin Dudley a big bowl of mistletoe berries.

"It's not really true, is it?" Rosie's voice pierced the queen's thoughts. Four of her maids were standing close, looking at her on the first landing of the newly garlanded staircase.

"What was that again?"

"It's only a superstition about the holly berries, isn't it?" Rosie prompted.

Anne Carey, wife of Elizabeth's cousin Baron Hunsdon, came to the queen's aid. "Obviously," Anne said, "it's pure folk custom that these more pointed holly leaves are male and the more rounded ones female." It was traditional to count whether more sharp-leafed or smooth had been gathered each year; whichever kind was in the majority supposedly decided whether the husband or wife of the house ruled the roost in the coming year.

"I shan't leave to chance," Elizabeth said, "who commands this dwelling or any other palace for the entire year. I don't give a fig how many sharp leaves of holly are hauled in here, a woman rules."

She basked in their smiles and laughter. They made her feel better, and she was greatly looking forward to the awarding of the new liveries to the kitchen staff. Finally, she began to buck up a bit.

With her main officers of her palaces, the queen processed toward the vast kitchen block. Behind her came the four chief household officials, the Lord Chamberlain, Lord Steward, Treasurer, and Comptroller, with some of their aides, laden down with piles of new clothes. She had sent for her former groom and favorite horseman, Stephen Jenks, because anytime she chose to leave her yeomen guards behind, she felt better with him in tow.

The royal kitchens of the Tudor palaces actually held three staffs that occupied separate areas. The hall kitchen served minor courtiers and household servants who ate in the Great Hall; the lords' kitchen provided for the nobles who sat just below the dais in the Great Hall; and the privy kitchen fed the queen and whomever she chose to have dine with her. This particular set of liveries was going to her privy kitchen staff.

The mere aroma from the open hearths and brick ovens pulled the queen fully back into the mood for Christmas. The bubbling sauces, spitted roasts, and plump pillows of rising dough being kneaded for pastries and pies made her nose twitch. In a long line stood her staff, Master Cook Roger Stout to lowest scullery maid and spit boy. The fancy livery was for those of the highest echelons and those who served at table, but everyone would receive at least a piece of cloth or a coin. Most gifts were given on New Year's Day, but the household staffs needed their new garments now to look their best these coming Twelve Days.

Elizabeth went down the line from pastry cooks to larders, confectioners, boilers, and spicers, giving a quick smile and word of praise to each with the varied gifts. "Is that everyone?" she asked the beaming Stout as he sent his staff back to their tasks. "I see there's a doublet left."

"I reckon it's for Hodge Thatcher, Your Most Gracious Majesty, as I noticed him missing. If he's nodded off, I'll skin him."

"More like poor Master Hodge is busy putting the skin and feathers back on the peacock for tonight," Elizabeth countered.

Hodge Thatcher was Dresser of the Queen's Privy Kitchen, which meant he "dressed" or ornately arranged the fancy dishes, especially for the feasts. It was no mean task to garnish and decorate soups, meats, and pies. On occasions when she entertained foreign ambassadors, he'd turned out many a finely refeathered roasted swan with the traditional tiny crown upon its head. For this evening he must reaffix the roasted peacock's iridescent coat and prop up the fan of feathers. She'd seen Hodge at that task once years ago, when he first came to serve in her father's kitchens. She glanced over at the hatches through which he inspected all food before it was carried upstairs to her table, whether she was eating in public or in private.

"His workroom is by the back door near the street, is it not?" she asked. Carrying the doublet herself, she strode down the crooked corridor while Stout and her entourage hurried along behind.

"Ah, yes, what a fine memory you have, Your Majesty," he cried, sounding out of breath, "for his is the last door before passing through to the porter's gate and so outside the walls. Allow me to ascertain if he is within and announce you," he added, but the door was narrow, and the queen poked her head in ahead of the others.

"He's not here," she declared at first glance into the dim room, lit by a single lantern on the cluttered worktable. She saw that the small area served also for storage; pots and kettles, spits and gridirons hung aloft on hooks and hoisting chains.

Then, amidst all that, the queen saw bare feet dangling head high. She gasped as she gazed up at a bizarre body, a corpse, part man, part bird.

Chapter the Second

Roast Peacock

Take a peacock, break its neck, and drain it. Carefully skin it, keeping its skin and feathers together with the head still attached to the skin of the neck. Roast only the bird, with its legs tucked under. When it is roasted enough, take it out and let it cool. Sprinkle cumin on the inside of the skin, then wind it with the feathers and the tail about the body. Serve with the tail feathers upright, its neck propped up from within, and a lighted taper in its beak. If it is a royal dish, cover the bird's beak with fine gold leaf. Carry said proud bird to the table at the head of a procession of lower dishes for to be sampled first by the monarch. Ginger sauce is best served with this fine and fancy bird.

AT THE SIGHT OF THE HANGING BODY SOMEONE CURSED; a few shrieked. The queen continued to stare up at the partly feathered corpse, which seemed to have grotesquely taken flight.

"Hodge? What the deuce!" Stout cracked out behind the queen as Jenks drew his sword and rushed past her. He looked behind the door and under the long table. As more people tried to enter, shadows from the single lantern danced and darted.

"No one's hiding here, Your Grace," Jenks said, standing at her elbow and sheathing his sword.

"Your Majesty," came her Lord Chamberlain's voice behind

her, "you must come out, and we will see to this—this great misfortune."

Ignoring him, the queen pronounced, "Master Hodge is dead, whether by his own hand or someone else's is to be seen. My Lord Chamberlain, send for Secretary Cecil and get everyone out of the room and doorway, for you are blocking what little additional light seeps in."

"Cecil, Your Grace?" the man repeated like a dimwit.

Elizabeth finally managed to pull her gaze from the terrible tableau. "Yes, send for Cecil, and now," she commanded, turning to face the wide-eyed, whispering group. "I do not want this noised about, to sadden or panic my people in court or city at this happy time of year. But leave me now, for I shall take a brief moment to mourn." Indicating only Jenks and Stout should stay, she closed the door herself.

"Let's get the poor wretch down first," Stout cried and reached for the crank on the wall that worked the chain pulley.

"Wait!" Elizabeth ordered. "Touch nothing yet, as there may be clues or signs of what has happened here, even in this grit under our feet."

"For some specialty like the peacock or boar's head, Your Grace," Stout said, staring at the floor, "he did some seasoning as well as dressing. It's probably just sugar or ginger."

"Jenks," she said, "fetch that lantern closer, and Master Stout, leave us and try to be certain untoward rumors of this do not spread—and keep your people at their tasks as best you can. I am relying on you." Nervously clutching the new doublet he had been given, her master cook hustled out.

Poor Hodge was attired, as far as the queen could tell by staring up into the shifting shadows amidst hanging vessels and utensils, only in his breeches and shirt. His arms hung at his sides; four neatly arranged, plucked peacock fantail feathers protruded from under each armpit. And, though the man's contorted face showed, his forehead and hair were covered by the sleek blue-green body and drooped head of a peacock whose roasted carcass sat yet upon the worktable.

The queen's neck ached from staring up, but she felt awestruck by the bizarrely dressed corpse. In lantern light, the feathers gleamed and glistened; the body seemed to sway. If it was not a reflection from the peacock's coloring, the little she could glimpse of Hodge's face and back was not only contorted but bluish. She wondered if, beneath the collar of his shirt and draped peacock skin, the man had a noose around his neck, which had choked breath and life from him.

She noted a tall stool tipped against the wall. Had Hodges hanged himself by stepping from it, or was there some other explanation—and hence a Yuletide hanging of a far different sort than she had hoped for on this day?

"I guess he could have committed suicide," Jenks whispered as if he had heard her thoughts.

"If he didn't," she replied in hushed tones, "in the strange way the body is displayed, we've got both a murder and a mystery. Someone may have meant to take not only poor Hodge's life but the joy of our court Christmas."

Ned Topside was glad to escape the palace to clear his mind and try to rein in his temper, but the cold air felt like a blow to his spinning head. No one had seen him lose control—at least only one, and that was settled.

"Watch where you're going, dolt!" he exploded at a man who bumped into him on the Strand. The lout was carrying a pitifully small Yule log and must already have drunk a good cup of Christmas cheer. Damn the capering numbskulls in the street who seemed so happy when he was at his wit's end.

He'd show Elizabeth Tudor a thing or two about replacing him as Lord of Misrule, and with her fair-haired boy Leicester, no less! He'd get back at her in spades for this last-minute trickery, after how well he served her. Now he was caught in the box of having to ask his old companions to play at court but admitting he was no longer the favored Lord of Misrule, and he had no idea how to save face by playacting any different.

And now, a pox on it all, he'd just learned his uncle and his troupe of players had left the Rose and Crown for a better situation at the Lamb and Cross, an old pilgrims' inn hard by St. Paul's, and that was a good walk in this cutting river wind when he'd told the queen he wouldn't be gone long. Hell's teeth, what did it matter now, since on a woman's whim she'd put the preening Earl of Leicester in his place to make all the final Yuletide decisions?

Ned tied his cloak tighter around his neck and heaved the last of the capon drumsticks he'd filched from the palace kitchen into the middle of the street, where two dogs leaped on it, growling at each other. Ned wiped his hands on his handkerchief and hurried on.

Meg Milligrew had vexed him today, too, he admitted, kicking at a pile of refuse, then cursing when it dirtied his boots. Well might she resemble the queen, because she was acting as haughty, and without the excuse of being royal.

"Out of my way there!" he commanded a group of unruly

urchins in his best stage voice. Why should they be allowed to bat their bladder ball in front of busy citizens as they passed through narrow Ludgate? Where were their elders? Did no one teach the youth of England to be responsible anymore? He used to have to toe his father's and his uncle's lines when he was a lad.

Ned could see the new roofs of St. Paul's in the distance. After a fire three years ago started by a lightning strike, the grand city cathedral had had its huge roof newly rebuilt. The Catholics, Protestants, and Puritans had all claimed it was God's warning to at least one of the other groups. The queen wanted "freedom of conscience" for her people, but she also wanted public loyalty to the Church of England. At least she didn't imprison folks and burn martyrs at the stake as her demented half-sister had. Women!

Still seething, he located the Lamb and Cross and entered the warm, crowded common room. As his eyes sought a familiar face, the mingled scents of food and fireplace assailed him. Why weren't people at home on this Christmas Eve day? Then, above the noise of talk and laughter, he overheard a snatch of conversation: ". . . and good speeches in tha' *Cloth of Gold* play today, eh?"

"Excuse me, my man," Ned interrupted the stranger, "but can you tell me where to find the actors of that play? Are they still hereabouts?"

"Being feted by the host, ri' o'er there," the man told him with a nod, sending a blast of garlic breath his way.

Despite his foul mood, Ned's heart beat harder as he made his way over to the table in the corner. Yes, his uncle, Wat Thompson, was there, and Grand Rand, as he used to call the pompous jackanapes Randall Greene, to whom his uncle inexplicably gave all the good parts—inexplicably until Ned discovered they were lovers. That was something no one could know, lest they be arrested and worse as sodomites. How Henry Stewart, Lord Darnley, got away with his male lovers at court was beyond him. The queen knew of it but for some reason looked the other way when ordinarily nothing escaped her notice.

"Ned!" his uncle cried, rising, when he saw him coming. "Well, I'll be hanged! My boy, it's been far too long!"

Ned felt his throat tighten. He'd come far from his rambling actor's days, but those times had not been all bad. He hugged his uncle and even shook hands with Rand Greene.

"I hear you did *Cloth of Gold* today," Ned told them and struck a pose as his voice rang out. " 'And can our dear English King Henry not make France's *Francois Roi* look the very shell of a man?' "

" 'For our fair English shall e'er outmatch any man with French blood in his veins,' " his uncle picked up the next line, and they clapped each other on the shoulders.

"And the lads?" Ned asked, referring to Rob and Lucas, who had played the girls' parts.

"This is young Rob grown from a stripling," Uncle Wat said, indicating a curly-haired young man, stuffing himself with bread sopped in gravy.

"No stripling but a strapping lad," Ned said, reaching over to ruffle his hair.

"Lucas left us when his voice changed, but we have a new lad, Clinton, from Coventry, who's always sleeping, that one. But how and why did you find us, my boy?" Wat asked, shoving over on the bench so Ned could sit, too. "Still in Her Gracious Majesty's Service, her principal player, are you not?"

"I am and more. These past six years she's held the throne, I've been her Lord of Misrule, too, though I've agreed to counsel my Lord of Leicester on how to handle the task, just for this year. So as not to humble his lordship, I've agreed to dub myself his aide, but the major decisions are all mine."

He looked from man to man as he spoke, trying to assess if they were following him—and believing him. They were the most rapt audience he had ever seen. And now, he thought, for the end of this little play, where he would summon the *deus ex machina* from heaven itself for their small-encompassed lives.

"And so, I've told Her Majesty—just for this special Twelve Days of Christmas—I'd like to try to work my old troupe into an entertainment or two for the court."

Amidst the smiles, cheers, and backslapping, Ned nearly cried. He knew how they felt. He recalled the elation of that day the queen, then princess, had invited him into her household because she favored his voice, wit, and charm. She always was one to take a fancy not only to talent but to form and face, so at least he felt safe asking these men to court—excellent players but no genius or Adonis here to usurp his place.

"Shall we come with you right now?" Uncle Wat asked. "We have but one more performance on the morrow, and they will surely understand we must leave by royal command."

"Come tomorrow after the play, uncle, and by then I'll have found a cubbyhole or two for you in the servants' wing. You understand, the palace is quite full up at Christmas. You must come to the servants' door off the street near the kitchen-block porter's gate."

"We will be there with bells on," Uncle Wat declared and stood, windmilling his arm to someone in the crowd. "In the excitement of seeing you and this thrilling invitation, I almost forgot."

"Forgot what?" Ned asked and followed his uncle's gaze to see a tall, square-jawed, blond man with clear blue eyes shouldering his way to them through the crowd. He was one of the hand-somest men Ned had ever beheld, and at that moment, with a sinking feeling, he discerned who he must be.

"A new player in the troupe?" Ned asked, his voice catching. He'd learned, last time he'd heard from them, that they were searching for someone well turned out to take his place, but ...

"Giles Chatam," his uncle said, talking out of the side of his mouth, "our new man from Wimbledon. All the ladies love him, and he's the consummate actor, too, if a bit ambitious. You know, refuses to be kept in his place."

The smile and welcome Ned gave the man was some of the most difficult acting he had ever done.

"But what's the dreadful message here?" William Cecil asked as he gazed up agape at the hanging corpse decked out in a fowl's coat and feathers. "Do you plan to summon the coroner, Your Grace?"

"I must, if only to have poor Hodge declared officially deceased and, on the official examination of the body, get a sec-ond opinion about whether this could be foul play."

At her inadvertent pun, the queen's gaze caught Cecil's. He shook his head as if in warning; she bit her lower lip.

"A second opinion?" Cecil said only. "Then you mean that in the midst of all your public activities, you, with our help, intend to investigate this? Your Grace, we have the Scots envoy MacNair hovering so he can report your every move to his Catholic queen, several ambassadors in town who will be at court, Bishop Grindal coming tomorrow for the service, a feast and public celebrations on which hangs the goodwill of the court and people..." His voice trailed off before he added, "In short, this seems a dreadful joke indeed, and much more than poor puns on hangings and foul play are afoot here."

"I'll fetch the coroner forthwith, Your Majesty," Jenks said so loudly behind his betters that they startled.

She had almost forgotten Jenks was here, but she could hardly ignore the fact that surely word of this would spread. They must act in haste to gather evidence before they sent for public officials. And she had an appointment soon with the ever disgruntled Earl of Sussex, which she wanted to keep. She intended to tell him she expected him to get on well with his rival, the Earl of Leicester, at least during this holiday season.

"You may send someone to fetch the coroner, Jenks, but not forthwith," the queen said. "We may eventually have to summon the constable, too, though their investigations aren't worth a fig unless they can find eyewitnesses to interrogate. They seem to trample some clues and ignore or misinterpret the rest."

"Which, I warrant," Cecil put in, "we'll need to search out should you decide to pursue this, or perhaps to summon the Privy Plot Council."

"When you came in, you, as usual," she told her trusted Cecil, "asked the right question first, my lord. What indeed is the message here? Though it is a mortal sin to take one's own life, and I am deeply regretful if Hodge was somehow so desperate he did so, I pray, despite the bizarre trappings, this can be proved self-slaughter. If not, the message, at the very least, is that someone dangerous and demented has come to spend Yule with us."

"These back chambers are close to the porter's gate and street door," Jenks said. "I suppose some stranger could have come in."

"We'll question the porter, of course, but random chance is highly unlikely. Jenks, fetch more lights in here," she said, and he hastened to obey. "Cecil, I have promised an audience to the Earl of Sussex and must keep that appointment. Besides, it will allow me to see how quickly news of this has flown about our court."

"Should I not be at your side with Sussex? His festering hatred of Leicester has made him difficult to keep in line lately. Military men like our illustrious Thomas Radcliffe, Earl of Sussex, don't know when to keep quiet or calm. They think life must be all assault, attack, and violence," he protested before his eyes darted to the corpse again and he shuddered.

"Ordinarily, I would take you with me, my lord, but I need you to oversee this dreadful situation. While I am gone, fetch Roger Stout back and have him survey this cluttered worktable. I pray you make careful notes of what is here and, more important, what may be missing. See that the coroner is summoned, then clear the table so he can examine the body here, while you are still in the room, silently making your own observations. After the banquet tonight, I will hold a Privy Plot Council meeting in my quarters, where you will report all you—and Jenks—have learned."

"Yes, Your Grace," Cecil said. "Leave it all to us, unless you can send Topside to help, too."

"He should be back by now, but I hardly intend to do nothing until the meeting. I will later summon Stout for more questioning. With his information and your close observances from this site—best send Jenks to speak to the porter, too—we shall decide whether to pursue the matter further or let the conundrum be buried with Hodge."

Jenks came back in with Roger Stout, each carrying two lanterns; the small room filled with light. Though the queen edged toward the door, she thought of two things she could not bear to leave unasked and went back to stand under the corpse again.

"Master Stout, what is that gritty material on the floor?" she asked, pointing. "I stepped in it, but I see other prints there, which I want well noted and drawn to size. It is not sugar or ginger, as you suggested before, for in this new light the grains look too dark."

Stout took a lantern closer and squatted to sniff at the fine reddish dust. "Yet it looks like a spice—cumin, I warrant, Your Majesty," he reported. "It's what the peacock's innards are always dusted with before it's served."

"And this stack of gold leaf?" she asked, moving away to lift from the table a thin slab of marble as big as her palm, upon which lay an inch-thick stack of fine sheets of beaten gold. She had seen it before even in the muted light of the single lantern but had been too distracted to pay it heed. Now it shone like a small, square sun.

"He must have stopped—or been stopped—in the very act of dressing the bird for your banquet table," Stout said, as he glanced at what she held. "You recall, Your Majesty, how the bird's beak is always covered with gold foil for Yule."

"So," she said, "whether or not Hodge killed himself, we do have another mystery. When such a small amount of gold leaf is needed for the beak, why did he have here enough to cover a rich man's effigy? And if someone killed Hodge, why was this pure gold not stolen?"

"Perhaps because, if a man kills himself," Stout ventured, "he is too distraught or despondent to care for worldly wealth. Or Hodge himself was going to abscond with it but in self-loathing at his planned evil—and for other reasons—took his own life."

"Or," Jenks put in, "the gold wasn't taken because the killer was in a rush to flee once he spotted it. He'd already taken time to hang the corpse and deck it out. And he didn't want to get caught with stolen royal property on his person."

"Or just the opposite," Cecil said. "Mayhap it was a murder well planned ahead of time, and the killer's motive has everything to do with the message, so he did not want to distract from that with what would be petty theft—petty not in what was stolen but petty compared to the murderer's true intent. Discern that and we have our killer."

The queen sensed her clever Cecil would say more, but he did not. Perhaps his deductions were for her ears alone. She too feared that this death did not just strike at Hodge but that, indeed, someone diabolically devious had killed the messenger in order to send the message.

Chapter the Third

ELIZABETH'S STOMACH FELT KNOTTED LIKE THE NOOSE that must have choked away Hodge Thatcher's life. With her Lord Chamberlain and other household officers trailing behind her, she beat a retreat from the kitchen block back into the corridors of the palace. The scent of suspended green garlands permeated the vast place, and servants were setting up the Great Hall for tonight's feast.

She was no doubt late for the audience she had promised the Earl of Sussex, but it wouldn't hurt to let him cool his heels. She was hardly in the mood for his rantings about Leicester's growing power at court and his influence over his queen. Had she not proved time and again that even those she favored would not be trusted overmuch?

"Oh, Your Majesty," came a woman's voice as Elizabeth ascended the grand staircase toward the royal apartments, "there you are!"

Margaret Stewart, Countess of Lennox, waited at the first landing, so she was trapped. That smiling face always looked like a mask to Elizabeth. Beneath it, the queen imagined, lurked the countenance of a woman who was at heart a treacherous harpy. Though Margaret was fifty, her former beauty still haunted her plump face, but now everything about the woman seemed overblown: her big body, broad mouth, large teeth, prominent nose, even the hint of red in her graying tresses, which peeked from her velvet cap—and her ambitions. Yet Elizabeth tolerated her, for the older woman was niece to King Henry VIII and so another of the queen's female cousins who were her cross to bear.

Margaret and Matthew Stewart, the Countess and Earl of Lennox, were Lord Darnley's parents, covert Catholics, and rapacious relatives of both the English and Scottish queens. Elizabeth knew the Stewarts were plotting to wed their heir to Queen Mary in defiance of her own apparent plans for Dudley. She had promised to let Darnley go to Scotland to join his Scottish father, then changed her mind more than once. At least that was how this web of intrigue appeared to everyone but Elizabeth and Cecil.

"Cousin, how are you on this Christmas Eve day?" Elizabeth asked, nodding but not stopping. Margaret lifted her skirts and charged, puffing up the stairs after her. Elizabeth waited at the top and held out her hand to stay Margaret where she was, four or five steps down. When Elizabeth was a girl and out of favor with her royal father, more than once Margaret had gloated to take precedence and to keep the younger woman in her place.

"Oh, did you wish to speak to me?" Elizabeth inquired.

"I will be brief, Your Majesty. May not my son go north after these holidays to visit his father in Edinburgh? You had said before that he could go. My dear husband is petitioning the Scot queen's council for the return of our lands, and Lord Darnley would be of great help in this endeavor."

Oh, yes, she'd wager, Elizabeth thought, that Darnley would be of great help there. Not only with those dour Calvinist Scots lords but with the pliable Queen Mary herself. Indeed, Elizabeth was planning on that very thing, but she wanted to be certain both the bait and the big six-foot fish were hungry for their reunion when the English queen finally let him go, apparently under duress.

But she said only, "I shall consider it, Margaret. You must excuse me, but we shall speak more of this later."

"I heard there will be no peacock on display at the feast," Margaret said as Elizabeth turned away. "That is, none but the one Leicester's rivals call by that sobriquet, 'the peacock.' "

In the shock of realization, Elizabeth could have tumbled down the flight of stairs. She was hardly surprised that word of her privy dresser's death was out and about, not even that Margaret too must hate Leicester, whom she perhaps still believed to be her son's rival for Queen Mary's hand.

A new thought struck the queen with stunning force. If Hodge Thatcher had been murdered and was intentionally decked out with peacock garb, the mockery and threat could be aimed at the controversial Earl of Leicester.

. . .

"If you intend to rant about my heeding Lord Leicester's advice upon occasion," Elizabeth began with Sussex moments later in her presence chamber, "I do not wish to take my time. You are beginning to sound like your own echo, my lord, but I would ask you one thing about that."

"Of course, Your Grace," he said. "Anything I can ever do to help with, ah, anything . . ."

Sussex was hardly an orator, but that did not keep him from commanding a large faction at court. And did the man not realize that his hand perched on his ceremonial sword always rattled it in its scabbard, and to a regular beat? It was like listening to a ticking timepiece until one became a lunatic. 'S bones, but the ache in her belly was growing, and in these precious holiday times.

"I am ever at your beck and call for all service," Sussex plunged on, sweeping her a bow with the offending sword lifted so it wouldn't scrape the floor.

Thomas Radcliffe, third Earl of Sussex, had been her Lord Deputy of Ireland and had led and fought bravely there if with little ultimate success, though it seemed no one made much headway in the Eire's fens and forests. His health had suffered, and he had petitioned to be brought back to court, a request she had granted. But since he'd returned, he'd spearheaded the anti-Leicester group more zealously than he had ever fought the Irish rebel Tyrone. If the queen had not been so fond of his kin, her lady Rosie Radcliffe, and had not had a soft spot, too, for his wife, Frances Sidney, he just might be heading back for another tour of duty.

Once bright blond but now graying and balding, Sussex still had fine military bearing at age thirty-eight. She did trust the man to keep state secrets and would not usually mind having him nearby—if he would only stop that damned sword rattling!

"Instead of your asking me whether I am heeding Leicester's words on such and such an issue," the queen said, "I wish to ask you some questions about him, and I ask you tell me true."

"About the earl—ah, of course," he said, hardly managing to cloak his surprise.

"As to those who speak ill of him—and I shall not mention nor request names—by what nicknames might they call him?"

"You don't mean like 'Robin'? I've heard you call him that."

"Hardly, my lord."

"Ah, I believe Your Highness knows he used to be dubbed 'the gypsy' because of his dark hair and eyes."

"And for his tendency to mesmerize certain people, namely me, I have heard."

"I suppose that could be part of why he was called so. Also, no doubt, the fact he came with little fortune to court but has managed to—ah, find such good fortune here, some might say through sleight-of-hand or even gypsy-like theft. Indeed, Your Majesty, those people of Romany are known for such."

"So I have heard, but that trait attributed to Leicester would be wrong. 'S blood, Sussex, the man loaned me money once when I was declared bastard by my father and did not have two groats to my name. When I was sent to the Tower, though I was innocent in a misguided plot to overthrow my sister, he was imprisoned there, too, and sent me flowers and kept my spirits up. I mention these things so that those who might dislike the earl will realize he is not some border reaver sweeping in to plunder something here."

He looked astounded at her passionate outburst. His sword in its scabbard even stopped its confounded clatter.

"Any other sobriquets?" she prompted, wanting to get back to the business at hand.

"Well—ah, you've heard, of course, he's widely called of late 'the peacock.' "

"Widely called? I won't ask by whom, but why?"

"Some observers think he tends to strut, Your Majesty. And no one—but the Tudor monarch, and rightly so, of course— tends to attire oneself as finely as he does. Certainly, I can't hold a candle to the gleam of his satins, silks, and gems. I heard Martin Bane, for one, say such display is, well—absolutely sinful..."

Though his voice had gone from a trot to a canter, when she narrowed her eyes at Bane's name, he stopped talking. "Forgive me if I overspeak, Your Majesty, but it was at your bequest."

"Yes," she said, almost to herself. "I myself have goaded Leicester with the term *peacock* when he vexed me sore. But I will not have sniping among my subjects in my court during this holiday time. Is that understood, my lord Sussex?"

"It is. Of course," he said and punctuated that promise with a brief rattle.

"Then what more do you have to say to me today?"

"Only that I am heartened to see how lovingly my dear cousin Rosie serves you as maid of honor, Your Majesty. That is all, for we Radcliffes are ever grateful for your leading and wise counsel."

"Who could not favor your Rosie?" Elizabeth responded, though she knew full well he'd hardly requested this interview for that.

"Ah, she is a lovely girl," he added lamely.

"Lovely in her heart, that is what I value," Elizabeth said as she moved toward the door to her privy rooms. "Those of us who were children of great loves—even if that love was lost," she added quietly, "are ones who care deeply for others, my lord. Perhaps I shall have Rosie tell her parents' story again during this Yuletide, for I refuse to let jealousies and hatreds so much as creep in at court right now. We shall have only camaraderie for Christmas, that is my decree."

But her words rang hollow in her head. She feared murder had been committed in the precincts of her palace. Whether or not it was aimed at the "peacock" Leicester, the attack on the queen's privy dresser could threaten her court or even her crown.

For the Christmas Eve banquet that would begin the Twelve Days of Christmas, the front half of the Great Hall was cheek by jowl with the most powerful nobles of the land. Larded in among them at the elaborately set trestle tables were ambassadors, envoys, church legates, and senior servants. For minor courtiers and, behind them, other household servants, the rear of the vast hall held similar tables, though not quite as sumptuously appointed.

At the front of the hall, at the dais table with the queen, sat those of most noble rank: Margaret Stewart and Lord Darnley; Leicester; Sussex and his wife, Frances; the queen's Boleyn cousin, bluff, red-haired Henry Carey, Baron Hunsdon, whom Elizabeth called Harry, and his wife, Anne; and, as a special honor, Sir William Cecil and his lady, Mildred. But anyone in the hall who believed such seating paired her off with Leicester was much mistaken.

At the queen's behest, the musicians in their lofty gallery were momentarily silenced, the hall was hushed, and Cecil stood to read the announcement they had decided on:

HER GRACIOUS MAJESTY DECLARES THAT THIS TWELVE DAYS OF CHRISTMAS SHALL BE CARRIED ON AS PLANNED WITH SEVERAL EXCEPTIONS. DUE TO THE MOST UNFORTUNATE DEMISE TODAY OF ROYAL SERVANT HODGE THATCHER, DRESSER OF THE QUEEN'S PRIVY KITCHEN, THE COURT WILL HONOR HIS MEMORY IN THESE WAYS: TO WIT, THERE WILL BE NO PEACOCK SERVED THIS YEAR; SPECIAL PRAYERS WILL BE OFFERED FOR HIS DEPARTED SOUL AT CHURCH SERVICE TOMORROW; AND THE BRINGING IN OF THE YULE LOG TO THE CENTRAL HEARTH IN THIS HALL WILL BE DELAYED UNTIL AFTER THAT TIME OF REMEMBRANCE. ALSO, FESTIVITIES UNDER THE AEGIS OF THE LORD OF MISRULE, THIS YEAR THE EARL OF LEICESTER, ASSISTED BY THE QUEEN'S PRINCIPAL PLAYER AND MASTER OF REVELS, NED TOPSIDE, WILL BE POSTPONED UNTIL THE DAY AFTER CHRISTMAS, THOUGH LEICESTER WILL THEN NOT RULE BUT MISRULE FOR THE REMAINDER OF THIS YULETIDE SEASON.

Murmurings and whispers assailed the queen's ears. At the Lord Chamberlain's nod, lutes, shawms, gitterns, drums, and pipes began to play again from the musicians' second-story gallery.

"I believe this is a fair blend of mourning and yet letting life—and Christmas—go on," Elizabeth said to Cecil, raising her voice to be heard. "I suppose they're vexed about waiting for the Yule log, but everyone gets so giddy over that I couldn't countenance it, even if Hodge's body will be held for burial until after Twelfth Day."

Hodge's death hardly seemed to stem the eating and drinking, she noted, though the queen's own stomach had not settled since she had seen the corpse hanging as if it were another piece of Yuletide holly to be cast off after the revels. She merely picked at her favorite dishes and settled instead for the sweet fruit suckets she loved. Her mind wandered from the conversation, even from Robin's, whom she had more or less forgiven once again for meddling where he was not bidden.

"I believe I will take some hippocras instead of straight wine," she told her servers, "just to help with digesting all this. The food was fabulous, of course, even prepared and delivered under duress." She saw their eyes light with pleasure as bright as their new livery before they hurried away.

Elizabeth's gaze caught Cecil's. He had not missed that she had hardly tasted the array of dishes. When the hippocras was proffered to her, she downed it, then excused herself early, though she told her Lord Chamberlain to announce merely that she was tired and all could stay at their places. She only hoped, despite the exhaustion of this day, that her master cook, Roger Stout, would have something to tell her about Hodge Thatcher's motives for possible suicide. She was no doubt clutching at straws, but if she received only one gift for the holidays, she prayed it could be that no murderer stalked her court.

Cecil also excused himself early and joined the queen just as Roger Stout was escorted into her otherwise empty presence chamber. "Will you write down pertinent facts, my lord?" she whispered to Cecil as Stout stopped before the table where his two betters were seated.

He appeared to be both flushed with excitement and drained

by exhaustion; she noted well that the new livery she had given him today looked pleasing on him, but for a fresh splotch on the left shoulder.

"Clifford," she addressed her trusted yeoman guard as he was about to leave the room, "draw up a chair for Master Stout, as he has had a doubly trying day."

"You are most thoughtful, Your Majesty," Stout said as he rose from his bow, "and I am most grateful." When both she and Cecil praised the meal, he told them, "If the many dishes were garnished well, thanks be to George Brooks, Master Hodge's 'prentice of long standing. With your gracious permission, I'll elevate him to the position of dresser *pro tem* 'til you name another."

"That will be fine, Master Stout," the queen assured him as he sat in the chair Clifford brought from the back of the room. When Clifford went out, the muted sounds of laughter and music floated to them from below.

"And now," she went on, "will you tell us anything you know that might indicate—despite the bizarre garnishing of Hodge's body—that the poor man might have possibly done away with himself?"

" 'Tis mostly from knowing his state of mind, Your Majesty."

"Say on."

"Hodge Thatcher comes from a long line of thatchers, I mean, those who thatch roofs, you see. Not unusual for a name to come from a long-tended family occupation. The thing is, Your Majesty, his father expected him to take over the trade, especially when the old man, his sire, slid off a roof—out by Wimbledon, it was—and broke his back. Can't move from his waist down, the old man."

"So Master Hodge felt guilty over disappointing his father?"

she summarized. Glancing over Stout's head she could see a portrait of her own father hanging on the wainscotted wall; she had paid it little heed for months, but it suddenly seemed to be staring at her. When she first came to the throne, she used to be ever aware of it. Sometimes the eyes even seemed to follow her around the room. Though her royal sire had more than once declared a woman could never sit on England's throne, she was certain her father would be proud of her—wouldn't he?

"Aye, guess that would be part of it," Stout said, pulling her back to the present. "But, you see, 'twas Hodge's dream to be a cook and in London, and when he worked his way up in the Tudor kitchens, he never would go home. His mother missed him sore, their only child, I guess. She died last year, and after that his sire would never take the coins Hodge tried to send, a most bitter, unforgiving man, he was, e'en afore his tumble from the roof. But then he got turned out of his home, and right afore holiday time, but a week or so ago, it were."

"And all this weighed heavily on Hodge's mind," she said. "He told you so?"

"Not only that," he said, nodding vigorously, "but I was thinking about that stack of gold leaf. Secretary Cecil here had me talk to the guards at the larder, where we keep the leafing for special displays under lock and key. Seems Hodge told them he needed the entire amount of it on hand to do not only the peacock's beak but legs and feet, too, special for the queen's Christmas, he told them."

"But I saw the bird's body was roasted with the legs under it and not leafed as usual," the queen observed.

"So did I, Your Grace," Cecil put in, "not that Hodge could not have stretched the legs out after it was roasted and leafed them over then. But still that stack of leaf was far too much for what he needed."

Hardly able to contain her excitement, Elizabeth stood and started to pace. Both men jumped to their feet so as not to sit in her presence. "Are you thinking, Master Stout," she asked, "that Hodge might have been intending to take or send at least some of that gold leaf to his father so that he might keep his home, or be well tended by someone? Perhaps he contacted his father or heard from him and—even partially paralyzed and homeless—the stubborn man would not accept charity from his son, not even at Christmastide. Hodge rued letting his people down and killed himself? Do I jump too far afield?"

"My thinking exactly, Your Majesty," Stout said, " 'specially 'cause of this."

He felt in the inside of his new livery doublet first on one side, then the other, until he produced a grease-spattered scrap of paper he carefully unfolded. When he held it out, Cecil reached across the table to take it from him and offer it to the queen.

"Open and read it, my lord," she said as her thoughts raced.

It was possible that Hodge had been despondent over his family problems, she surmised, gripping her hands together. Perhaps when he decided to kill himself, on the spur of the moment, he decked himself out to show whoever found him that he had lived proudly in his place as royal dresser and garnisher, however much his father criticized his chosen trade. And perhaps he had left behind a suicide note.

"I am having this writ by the sexton of the church," Cecil read, squinting at the folded paper and tilting it toward the bank of beeswax candles on the table. *"Money cannot replace nor buy the time you did not spend with us, come to us, and help me in the proud trade of your forefathers. You*

made your fancy bed with cooking for the family that ruined the true church. You chose their table finery and all that, so lie in it, that bed you made. You cared not a fig for us, and naught can make up for that now your mother's gone and I be like this, not even half a man and that without a home."

"So cruel, for all of them, and at Christmas," the queen whispered, stopping her pacing so fast her skirts swayed. She felt a sudden chill and clasped her elbows in her hands. Hodge's family had hated hers, but Hodge had chosen loyalty to the Tudors. Though this was not the suicide note she had been expecting, sadly, self-slaying seemed entirely possible now.

"The note's not signed," Cecil said with a catch in his voice.

"I warrant it did not have to be," she said. "The way it is worded could have sent him off the edge of despair. To lie in that bed, which his father cursed, perhaps Hodge defiantly became that peacock, which was fine looking, though it was dead."

"Aye, he was always proud of how he dressed the peacocks, swans, boar's heads, too," Master Stout said. "But maybe how gay and glad we all were in the kitchens that day made him think how wretched he was, so he climbed up on that stool, brought the chain pulley down a bit, and did the dreadful deed right then."

The three of them stood silent until the queen thanked Master Stout. He bowed and left the room, saying no more.

"You're no doubt much relieved," Cecil said from the other end of the table.

"I am. My stomachache is even better. It all fits. Perhaps now I will not call the late meeting of my Privy Plot Council, and we can all get back to normal after the prayers for the poor man's soul tomorrow. He won't be buried in hallowed ground now, but I will have Stout send a message to that unforgiving father of his. What? Why are you looking at me that way, my lord?"

"I am tempted to tell you all is well, but you have not yet heard some other things I have learned from your commanding me to observe the coroner's work and the scene of the death."

Her hopes plummeted; her stomach cramped again, despite that hippocras she'd drunk after dinner.

"When I appointed you my chief advisor, Cecil, I charged you to always give me true counsel, whatever the risk or cost."

"Then you'd best call that meeting, Your Majesty. More than that booted print in the cumin under Hodge's body suggests that foul play was indeed afoot."

Chapter the Fourth

Maids of Honor

Make pastry enough for a double-crust pie. Preheat brick oven by burning wood or coals inside, then raking them out. Roll out pastry and cut in rounds, then fit in small bun or tartlet tins. Prick pastry with fork tines. Bring to near boil ½ pint fresh cow's milk with 4 level tablespoons of white breadcrumbs (2-day-old bread is best). Remove from heat and leave for a few minutes. Into that mixture beat 8 teaspoons butter, cut in cubes. Beat in 2 tablespoons sugar, grated rind of 1 lemon, and ¾ cup ground blanched almonds. Although the mixture has some texture, be sure it is not lumpy. Beat in 3 good hen's eggs. Half fill the pastry shells and bake for 15 minutes or until pastry has pulled away from side of tins and filling is golden brown. Carefully lift pastry from tins and cool before eating.

IT WAS NEARLY ELEVEN O'CLOCK THAT NIGHT WHEN THE queen opened the hastily called meeting of her Privy Plot Council in her presence chamber. "I am not certain that we even have a murder to investigate," she explained, "but considering the holiday season and all that depends on its going well, we'd best at least put our heads together on Hodge Thatcher's strange demise."

She glanced around the table. Cecil sat next to her, frowning at a written report under his folded hands. Across the table, Meg Milligrew was wide-eyed; Jenks, beside her, looked intent, too. At the far end of the table, Ned Topside seemed glum and distracted when he should have been happy, for he had told her he'd found his old players' troupe and they were coming to court tomorrow.

On Elizabeth's other side, Harry, Baron Hunsdon, was disturbed by being so suddenly summoned from the festivities, but then he was the one among them who knew nothing of these events yet. He was probably alarmed because each time her covert council had struggled to solve a murder, deceit and danger followed. The queen rued Kat's absence, but she needed her sleep and should not be disturbed by unrest. Elizabeth longed to invite her maid of honor, Rosie, to replace Kat in this company, but if a murderer were out to disgrace Robin, her little band would have to investigate Rosie's kin Lord Sussex—along with about half the court.

The queen concluded her opening remarks with "Now that I have summarized for you the case for the poor man's suicide, my lord Cecil will present the other possibility."

"Granted," he began, "some of the physical evidence at the scene of death could be attributed to a suicide. Hodge could have half undressed himself, for his breeches, doublet, and shoes were found under his worktable. The coroner informed me that, for some reason, suicides sometimes take off their shoes, and Hodge was barefooted."

"On the other hand," the queen put in, "his disrobing could mean he was getting ready for his new livery and therefore expected to live."

"After all," Ned said as if rushing to her aid, "Her Majesty's interview with Master Stout tips the scales toward suicide."

"I'd like to believe that, too," the queen said, "but you are not, Ned, writing the script for the meeting as if it were some play."

Ned frowned and shifted in his seat as Cecil went on. "Also, the man could have climbed on that stool and slipped the knotted noose around his own neck, having donned the skinned coat of the peacock and having stuck those tail feathers carefully under his armpits. However, to be fair, before I proceed, let's listen to someone who came upon the death scene before I did."

"Jenks?" Cecil said, turning his way. "Anything to add at this point before I list the evidence to suggest we are dealing not with suicide but with assault and murder?"

"I found it hard to believe," Jenks said, "that when that noose—made of twisted twine, more or less a thin but strong rope really, was the same sort he used to truss up birds or boars for roasting—now, what was I going to say? Oh, that I find it hard to credit, if Hodge hanged himself, that he didn't flail around in choking to death and ruin the way those feathers stuck out, spaced just so," he concluded with gestures.

"Another good point," the queen said. "If he didn't struggle, he must have wanted his own death—and to be arrayed like that."

"Or if someone hanged him," Cecil countered, "the culprit held his hands in place or rearranged those feathers after the final struggle. Neither I nor the coroner saw ligature marks on his wrists or arms to suggest someone had him tied while he died, then removed such ties. But wait—here is the report I had the coroner write out and sign, and it is most compelling."

The queen noted that everyone seemed to take in a deep breath and go as still as a statue. All turned toward Cecil.

"I won't read you all the petty details and the Latin medical phrases," he said, "but to put it briefly, Hodge was knocked hard enough on the head to fracture his skull. The four-inch-by-eight-inch wound on the top back of his pate," he went on, pointing at his own head, "was no doubt received before he either stepped up on that stool—or was lifted up to be hanged from a rope attached to the pulley chains."

"He hardly took a hit like that," Jenks said, "by bumping into one of those hanging kettles, however big some are. They all hang high."

"And," Meg added, "it's not likely he got a knock on the top back of his head accidentally falling. Not and then climbed up there, like he was out of his head, for such a blow would make him dizzy at least, stun or knock him out at worst. If someone hit him, someone must have helped him up on that stool."

"Agreed," Harry put in, as if coming to life at last. "It's highly doubtful that the man would hit himself to make it look like an attack. If it's not a crime of passion, it sounds like a crime of planning."

"I fear so," Cecil said. "He was probably hit by the man who left a boot print in the spilled cumin grit on the floor—his murderer, who helped him look as if he might have hanged himself."

The queen listened with a heavy heart; yes, it must be a murder, one she could hardly ignore. Literally from up his sleeve, Cecil produced a second paper and unfolded it to show the sketch of the boot print she had requested.

"To size as well as shape?" she asked, gripping her hands hard in her lap.

"It is. Though it may not belong to whoever hit Hodge, gave him a hoist up, and knocked over that stool, it's a place to start."

"Was there blood," Harry asked, "on his skull up under that peacock skin?"

"Indeed, though it seems the bird skin acted as a sort of bandage to mat and pool the blood," Cecil explained. "Yet I doubt that the skin was placed on his head as an afterthought to hide that blood. It all seems diabolically designed. I believe the murderer slipped into Hodge's workroom with the intent to kill and display his victim, but for what purpose or motive I do not know."

"That," Elizabeth said, "is what we must learn to find the killer."

"By the way," Cecil added, turning over the coroner's report, "I've sketched something here I believe is as significant as the boot print."

"What's that, then?" Meg asked as they all gazed at the strange shape.

"I warrant it's the circumference of the head wound," the queen answered for him.

Jenks leaned forward, frowning at the sketch of the oblong wound with rivulets of blood or some crude pattern roughly drawn in. Ned quickly rose from his seat and leaned close to see.

"Yet his face was bluish," Elizabeth went on, "which means he did indeed strangle or suffocate from the noose—but after he may have been stunned enough to be lifted up there and dressed with the peacock regalia. If he were dazed, that could also explain someone's being able to hold his hands at his sides while he weakly struggled and so died, but without disturbing the symmetrical arrangement of feathers under his arms or making ligature marks."

Cecil nodded. Harry seemed silently thoughtful, and her servants still wide-eyed. Only Ned looked as if he'd like to argue, but for once he said nothing.

"Then I must cut this meeting short," the queen said, rising and scraping her chair back. "Cecil, Jenks, and I must return to the site of the murder instantly to search for what could have caused this mark—the first of the two murder weapons, in effect, if we count the noose, too."

"I looked around as best I could while the coroner worked," Cecil said as everyone rose. "Whatever caused this blow, Hodge's murderer must have taken it with him."

"I suppose it has to be a him," Meg put in as Jenks squeezed her shoulder and hurried after the queen, "because a woman probably couldn't lift him, but she could wear a boot like that. Are we going to check the boot soles of everyone to see if one fits that shape or has cumin stuck in the cracks of it, Your Grace?"

"That would be fruitless with so many at court. The culprit could merely change boots, though the size of the foot may help us to narrow down possibilities later. Meg, I can't ask my maids for a cape this late, or they'll know I'm going out. Lend me yours, if you please. My lord Harry, best go back down to join your wife and keep an eye on things below. If anyone asks how I am, report that I am fine but resting until tomorrow.

"Cecil, Jenks, and I," she went on, stopping in the door to her chamber, "will go down my privy staircase to the river, out and around to the kitchen court, and in that way, to avoid everyone still lingering about the Great Hall or gadding about in the corridors. Meg and Ned, you will stay here and, if something demands my presence, Ned, hie yourself to fetch me, while Meg speaks for me through the door as if I am too tired to come out."

As the queen took Meg's squirrel-lined wool cape, Elizabeth realized her herbalist did not look as happy as usual to play queen, even if only for Ned's eyes. Perhaps, for once, she didn't want to be alone with him, she thought as she hurried toward her bed-chamber, where her father's old privy staircase could be entered behind an arras. Jenks didn't look too happy to be leaving Ned and Meg behind, either.

The slap of chill night wind shocked the queen at first. Meg's cloak was thin compared to hers. She must give the girl one on New Year's Day to ward off the sting of winter. At least this had a hood to pull up and gather close about her neck.

They had not brought a lantern, for they knew the palace windows overhead would light their way, and a nearly full moon shone off thin snow and thickening river ice. The queen's stomach growled, as if in foreboding; she realized she should have eaten something more, however unsettled she'd felt.

"The Thames is near frozen clear across," Jenks said. "We'll have that Frost Fair for certain."

The lights of Lambeth Palace, home of the Bishop of London and Martin Bane, when Bane wasn't at court protecting their interests, shone across the expanse of ice. Lambeth had its own barge with oarsmen, but with the Thames gone nearly solid, Elizabeth realized that the churchmen must have been traveling rutted roads and crossing crowded London Bridge. They'd be happy enough to soon use a cart or sleigh. When ice must be traversed, horses wore studded shoes, and wheels had nails pounded through them for traction.

Before the river tidal flats began, though they were but frozen mud now, a small path wended its way around the palace's stony skirts, and they followed that. One more turn and they could see the torchlit porter's door that guarded the kitchen block from the public street on the other side of the walls.

"That reminds me," Elizabeth whispered. "Jenks, did you

inquire from the day porter if anyone unusual came in or out of the kitchen-block gate this afternoon?"

"Yes, Your Grace. No traffic for once. All the Twelve Days supplies were already in, he said, and no one wants to leave where all the good times are—that's how he put it. Except for Ned."

"Ned put it how?"

"No, I mean, Ned went out the porter's door this afternoon, looking most distraught, too, didn't even answer the porter's 'heigh ho' to him. The poor man—the porter, Your Grace— thinks Ned's really the hail-fellow-well-met he plays in the comedies."

"Why would Topside be going out this back gate today?" Cecil asked sharply.

"He learned his old troupe of players is in town," Elizabeth explained, "so I gave him permission to invite them for a performance or two before all this happened. And he was vexed because I named Leicester as Lord of Misrule. Cecil, get us past the porter, won't you, as I have no wish for him to know it's me."

He walked ahead and knocked on the bolted door; his words floated to Jenks and the queen. "My lady and I have been walking by the river with a guard, but it's far too cold. We want to get back in by the kitchens, get a bit of warmth from the big hearth fires."

"Oh, my lord secretary, certes," the man cried and rattled his keys overlong opening the gate. With Elizabeth holding her hood close to her face, the three of them hustled past before he caught a glimpse of anyone else. Icy wind even here in the courtyard swirled up Elizabeth's skirts, but once inside, it was warmer, almost steamy with mingled, succulent smells. Despite the work they'd come to do, the queen felt even hungrier.

"I told Stout to seal off the dresser's workroom and let the man who replaced him work elsewhere for a few days," Cecil said, "lest we should need to return like this."

"Good planning, my lord," she said. "Jenks, go find Stout and tell him that we're here and why—and bring back some lanterns again."

He hastened to obey while Cecil unwrapped the thick twine stretched across the door from latch to hinge. Neither rope nor string, it looked to be the same sturdy stock that had been used in multiple strands to make the hangman's noose. Cecil opened the door. The darkness within seemed profound, almost a living, breathing being. In the pale slab of light from the hall sconce, the queen's eyes adjusted slowly. She imagined she could see the corpse still hanging amidst the pots and chains, a man sprouting feathers as if he could swoop at them.

She jumped as light leaped in behind her and Cecil. Jenks held one large lantern, and her master cook two more.

"Your Majesty," Stout said, "I had no idea you'd be back and at this hour. The staff is yet cleaning up and having a bit of our own feast, though there's a pall on things from what happened here. Still, you said, Yule will go on."

"You are doing what is right, Master Stout. I simply wanted you to know we are here. Please return to your people without divulging my presence, and I'll send Jenks for you if I need you further. By the way, did you hear the coroner say Hodge had a head wound?" she asked as he set his lanterns on the table and started for the door.

"I did," he said, turning back, "but assumed it was made by his bumping against or falling on something—a corner of his work-table or a fancy bowl, though I overheard the coroner say it seemed to resemble a fancy sword hilt, one molded or sculpted, but I deemed the latter quite impossible."

"I appreciate your help and discretion in this delicate matter. There will be nothing more right now," she told him, as she recalled the constant rattle of Sussex's ceremonial sword. The problem was, Elizabeth thought, not so much that Master Stout was clever only in the kitchen but that he could not conceive of evil in his narrow realm as she could in her broader one.

The three of them thoroughly searched the room for what might have been used to hit Hodge. They found nothing telltale or unusual on the floor, worktable, or shelves, or even aloft in the hanging kettles and pots she had Jenks peer into while he stood on the very stool the murderer had perhaps used to tie the noose and hoist Hodge.

"What was that low, growling sound?" Jenks cried, looking under the table again. "Not the wind?"

"It's my stomach," the queen muttered. "I should have eaten more at dinner, and that hippocras helped me not one whit."

"This search is a dead end," Cecil said, "if you'll excuse the pun."

"We must conclude that the murderer took the weapon with him," Elizabeth said with a sigh. "If we find it, we may find our man, but exactly what are we looking for? If only we still had the body, I'd take a close look at that blow myself."

"If you're up to it," Cecil said, "we could go look, as the corpse is not far from here. You never asked me where we had the coroner stow Hodge, so I didn't think you wanted to know. The ground's so frozen, he can't be buried until it thaws, though, at least, it sounds now as if the poor wretch is headed for a grave in hallowed ground instead of some potter's field with self-slayers."

"Then where is he?" she asked. "Surely, not in the palace proper and not in my kitchens!"

"In the boathouse on the riverbank."

"Is it locked or guarded?"

"A guard would freeze out there. It's barred and locked, yes, with all your barges off the ice now, but I still have the extra key," he said and, with a taut smile, produced it on his jingling chain of them.

"Bring that largest lantern, Jenks," she said, redonning Meg's cloak, "and, my lord, we'll need another." As they went out into the corridor, Stout stood there with a laden tray.

"I've been waiting to offer you a late-night repast when you emerged," he explained, his eyes darting among the three of them in the light of the two lanterns they carried. On the tray were tankards of beer, no doubt much like the ones the staff was enjoying now, and a little plate of cheese tarts—no, they were those lemon custard ones everyone called Maids of Honor she'd passed over earlier this evening.

"I know you like these, Your Majesty," Stout said, "and you did not eat a great deal at the Christmas Eve feast."

She merely nodded and, despite their terrible task ahead, reached for a tart. Murder or not, she was famished, and it both annoyed and touched her that even her master cook knew that she had not eaten much this eve. Would she ever become accustomed to the way her people watched her every move as if she were the head of a massive family?

At that thought, a shudder swept her. Despite the fact that Hodge Thatcher's family had obviously hated the Protestant Tudors for "ruining the true church," as the note put it, Hodge had chosen loyalty to her. Since this was indeed a murder, she must try to solve it for the memory of the man himself and not only to assure the safety of her court or crown. Any crime that struck at one of her people, cook to clerk to courtier, must be solved and punished.

Cecil and Jenks also took a drink and downed a tart—actually, Jenks ate three. When Elizabeth indicated she'd have no more, Master Stout wrapped up the rest of the pastries in a cloth and handed them to Jenks.

"They say, you know, Your Majesty," Stout said, turning back to her with the hint of a bow, "that your mother when she was maid of honor made these tarts for your royal sire."

"I've heard that, Master Stout, but don't credit it a bit. More like they were concocted by some clever pastry cook who knew he could charge more for them if they could be tied to such a tale. My royal father only favored massive portions, so these are much too dainty and delicate for him—or most men," she added as Jenks's big paw managed to crush another tart to crumbs before he could get it in his mouth.

Meg stood at the oriel windows of the queen's bedroom and watched the moon glaze a path on the white Thames. "It looks pretty but so dreadful cold out there," she remarked to Ned, who was seated at the queen's table as he had been yesterday, once again writing furiously.

"Chilly in here, too," he muttered.

"With this hearth blazing?"

"I spoke metaphorically, Mistress Milligrew—ah, I mean, Your Most Glorious and Gracious Majesty," he said, looking up. "If you keep up the way you've been treating me, I shall dub you 'the Ice Queen' and write you as such into the Christmas entertainment I am planning for my troupe's arrival tomorrow."

"If I'm treating you cold, it's only because you've treated me that way."

"Really?" he said, tossing down his quill. "Did it ever cross *your* mind that I might have a few important and weighty things on *my* mind this season? And now, the queen's off on a hunt for a murderer, and who needs that complication?"

"You're just angry because you're not Lord of Misrule this year and can't get by with all your high-and-mighty decrees as you always have, going about masked, kissing all the girls, the ladies, too——"

"Aha! Do I detect green eyes?"

"You're the one with the green eyes, and you know well enough how to use them. No, I'm not jealous, just in love with a man who, by comparison, makes you look pretty bad. As for *your* foul mood, *you* ought to be happy the queen's taking your old fellows in for the holidays."

"Happy as a hawk in a windstorm," he groused. "One member of the troupe is new and untested, and a bit of a climber, I'm afraid, and I'm going to have to take some of my precious time to keep a watch on him."

"Hm," she said. "Takes one to know one, so——"

She stopped talking midthought as Ned rose and came quickly to stand behind her at the window. She spun to look out again so he wouldn't be pressing her, face to face, against it. He leaned a hand on the deep sill as if to block her in or embrace her, but she saw he was craning his neck to stare out the window at something down by the iced-in barge landings.

"Just keep an eye on him yourself, name of Giles Chatam," Ned said, his mouth so close it stirred the hair at her temple and warmed her ear.

"You mean he's a ladies' man, too," she goaded, "and you don't think I'd be safe around him?"

"I mean he's likely to be disguised half the time because I'm writing him parts where he's masked and cloaked, dark parts, the villains."

"While you play the innocents and heroes, I suppose," she said and managed a laugh. "Best be careful, Ned Topside, queen's master player, or all your friends will see right through you," she scolded and, most unqueen-like, pushed him back and darted to the table to read the playlet he'd written.

"I'm going out," he announced, hard on her heels; he snatched the paper before she could read it.

"But you're to stay here."

"I'll be back directly, but I've got to use the jakes and can hardly borrow Her Majesty's velvet close stool, now can I?"

"How do you know about something as privy as her close stool?"

"Let's just say," he muttered, "she's as good as dumped me in it lately."

"Ned Topside!"

"Stop fretting. My stomach's just upset by something I ate at dinner, and it's ruining my disposition, too."

Meg wondered if he actually had a wench to meet. He didn't look ill. She knew he was vexed with the queen, but that gave him no leave to ignore her wishes. Hands on hips, Meg watched Ned walk away, open the door, duck under the yeomen's crossed halberds before they could react, and disappear at a good clip down the hall.

The door to the boathouse moaned mournfully, but the interior provided shelter from the cutting wind as the queen, Cecil, and

Jenks stepped inside. The large wooden structure sat upon rows of sawhorses and four-foot stilts along the river bank, but the entrance was level with the smaller of the two barge landings. Not only were the valuable rivercraft being kept under lock and key; the thick double doors were barricaded by a large beam bar the two men had lifted to get in.

Their two lanterns illumined the queen's massive state barge sitting high on tree trunks where it had been rolled in. Two other passenger barges and several working boats were hulking shadows in the depths of the low-ceilinged building. The single small window at the back overlooked the frozen river.

"Over here, in this far corner," Cecil said and started away. Elizabeth followed, then Jenks with the second lantern.

Floorboards groaned under their feet; the entire edifice creaked from the cold like old bones. Elizabeth and Jenks slowed their strides when they approached the ten-foot wherry in the corner. A sliver of moonlight sliced across the boat's prow.

"I had him laid in here like a mummy in a sarcophagus, so we'll have to unwrap his head," Cecil said, leaning over the side of the boat.

As Elizabeth stepped closer and looked into the ribbed hull, she wished she hadn't eaten even one little tart. In this cold, no odor emanated from the body, but the sight of the shrouded form shook her deeply. Cecil's mummy comparison aside, Hodge was laid out lengthwise in the boat, as if he were about to be launched for a fiery Viking funeral.

"Your Grace," Cecil interrupted her thoughts, "if you can hold a light for us, we can unwrap the top of his head, keeping his face covered."

"Yes, good idea," she said, taking the lantern Cecil held.

Jenks put down his lantern and little bundle of pastries on the wherry's single seat and climbed inside the hull to support Hodge's shoulders while Cecil opened the shroud from the top; they worked together to turn the body so that the back of the head was visible.

"Definitely struck from behind and with a downward blow," the queen observed, her voice sounding as shrill as did the wind through the boathouse chinks and cracks. They all startled at a distant hollow boom followed by a crackling sound.

"Just river ice settling," Cecil said. "It will be solid soon, but back to business. Hopefully, he never knew what hit him."

"But we must discern exactly what did," she said, "for it is our best hope to solve this riddle. There—hold him a moment just like that. Yes, I see the shape of the blow." Holding the lantern in one hand, she rested her other on an oarlock and bent closer. "But his thick, blood-matted hair keeps us from clearly discerning whatever pattern was on the weapon," she observed. "The coroner at least should have washed his head there. I wish we had some sort of lather to shave that spot for a close look."

"I could go fetch some and a razor," Jenks offered.

"No, I think that won't be necessary. Since the coroner is finished with the body, and we are the ones who will bury him when there's a thaw, I don't think anyone will even notice what I intend. Jenks, let me borrow your knife and those Maids of Honor, if you please."

Both men held the corpse while Elizabeth proceeded to smear the custard filling over the area on Hodge's head obscured by blood and hair. Carefully but awkwardly, her hand shaking, she began to shave his matted hair away.

"I can do that, Your Grace," Cecil said.

"Just keep holding him. I'm going to use this cloth to wipe it off, and then we shall all see what pattern of murder weapon lies beneath."

Her belly cramped from leaning into the boat as well as from her stomach-churning task. At least Cecil's sketch had captured texture as well as shape: Whatever had hit Hodge from behind had dented in his flesh and skull in a pattern. Within the outer form, there was a sort of band or belt with what might be an insignia in the middle of the band.

"A coat of arms or design, even a short word?" she asked, shifting the lantern to try to make the contours of the wound stand out in shadow. "If only we could read it!"

"As the coroner suggested, made by a sword hilt?" Cecil said. "Or by a large kitchen utensil?"

"That brighter light's better," Jenks observed, and Elizabeth nodded until her stomach cartwheeled again.

"What light?" she asked. "No one's moved a lantern, and the moonlight can't shift that fast. Could someone have a light outside?"

She tore her gaze away from the corpse. Through the single window of the boathouse, moonlight flooded in. No, it could not be that, she reasoned, for this was golden, warm light, not that of the winter moon.

"Someone must have lit a fire outside on the ice," she said. "We'll be seen leaving here and going back to the palace."

Both men looked up as she hurried to the window, then scrubbed at the swirling frost patterns on it so she could see out. She suddenly recalled how Hodge, lying in the boat, had looked as if he were about to be launched for a Viking funeral.

"We must run!" she cried. "I wager someone's lit a fire under us!"

Jenks dropped the body and vaulted from the wherry. Grabbing a lantern, he ran to the door and rattled it. "It's locked or barred from outside!" he shouted. "We're trapped!"

Chapter the Fifth

Mince Pie Mangers

This Yuletide variation of mincemeat pie should be baked in a rectangular crust, in the shape of a manger to recall the birth of the Savior. But the following recipe for the filling must be made months ahead so it can ferment. Mixtures of spices and liquors well preserve perishable meats and fruits.

Grind or crush (some use large stones for this mincing) 1½ pounds boiled beef, ½ pound suet. Combine with 4 cups beef broth and the following: 1½ teaspoons salt; 2 pounds apples, peeled, cored, and chopped; 3 cups brown sugar, tightly packed; 2 cups raisins; 1½ cup currants; 2 teaspoons powdered cinnamon; 1 teaspoon each of powdered mace, cloves, and nutmeg; 2 cups finely chopped candied rinds; 2 lemons with rind, ground up; 3 oranges with rind, ground up; 1½ cups cider; 2 cups of red or white wine, such as Rhenish or sack. Seal and age at least 3 months.

"WILL ONE OF THESE SMALL OARS FIT BETWEEN THE doors to lift the bar?" the queen asked Jenks as she and Cecil rushed to join him at the entrance to the boathouse. "I doubt if someone has the other key to lock us in. It's probably just barred." But she saw that the crack between the doors would take nothing wider than a sword, and such would never lift that heavy piece of wood.

They could smell smoke now, curling through the floorboard

cracks; they could hear the crisp crackle of flames. Surely, the queen thought, on the open riverbank in the cold of night, a fire had not been set by vagabonds trying to keep warm.

"Someone will see the blaze and come running!" Cecil cried, then began coughing in the thickening pall of smoke.

"But maybe not in time!" Jenks shouted. "I can break the window, but it's high up from the ice."

"Yes, break it!" Elizabeth ordered.

The men lifted a large oar from the state barge and smashed the window. Cold air and smoke belched in but, God be thanked, no flames so high yet. The men ran the oar around the small window, knocking out the panes of thick glass and their diamond-shaped metal frames.

"I'll drop down first to be sure no one's waiting," Jenks said, ripping off his surcoat. She thought he would discard it to keep it from catching fire, but he laid it over the jagged sill of the shattered window. Just behind their feet, tongues of flames flicked through the floorboards.

Drawing his sword and using only one hand to drop, Jenks went lithely out the window.

"All clear!" he shouted up. "No one!"

"All at tables and revels," the queen muttered, but she sucked in smoke and began choking, too. Her skirts and cloak burdened her, so she threw the cloak out first, then divested herself of layers of petticoats and heaved them out. With Cecil's help above and Jenks's below, she climbed out, dangled, then dropped the short way. Jenks half caught her, but the bank was slick with frozen mud; she sat down hard and sprawled out onto the river ice. Jenks came sliding after her, but she told him, "I'm fine. Help Cecil!"

He was soon out the window, too. " 'S blood," she cursed as the two men helped her climb the banks with her gown hems dragging, "I'll have the head of whoever set that blaze. And, I warrant, we'll find it's a villain who's as adept with nooses as with firebrands."

Even the voices of the boys' choir from St. Paul's, echoing so sweetly in the chapel at Whitehall, could not calm the queen the next morning. At the beginning of the Christmas service, as she had requested, a prayer had been offered for Hodge Thatcher's soul, though it had not been announced that someone—perhaps someone here in the congregation—had killed the man.

Not only did Elizabeth have a murder on her hands, but she was blessed to still be alive herself. Last night, Jenks had summoned help to fight the fire while she and Cecil had beat a hasty retreat back to the privy staircase. But with the river frozen, water to douse the flames had been slow coming. The building, with Hodge's body inside, had burned to its footers. Only the state barge had been saved, rolled out at the last minute because it sat so near the doors.

A hue and cry had gone out for the vagabonds who were supposedly to blame, but the queen believed Hodge's murderer had set the fire, at best to warn her, at worst to roast her like the Christmas peacock or suckling pig. Unfortunately, the press of people trying to put the fire out had trampled any other boot prints they might have matched to the one Cecil had sketched.

Elizabeth shifted in her seat. The service had gone on for nearly an hour already, most of it with Bishop Grindal's droning sermon.

"The holy scriptures of this blessed morn are, of course," he intoned, "readings of the nativity of our Lord."

His shrill voice roused her from her exhaustion and agonizing. However did this man come so far with that voice, she wondered. There were many fine, deep-voiced ministers she had known, but this one had talents and powers to rise above his greatest weakness.

As if he were a politican and not a prelate, the silver-haired, portly bishop had a habit of seeming to smile no matter what he said; sometimes it seemed his plump face would crack open like a porcelain ball. It was ironic that Grindal always looked quite smug and jolly compared to his chief aide, Martin Bane. Thin and black-garbed as a raven, Vicar Bane stood beneath the pulpit as if he were some sort of enforcer of whatever his earthly master might decree.

Elizabeth felt hemmed in with the Earl of Sussex on her right hand and the Scots envoy, Simon MacNair, on her left, though she had invited both men to those seats. Margaret Stewart and Lord Darnley were also in plain sight, across the aisle in the front row. Behind her sat Kat and Rosie. Robin, fuming at not being asked to sit next to her, was on MacNair's other side. She must tell Robin, at least, what had really happened to Hodge. He and everyone else here today knew he had enemies at court, but not that one particular person had stooped to both mockery and murder—and perhaps even attempted a fiery assassination of the queen.

"So it was while they were in Bethlehem, the days were completed for her to be delivered. And she brought forth her firstborn Son, and wrapped Him in swaddling cloths, and laid Him in a manger.

"That humble manger," the bishop continued, looking up from his text, "must be a reminder to us of humility. It is wrong to pursue overly lighthearted practices at this season. For instance, I speak to those who allow your mincemeat pies to be fashioned in the shape of the manger and brought to your feasts and who then celebrate with great abandon. And is it not pure, pagan superstition that a person will have as many happy months in the upcoming year as mince pies one tastes?"

Mince pies, Elizabeth thought. Bane had called snowballing profane yesterday, and now Grindal was scolding about mince pies? Did they not see the important things in this holiday season? Did they not know the large political and social as well as religious issues she faced, which made snowballing and pies mere trifles?

"Have not some of you," he plunged on, "even decorated that pie with springs of holly or the pagan mistletoe? Have I not heard that some have placed upon such a pie the pastry form of a babe, which was then devoured with said pie?"

Elizabeth had given him no leave to scold her people for age-old traditions of the day. He and his spokesman Bane presumed far too much of late. Not daring to look her way, Grindal continued reading,

"Now after Jesus was born in Bethlehem of Judea, behold, wise men from the East came to Jerusalem, saying, 'Where is He who has been born King of the Jews? For we have seen His star in the East and have come to worship Him.'"

Though she was tempted to stand and order Grindal to stick to such readings and not his own rantings, the queen settled back in her seat again. She wanted nothing to ruin the beauty or sanctity of this day. Already the season had gone awry with Hodge's death and the Christmas Eve tradition of the Yule log being postponed until today. Still trying to find a compromise between mourning for a death and rejoicing in the Lord's birth, she had asked that a religious mystery play be performed tonight and had postponed the Lord of Misrule's antics yet again.

"That star was a sign to the wise men of that day," Grindal said. "And today, do not those who are wise read the signs of the times, too? When lightning struck the dome of St. Paul's three years ago and caused the fire, some said it was a sign that God Himself was displeased with the indulgent, extravagant way that some ornate, Catholic practices were yet clung to in this land while it is claimed such things are purged and purified."

"And," the queen muttered only loud enough for those around her to hear, "some said that fire was God's displeasure with a radical, Puritan-leaning bishop who can do naught but criticize and carp!"

Simon MacNair, despite the fact he represented the Catholic queen of Scotland, murmured his approval of her words.

"And have we not now had a like sign?" the bishop went on, while Vicar Bane nodded as if his head were hollow and set on a stick. "The fire which destroyed the royal boathouse last night seems a warning against too much levity or frivolity at court this time of year. And the death of the man in the kitchens who was to decorate the peacock—one wonders if we are not harkening back to the pre-Papist church days of yore when the pagans had a human sacrifice—"

"What?" Elizabeth cried. "We harken back to no such thing!"

Pews creaked and satins rustled as heads snapped her way. Bishop Grindal seemed momentarily cowed, though his lackey Bane looked furious at her interruption.

"I'll not have my London bishop prophesying or pronouncing

judgment on the court and Christmas!" she went on. "You are not here to cast a pall but to give your blessing. Choir, another song, something for a recessional. Let us have 'Good Christian Men Rejoice,' for that is what we should all do on these Twelve Days, beginning with the bringing in of the belated Yule log to the Great Hall forthwith. Though there will be no mumming this evening, we shall view a mystery play by a visiting troupe called the Queen's Country Players. Bishop, will you dismiss us with your blessing?"

Elizabeth of England stood, glaring at Grindal and Bane. Everyone else rose. His voice still defiant, Grindal pronounced a blessing on them all. The queen barely let him get out his *Amen* before she bade Robin escort her out.

Elizabeth cheered with her courtiers and servants as six men dragged the huge Yule log into the Great Hall. It vexed her that Bishop Grindal—who had, she'd heard, hastily departed the palace, leaving Bane to oversee things—had been right about one matter: She'd read in some history book that in olden, pagan days, this part of the festival had included a human sacrifice.

The log was actually a tree trunk, marked a year before, on last Christmas Day. Though the lengths of logs varied by the status of households and the size of hearths, any of the queen's palaces could take one of ten feet. Her arm around Kat's shoulders, Elizabeth watched it drawn along the floor to impromptu singing and some dancing to carols played by the musicians in the gallery overhead.

"Oh, prettily decorated!" Kat cried in her excitement and clapped her hands like a child. "I haven't seen one that gaily done with garlands and ribbons for years!"

"I am happy that you are happy, my Kat," Elizabeth told her.

Everyone followed the log as it was rolled and lifted onto andirons; burning brands were thrust under its middle.

"Wait!" Robin cried. "Who has the piece of it kept to light next year's log? As Lord of Misrule, it is my duty to keep it safe."

"I see you have studied your duties well," Elizabeth called to him over the hubbub. He did not look so angry at her now. Robin had always liked being the center of attention, and she did not mind sharing that with him today. It warmed her to see everyone so merry, though the smell of smoke and the sight of flames recalled too well her nightmare in the boathouse last night.

"I have indeed studied my duties well, Your Majesty," Robin said, suddenly kneeling at her feet. Sussex, evidently not to be surpassed by his nemesis, knelt, too, only to have his wife, Lady Frances, giggle and hook some holly behind his ear.

"All right," Robin said, rising and clapping, "let's hear more singing, not from the fine boys' choir this time, but the likes of you revelers!"

With Robin himself leading, the crowd broke into "The Yule Log Carol." Even Kat's trembling voice swelled, Elizabeth's bell-clear one, too, and several fine ones she did not recognize until she turned and saw Ned had brought his band of players into the hall with him. They were singing out strong from the dais that would soon serve as their stage:

> Part of the log be kept to tend
> The Christmas log next year.
> And where 'tis safely kept,
> The fiend can do no mischief here.

"The fiend," Cecil said suddenly in her ear, "may have not done his worst yet. Your Grace, have you told Leicester about Hodge, or do you want me to explain to him that he must have a care for himself?"

"I shall tell him as soon as this is over, but now I wish to welcome Ned Topside's friends."

She motioned for Rosie to stick close to Kat and, still smiling and greeting one and all, made her way to the dais. Ned saw her coming, elbowed one man and said something to the rest out of the side of his mouth. They all bowed grandly, one at a time in order, like pins going down on the bowling green.

"It has been some years since you have helped me with the poison plot which threatened our person," she told Wat Thompson and Randall Greene.

Ned introduced the others, including a fair-haired young man who radiated confidence to match his comely face and fine form. "Giles Chatam, Your Grace," Ned introduced him last, almost as an afterthought.

"Your Most Gracious Majesty," Chatam said in a deep baritone to rival Ned's, "I am neither of those traits my name might suggest. I am not chatty and have no guile, for only loyalty and hard work lie behind this smile."

"Stow the poetry 'til later," Ned muttered, but Giles's smile was nearly as bright as the Yule log flames now fanned to life.

"I did not realize others in your old company were as clever as you, Master Player Topside," Elizabeth said, still regarding Giles Chatam. "I look forward to the mystery play and other performances."

As they swept her bows again, she realized that Giles reminded her of Ned when she first took him in, but without that cocky nature. Perhaps she should talk to Ned about Giles joining him as court player, but then, she'd best see how well the young man did performing first.

As the afternoon wore on, the queen saw that Martin Bane still lurked about, like a harbinger of doom. She glimpsed him shove a paper up his sleeve when she looked his way; he was probably writing notes for the bishop about what everyone said or did. If Bishop Grindal had not been popular, especially for helping to rebuild the burned roof of St. Paul's with some of his own funds as well as hers, she might consider dismissing him and Bane, despite the upheaval that could cause. She was sorely vexed they didn't approve of her Christmas. Surely, churchmen would not stoop to something low and immoral to make their dire prophecies of Yule come true.

When she could slip away, she summoned Robin to her presence chamber from the festivities still going on in the Great Hall. "Is there some problem with the performance this evening?" he asked. "I've entrusted most of it to Topside, and I'll take over the events of the morrow with the traditional fox hunt on St. Stephen's Day."

"Yes, I'm sure planning that is far more to your liking. Will we be able to ride the ice to Greenwich Great Park?"

"For one last day, we'd best take the bridge," he told her, sitting beside her on the window seat as she indicated. "We can't be too careful, you know. But what is it then, my queen?"

"What you can do for me is to be very careful yourself," she told him, not protesting when he took her hands in his big ones. They were warm; Robin's hands were always warm, and hers, especially lately, were always cold.

"Careful as Lord of Misrule? In what way?"

"I'll not have you tell others, but I must warn you in good faith that your person, perhaps your life, could be in some peril. Did you hear how my privy kitchen dresser was decked out when he died?"

"Holding peacock feathers from the bird he was preparing?" he asked.

She wondered if such slight misdirection had been noised about or if Robin, enmeshed in his own cares and concerns as usual, had just not paid enough attention to take the full meaning. "Listen to me, Robin," she said, gripping his hands hard. "Hodge Thatcher was struck on the back of the head, then trussed like a peacock and hoisted up to hang by a noose. I believe he did not take his own life but it was taken from him. And since he was arrayed as a peacock, Cecil and I have construed the message may have been a blow at you."

"Aha." He went ashen, no doubt not realizing how hard he pressed her hands. "Could Sussex have hired someone?" he asked suddenly. "And, forgive me, my queen, but Margaret Stewart and Darnley both detest me, as no doubt Mary of Scots does from afar. I am not exactly the best-loved man in the palace. I was settling into the Lord of Misrule role, hoping some would come to see me in a more lighthearted way—to think better of me."

She tugged her hands free and stood; he jumped to his feet beside her.

"We could be reading too much in, of course," she said, "but I wanted you to know and guard yourself well."

"Yet I suppose," he said, wringing his hands most unlike himself, "you could be reading not enough in. If I were you, I'd have a care, too, for the murder was of one called 'the queen's dresser,' the man who decorated everything you ate. Christmas delights or not, best have someone watch and taste your food. And since the word *dresser* has a double meaning and Rosie Radcliffe sometimes helps you don your garments, tell her—unfortunately, Sussex's fond kin—"

"I'll not have Rosie disparaged, I don't care who her kin are. I trust her with my li—"

"That's exactly what you are doing. I beg you to at least have her and someone else search your gowns for venomous barbs or some such. Someone as devious as you describe could have all sorts of harm in mind. And I wouldn't put it past Vicar Bane to try to prove God's wrath on us, either."

"I've long known he bore watching, but your points are well taken. We must all be wary, but we shall not be frightened out of a happy Christmas!"

Just as the early winter's darkness fell outside on Christmas Day, they held the mystery play in place of the more raucous mummers' one with all its maskings and elaborate costumes. "Mysteries and moralities," the common folk called these simple dramas, which were once trundled about the countryside on carts or performed by trade guilds in the cities. The playlets seemed quite staid and old-fashioned now, but Elizabeth knew Kat recalled such with fondness. And the biblical message might serve to calm Bane and any other Puritan elements about the court, even though the plays had been popular under the Papists of England.

As these were traditional scripts with but a few variables in speech, costume, or staging, many people, at least those who had reached the lofty age of forty, knew the plots and words by rote. Though the queen had seen these done only in her sister's days on the throne, she too knew what was coming.

With Ned cast in the main role as the evil King Herod, the players presented the drama in which the three wise men went to the king's palace to ask for directions to the place where the Savior was born. King Herod, however, was a deceitful liar who wished to kill the newborn babe. So the angel of God appeared to the wise men in a dream and told them to avoid Herod on their way home. The result was that Herod gave orders for many children to be slain, though that was only told in speech, thank God, and never reenacted.

"Did they have to do a play where the ruler turns out to be a killer?" Elizabeth groused quietly to Cecil as he suddenly appeared beside her at the forefront of the standing audience. "I favor that new blond actor, and he's rightly cast as an angel, at least," she said with a little grin. "But I think Ned needs a dressing-down for playing the monarch that way. Forgive me, my lord, but, Christmas or not, everything seems a conspiracy to ruin my holidays."

They walked slowly off to the side of the crowd, so they could talk without whispering. "Then I hesitate to tell you what I've come for, Your Grace." Her belly knotted again as he went on. "There is someone come to court to see your chief cook, but I believe you will want to meet the visitor."

"Stop riddling, for I've had enough of that."

"Hodge Thatcher's crippled father, Wills, has been brought clear from Wimbledon on a cart with nail-studded wheels on the edge of the frozen river. It seems Roger Stout sent him a message of his son's sad demise."

"Why should I see him, the bitter man? Or do you mean he's asking for his son's body?"

"I'm afraid so. He's broken, grieving. Somehow the two men who brought him carried him into the corner of the hall back there," Cecil said, nodding toward the screened entry to the kitchens, "where he saw the mystery play being performed. But the thing is, he says he sent word to a friend visiting London who used to live in Wimbledon. He asked this friend to go tell Hodge in person that he regretted that cruel note he sent—the one we evidently read last night."

"Wait," she said, gripping Cecil's sinewy wrist. "You're saying Hodge was to have a visitor sent by his father, a man who might have arrived the afternoon he was killed and so could know something about his death?"

"That's it, though neither you nor Ned Topside will want to hear the visitor's name," Cecil said, raising his voice to be heard over applause.

"What does Ned have to do with that—or I, either?"

Cecil nodded toward the kitchen entry again. "It seems Hodge's visitor is the angel in the play. Hodge's father thought Giles Chatam was playing at an inn and was surprised to see him here at court, but there you are—perhaps a witness, a fallen angel fallen right in our lap."

She did not laugh at his wordplay as her mind raced. "Then, too, the visitor could have killed Hodge," she muttered, smacking her hands into her skirts. "I'll see this Wills Thatcher now," she added, starting toward the kitchen entrance, "and then the bright and shining Master Chatam after he ascends back into heaven in this mystery play."

Chapter the Sixth

Mulled Cider

For the universal benefit and general improvement of our country, our love for cider shows the Englishman's favoring of wholesome, natural drinks, even in a preference to the best beer from hops. To make, put 12 cups Kent cider in a large pan or kettle, add 1½ teaspoons whole cloves, 1½ teaspoons whole allspice, 6 sticks of cinnamon, and 1½ cups of brown sugar. Add 1 bottle of fermented cider, which can be strengthened also by freezing. Bring to a boil, stirring gently to dissolve the sugar. Simmer for a quarter hour to blend flavors, then discard spices. If possible, serve in heated pewter tankards. Makes at least 18 drinks. If served at holiday time, include slices of apples and a piece of toasted bread and drink the toast!

THE QUEEN SAW THAT WILLS THATCHER LAY ON A PALLET in the privy kitchen, his paralyzed legs draped with a woolen blanket. His carriers had put him on a work-table, so that he was easier to see and hear or to keep him off the cold flagstones. Her master cook, Roger Stout, spoke with the wizened old man, and someone had fetched him something to drink. Evidently no one fathomed the queen would come into the kitchens again, for no one so much as looked her way until Harry Carey, who escorted her with Cecil, cleared his throat.

Amidst a gasp or two and quick bows, the place went so silent she could hear something bubbling in its kettle on the nearby hearth. Only Master Thatcher could not bow; Elizabeth's gaze snagged his before his eyes widened. His face was wrinkled and ruddy, perhaps from being out in the cold all the way from Wimbledon.

"This is your queen, Her Royal Majesty, Elizabeth," Harry announced to the old man, "come calling with her condolences."

"Majesty," Wills gasped, raising himself on one elbow in an attempt to roll into some sort of bow. He lowered his gaze, yet when he looked up again, his eyes were wide as platters. "I—you, here?"

"Whatever you thought of your son Hodge's trade, Master Thatcher," Elizabeth said, loudly enough for all to hear, "he was of good cheer and of much service to me. And he was most loyal. Should I thank you for teaching him those fine traits?"

"I—Majesty—I heard he died. Since then I regretted each hard word 'tween him and me, I did."

"So it took losing him to make you love him?" she asked.

"More like, it took Christmas, Majesty, my first one alone. I rue each day I didn't take pride in my boy. Aye, it's too late to say so to him. But I come for his body now, to bury him at home, near as I can get him to his mother's grave, though he'll have to lie in unhallowed ground, a suicide."

Elizabeth's eyes met Master Stout's; few yet had heard that Hodge had been murdered or that his earthly remains were now burned bones and teeth Jenks had raked together and put in a small wooden box. Stout knew these things but had evidently not yet told Master Thatcher.

"Leave us now, all of you but Secretary Cecil and Baron Hunsdon," she commanded quietly. "Master Stout, see that the men who came from Wimbledon with Master Thatcher have hot cider."

When the kitchen was quiet and Wills Thatcher, propped yet on his elbow to turn her way, waited, she told him, "Several things I must say about your son, and ask that you keep these confidences—and steady yourself for a shock." Looking astounded, he nodded.

"Firstly, Hodge did not kill himself over your harsh note, though he did read it. Indeed, he did not kill himself at all."

"He—ill, or his heart failed? At his age?"

"The thing is, you see, you must not blame yourself for causing his death. Hodge did not die by his own hand. I regret to inform you that your son was murdered, why and by whom we do not know, but I—my people—will discover."

The old man sank back flat on his pallet. He sucked in a ragged breath and stared straight up at the lofty, soot-stained ceiling. Tears tracked from his eyes, but she sensed he was both relieved and grieved.

"Forgive me for asking such a thing now," she went on, trying to keep her voice controlled, "but Giles Chatam from Wimbledon—you and Hodge knew him, and you sent him to your son?"

She waited while he composed himself. He struggled to sit, so Cecil and Harry stepped forward from the shadows to help him off the table and into the only chair. Elizabeth sat on a bench facing him. Again, the old man looked stunned at her proximity.

"Aye," he whispered at last, after a swig of the mulled cider Cecil fetched him. "Friend of the family, Giles's parents were. His father a glover, kept the whole town in gloves." Wills sniffed hard, took another sip of cider, and went on, "I thatched their house, and the lads ran about together for years. Both of them had a fanciful side I could never fathom . . ."

"Take your time, Master Thatcher. So Hodge and Giles were longtime friends?"

"Aye, 'cept when they both fancied the same girl. Had a bad row over that, and she up and wed someone else. Then Giles's parents perished in a house fire—don't know how it started middle of the night."

"A fire? His parents were trapped and died in a fire, but he was safe?"

"He got out somehow, that's all. Took it terrible they were both lost in the blaze, he did."

Elizabeth looked at Cecil, but he merely raised his eyebrows; Harry remained unmoved, but she didn't expect him to follow all this as her brilliant secretary evidently had. Besides, Harry had not almost been roasted alive last night.

"Go on, please, Master Thatcher," she urged.

"After the fire, we took Giles in for a few years. Hodge had already gone to make his fortune in London. Then Giles left with that acting troupe to wander far and wide. But, aye, I had the sexton write a letter to the inn where Giles sent a note he would be in London. Always wanted to see London, that boy. I had the sexton write Giles to go visit Hodge here, try to patch things up—for him and me. I never should of sent that cruel letter, and it was Christmas . . ."

"So all should be forgiven at Christmas," the queen said, rising with a sigh. "Master Hodge, I shall see that you have food and a warm place to stay until your friends can take you home. But one blow more, I'm afraid. We stored Hodge's body in the royal boathouse on the river, and a fire struck there, too. I regret to tell you that Hodge's body burned with the edifice last night, but we have carefully collected his remains, and you shall have them in a box to take home with you to bury in holy ground near his mother's grave."

Wills had slumped, then straightened his shaking shoulders. "I thank you for doing your best for him, Your Majesty," he said, his lower lip trembling. "Is—is there anything else?" he asked, and she could almost see him cringe.

"Only that your son left you a purse of coins to keep you well. How much was that Hodge had lovingly saved from his wages working for me and my family, Lord Hunsdon?" she asked. She almost quoted to the old man from his spiteful letter about her family ruining the true church, but she held her tongue. After all, it was Christmas, and that's what had melted old Wills's heart.

"I'm not certain, Your Grace," Harry managed with a straight face, "but he'd saved a goodly amount." Cecil nodded solemnly.

"Then you must see to it," she told Harry, "that Master Thatcher receives Hodge's purse before he goes home on the morrow. I am sorry for your loss, Master Hodge, and wish you well."

She walked from the room back to her own problems, but not before she heard the old man say in a choked voice, "No wonder my boy served the Tudors so well. Aye, God save that queen!"

Elizabeth gave orders for Wills to be tended to and, with Cecil in her wake, cut back into the corner of the hall. The mystery play had ended, and everyone was eating and milling about again. Occasional laughter pierced the buzz of a hundred conversations.

"Harry," she said, "please send Ned Topside to me at once, over there in the corridor, then rejoin your lady and the others. I rely on you to help keep people happy and to keep me apprised if they are not. My lord Cecil," she said, turning to him as Harry bowed and departed, "we shall see what our new player Master Chatam has to say about his visit to Hodge yesterday—and about the fire that evidently trapped his parents while he himself escaped. Some people, I've heard," she said, rolling her eyes, "are fascinated by fire, and right now, I am, too."

"Oh, Your Grace," Meg Milligrew said as she came down the hall behind them, "there you are. I went upstairs to get a few more sprigs of mistletoe. Someone's been taking not only the berries but the entire little branches out of the kissing balls, probably intending to use them privily later. I wish it was Jenks, just lying in wait for me!" she said, and laughed. Her face flushed; she looked happier than the queen had seen her lately. In the new year, perhaps there should be a marriage, Elizabeth thought, and not that of the queen, the one her people and Parliament would like to see.

Ned appeared, still in kingly costume, holding his tin crown, and out of breath. "Your Majesty, you wished to see me?"

"Rather I need to see your mystery angel."

He looked surprised, then alarmed. "Giles Chatam? Why— what's he done, if I may ask?"

"Hopefully nothing, but it turns out he not only grew up with Hodge Thatcher, but they both loved the same girl."

She saw Ned's eyes dart to Meg, then back to his queen. "But he was with the players. You aren't going to ask him if he killed Hodge like some jilted, lovesick swain, are you?"

"Not directly, but Hodge's father has just informed us that he asked Giles to visit Hodge, and who knows it wasn't yesterday afternoon?"

"My uncle would know, the other players, too," Ned countered, his usually controlled baritone voice rising.

"Precisely, so you are to circumspectly and individually question them about Giles's whereabouts yesterday and anything else they might know of his doings, including whether there have ever been fires set near where they've been traveling with him."

"I'll do all you ask, of course, Your Grace," Ned said, turning this mock crown round and round quickly in his hands, "but I would not have brought the troupe to court if I could not vouch—at least my uncle will, I'm sure—for the whereabouts . . ."

"Ned," Meg cut in so stridently that everyone turned to her, "you know people can slip out sometimes and not be where they're supposed to be, and no one knows it."

Ned glared at Meg and spun back to the queen. "You'd like to see Giles first thing tomorrow," he asked, "before everyone leaves for Greenwich for the fox hunt?"

"I want to see him first thing right now. See that your friends are settled in for the night, then bring him up to my presence chamber—and don't tell him why."

Ned bowed and hastened to obey, but his words floated back to her. "This will go to his head, really go to his head."

"That's the pot calling the kettle black," Meg muttered.

"And to what were you alluding," the queen asked, "about Ned's not being where he should have been?"

"It was just what Ned calls a figure of speech," the girl said, looking quite caught in something.

"Meg, tell me now."

"I don't mean to tattle," she blurted, "but he slipped out last night from your chambers when he felt sick over something he'd eaten, that's all."

Robin could have been right, the queen thought. She had to have her food watched. She'd had a bad stomach, and evidently Ned had, too.

"How long after Her Grace and I left did he depart," Cecil asked Meg sharply, "and how long was he gone?"

Now Elizabeth stared him down. What was he thinking?

"Don't exactly know," Meg said, tilting her head and looking thoughtful. "He just ran to the jakes. Later he said he threw up his food, then stepped outside to clear his head. Came back up out of breath and looking all windblown and feverish after maybe a quarter of an hour, so I dosed him with a bit of the chamomile I keep for you, Your Grace, for your stomach upsets and to soothe your temp—I mean, in case you get upset—an upset stomach. And if you let on I told you all that, Ned'll skin me sure."

"Those of us in the Privy Plot Council must not keep secrets, at least not from your queen," Elizabeth said, patting her arm. "Best go tend to that mistletoe now."

Meg looked as if she'd say more but obeyed. "Cecil," the queen said as they started down the corridor toward the main staircase and her yeomen guards fell in behind, "what are you thinking about Ned Topside?"

"The same thing you should be thinking, Your Grace," he dared, "but probably won't admit."

"That he left the palace by the kitchen porter's gate the afternoon Hodge was killed, and so passed directly by Hodge's workroom?" she parried. "That he left Meg alone when he was bid stay with her last night about the time the fire was set?"

"The truth is," Cecil whispered out of the side of his mouth so even the guards would not hear, "we must suspect everyone in this."

"Ned? Ridiculous!" she cracked out. Motioning her yeomen to stay back, she turned to face Cecil halfway up the sweep of garlanded staircase. "You have always preached such rampant distrust to me, my lord. From the first, during the poison plot, you told me to trust no one. But haven't we learned the hard way that we must have faith in people like Meg, like Ned? When everything went wrong at Windsor the year Robin's wife died so strangely, you warned me not to trust Robin, either, but he was surely innocent of her death!"

"So it seems."

"Seems? And everyone thought I should suspect my dear Kat just last summer when the maze murderer stalked my gardens. Ned has been with us through thick and thin."

"Your love of and loyalty to your people are ever admirable, Your Grace. But remember what I taught you, the legal term *cui bono?*"

"Who profits for himself—who has a motive?" she translated before he could. "Do you really believe Ned would be so vexed by my replacing him with Leicester as Lord of Misrule that he would kill an innocent privy kitchen dresser of his queen to ruin the holiday season?"

"Hard to fathom, but I know one thing. Ned's a consummate actor—probably this Chatam you're about to question is, too. At this season of the year when love and good cheer should fill our hearts, it's hard to accept that bad blood could course through some, but that may very well be the way of it."

"I know," she said angrily as they started to climb the stairs again. "Curse it, but don't I know."

• • •

"But I never received Old Wills's message to visit Hodge," Giles Chatam told her. Unlike Ned when he talked, the young man stood very still with a minimum of flourishes and gestures to detract from his facial expressions. Somehow, that made him seem more sincere than Ned.

"May I not tell Master Thatcher so myself lest he blame me for not delivering it?" he cried.

"I believe he is departing at first light for Wimbledon tomorrow," Elizabeth told him, "but, of course, you may explain to him."

"I overheard whisperings about a servant's death but had no notion it was Hodge," he said, his voice earnest and his face crestfallen. "I was hoping to look Hodge up tomorrow—I just didn't think it could be him."

"Have you called on him when you were in London other times?" she inquired. Cecil sat at a table in the corner, supposedly absorbed in his own business but, no doubt, taking notes. She had sent Ned out of her presence chamber, much to his obvious dismay, so she had kept her yeoman Clifford in the back of the room as a guard for this interview.

"In truth, there were no other times, Your Royal Majesty, for this is my first visit. That's why I go out and about every spare moment I can. It's a wonderful city, and I want to see all the sights—London Bridge, St. Paul's, the Abbey. But to perform for you and see Whitehall from the inside—it's more than I ever dared to dream."

His eyes were clearest blue, his forehead flawless. His demeanor was deferential yet not menial, polite but refreshingly un-political. She liked him very much, his talents, too.

"I understand you have been an orphan for years, the result of a tragedy."

"Sadly, yes," he whispered. His gaze, linked with hers, did not waver. "As Master Thatcher may have told you, a fatal fire broke out, the result, I fear, of my mother's carelessness with the Yule log embers. That is why I thought you had summoned me here, Your Majesty—I mean, that I was nearly crying when the play began in the Great Hall, because everyone had fussed so over the log being brought in, and it reminded me of my Christmas losses. I thought you would tell me I did a wretched job tonight as the Lord's mes-senger angel when I was in truth so distraught . . ."

Those crystalline blue eyes teared; he bit his lower lip and sniffed once hard. She ached to comfort him. To have each joyous Christmas bring memories of tragedy was tragedy indeed. Espe-cially considering how things were going during this Yuletide, she sympathized with this poor young man completely.

Elizabeth felt safer out among crowds of cheering people the next morning than she had inside her own palace. She had covertly appointed both Roger Stout and her cousin Harry's wife, her lady in waiting Anne, to keep a good eye on the preparation and pre-sentation of royal food and drink. Just after daybreak, her gaily attired entourage set out for the traditional fox hunt for this December 26, St. Stephen the Martyr's Day.

They made their own music, for many had strung bells on their reins. The queen, riding sidesaddle on her white horse, had jingling rings on her gloved fingers and bells on the toes of her boots. Even the crunch of the hundreds of hoofs on a dusting of new snow and their mounts' snorting of frosted air seemed musical.

Twenty of her mounted guards with flapping pennants on poles preceded her, and twenty brought up the rear of the parade. Down the Strand, through Cheapside, and across London Bridge, the yeomen shouted, "Make way for the queen! Make way! Uncap there, you knaves!" When she heard the latter, she sent immediate word for them not to order her people to uncap today, for the wind was chill. Yet most men did, and women cheered, and everyone huzzahed her passage.

Robin rode just behind her bedecked horse, then Sussex and her other earls and counselors—though Cecil had stayed behind to work—then barons like Harry, mingled with her maids of honor and ladies who had chosen to brave the brisk day. Simon MacNair and, unfortunately, Martin Bane were in attendance; Margaret Stewart and her son Darnley, too. Kat had come along, though the queen feared she'd catch the ague and had ordered the old woman bundled to her nose. Her dear former governess was enjoying each event of the season, and that warmed Elizabeth as had little else since Hodge's corpse was found.

She had brought none of her servants this day, but for Jenks. Of course, some kitchen help had been sent with Master Cook Stout ahead to Greenwich with supplies to pitch tents and prepare food and mulled cider for after the hunt.

Elizabeth loved Greenwich, the palace where she had been born, and visited it often, especially in the summer. Graced by two hundred acres of pasture, wood, heath, and gorse, and stocked with deer and other game, the Tudor redbrick edifice lay but a short barge ride east of London on the Thames, or a longer, harder ride ahorse.

But for a few green firs, the trees of Greenwich Great Park stood bare branched, all the easier to ride through and see one's prey. For some reason, the fox was the traditional St. Stephen's Day quarry. Perhaps, someone had mused once, that was because its coat was Christmas red and easier than deer or boar to spot against the snow. And, in the tradition of goodwill at Yule and in honor of the martyr, unless the hounds had mauled the beast, the St. Stephen's Day fox was always let go.

"Were the packs of hunt dogs sent ahead, too, Your Majesty?" Simon MacNair asked, suddenly riding abreast with her.

"The royal packs," the queen said, pointing back across the river at an island, which was completely iced in, "are kept in kennels directly over there, Sir Simon, which, in this weather, are even warmed. The place is most aptly named the Isle of Dogs."

"Ah," he said, squinting into the sun off the snow. Robin and Sussex rode closer on her right side, perhaps to eavesdrop on what the Scots envoy and their queen could be discussing. "But, Your Majesty," MacNair went on, "to prepare myself for my stay here, I've been reading far and wide about your realm, and I believe I saw the Isle of Dogs was named for the ghosts which haunt it yet."

Elizabeth shook her head, but Kat's voice cut in. "I've heard that tale, too, a sad one of lost loves and lives. A young nobleman and his new bride drowned in a marsh there, and their hunting dogs kept barking, barking until their bodies were found. And even now, years after, the hounds still bay, and the ghosts still call them to the hunt."

"There, you see!" MacNair said.

"Kat, I did not think you'd be a purveyor of such stories," Elizabeth chided. "The night howls people hear on this stretch of river are my hunt hounds, not some phantom menace."

"But a better story, you must admit, Your Grace," MacNair said, and she noted that, for the first time, he had used the more familiar form of address for her. Fine, she thought. She wanted to win this man over, but even if she did, she knew his loyalties lay with his Scottish queen.

"Since you seem to have a fanciful nature, my lord," she told him, "after the hunt, I shall show you the old Saxon graveyard in the forest, for small mounds still mark the site. You and my dear Lady Ashley can keep an ear cocked for what those spirits have to tell us."

They all managed a laugh, and soon the hunt was on.

The hounds, which had been brought across from the Isle of Dogs in small caged carts over the ice, seemed to scent the fox at once. They took off in a brown streak of tails and barks with the hunters' horses following.

Fox hunts were truly about the ride and the chase, not the capture. Elizabeth loved to ride fast and free and all too seldom did so anymore, especially in the winter. How this custom of fox hunting on the day named in honor of the first Christian martyr, who was stoned to death, had gotten started she'd never know. But at least it got everyone out of the palace for the day. She was even hoping it would clear her head so she could decide whether to dismiss the Queen's Country Players or keep them around with Giles Chatam under close observation. Why not, since the others she suspected of trying to mock Dudley, burn her to bits, and ruin Christmas were all her guests?

She leaned forward, urging her mount on as others tried to stay with her through the trees. If she or someone just ahead— and few dared ride ahead—bounced branches, little cascades of snow flew in their faces. Her horse's hooves beat faster, her bells rang madly as she pursued the fox and hounds.

Her thoughts pounded just as fast and hard. The murderer and would-be murderer was surely someone who hated Robin and perhaps her, too. The Stewarts did, of course, and MacNair wanted Mary of Scots on her throne. Sussex hated Robin but surely would not want her or Cecil dead, though he could want to throw a good scare into her so that she would heed his advice to marry and produce a Protestant heir.

She could not believe that a churchman like Martin Bane would traffic in murder, though it was obvious he and Grindal wanted to warn her to stop her celebrations at any cost. They might think she was a bit of a pagan herself, but they could never stomach the Papist Queen Mary if Elizabeth were gone. And the handsome, talented Giles Chatam? He might have a motive to harm Hodge, but to sneak out and try to kill his queen, who just might make his career? Or had he learned where the body was and, without realizing they were inside, tried to incinerate even the remnants of his rival forever?

"There!" someone shouted. "There it goes! It's circling, trying to lose the pack!"

The hunters wheeled about and thundered back toward the river through thicker trees. As they burst into a clearing, they were nearly to the pavilion tents where food and drink were waiting.

The fox charged right through, and, though most of the horses were reined in, the hounds and several mounts snagged tent ropes and upturned tables and food. Servants screamed and scattered, then all was silent once again but the distant baying of the hounds.

Elizabeth could not decide whether to laugh or cry. She pulled up and surveyed the chaos.

"It seems even your portable kitchens are in disarray this season," Harry said, reining in beside her.

"Oh, oh, Your Majesty, sorry, just so sorry!" Roger Stout called to her. The man appeared to be actually pulling his hair out while others bent to retrieve roasts or bread loaves that had rolled into the snow. "And here the gift that boy left for you took a tumble, too!" Stout cried.

"What gift and what boy?" she said, urging her horse closer.

"A special holiday gift for the queen, that's what he said. Ah, here, a heavy box it is, too, over here where it fell off the table."

Elizabeth dismounted before Harry could help her down. Jenks suddenly appeared and slid off his horse; Robin on foot, Sussex, and MacNair came closer. Across the way, still ahorse, Vicar Bain watched at a distance as if he were hiding behind trees. Margaret Stewart and Lord Darnley reined in. Snow pockmarked from the headlong rush of fox, hounds, and mounts crunched under the queen's jingle-belled boots as she walked slowly over to the box, a plain wooden one, bound with a leather belt. It looked the mate to Meg's herb box she'd given up for Jenks to use as a place for Hodge's mortal remains.

"Shall I open it, Your Majesty?" Jenks asked.

"Of course," she said, smiling at the little crowd growing

around her as more hunters straggled back. "Nothing like an early gift for New Year's!"

Jenks pulled off his gloves, and his cold fingers were stiff loosening the leather belt. When he opened the box, so many courtiers crowded around that they almost shut out the light, and the queen put up a hand to hold them back.

A piece of paper lay folded across the box's contents with large-lettered words on it. *"HANGING MEAT, ROAST MEAT, MINCE MEAT,"* Jenks read aloud. "That's all it says. No, here in smaller words, *Stones for murdering martyrs.*"

"What?" the queen demanded, her voice shrill. She leaned forward to see what the box held, then gasped. It was filled with stones, just plain rocks, at least a dozen of them, rough and bumpy. No, one, near the bottom, was completely covered with gold foil.

"Find the boy who brought these here!" she commanded, and another hunt was on.

Chapter the Seventh

Christmas Tussie-Mussies

Not only do dried garden flowers keep the scent of summer in the dark and dreary months, but they may well help ward off diverse diseases and cheer one's spirit. In the growing months, gather and dry such sweet-smelling flowers as you favor, lavender and roses, of course, not forgetting to include those which have not only scent and color but curative powers. The latter may include sweet marjoram for over-sighing, basil to take away sorrowfulness, borage for courage, and rosemary for remembrance, especially of joyous Yuletides past. Gather the dried blooms into small bouquets adorned by lace or ribbons. Strew the crushed or unsightly petals about on floors or table carpets or in coffers for delightful odors during the Twelve Days and thereafter.

"PUT THOSE STONES HERE, YES, RIGHT ON THIS TABLE carpet so they don't get chipped," the queen ordered Jenks. Lugging the box of them, he followed the other Privy Plot Council members into the queen's chamber at Whitehall before dawn the next morning. Ned quietly closed the door on the yeomen guards as Jenks tipped the box on its side to dump them.

"No, pick them out carefully," the queen commanded, perching on the edge of her chair, "here where we can see them in window light. I'll not have mishandled what may have been used to kill Hodge Thatcher, especially that gold-foiled stone."

"Yet we may be foiled indeed," Ned whispered to Meg.

"I heard that," Elizabeth said, "and am in no mood for puns or jests. How I am to smile my way through the holiday festivities this night I do not know."

"On the other hand," Ned replied, "since this is St. John the Evangelist's holy day, we can hope to have our murderer's head on a platter instead of that boar's head tonight."

"If I were Salome," she muttered, "I would gladly cast off my veils and dance all night to have it so, but to the business at hand. Cecil, please take out your sketch of Hodge's head wound, then each of us must take two stones to study to see if one fits the approximate pattern of the drawing."

He did as she asked, also producing the boot-print sketch from the scene of Hodge's murder. Elizabeth took the gold-foiled stone, which was completely covered with what appeared to be the same thin foil that had been on the table at the scene of the murder. Jenks, Meg, Harry, Cecil, and Ned did as they were bidden with the others. Evidently hewn from a larger piece of rock, the stones were of rough, pitted texture about the size of a man's fist.

"You might know, the boy who delivered these to me at Greenwich escaped just like the fox," Elizabeth groused, "nor could Jenks locate a site on the grounds which could have provided them." She shook her head. She'd hardly slept again; a headache as well as a churning stomach sapped her strength and concentration. "But I vow that, whatever it takes," she added, looking at each of them in turn, "whoever is playing this clever game with our Christmas will be caught and punished."

"The number twelve here may be significant," Cecil mused. "Symbolic of the Twelve Days of Christmas?"

"Pray God," Meg put in, "there are not worse gifts to come."

"But what's the flowery smell?" Cecil asked. "It's not coming from the box, is it? It's not my papers," he added, lifting both sketches and sniffing at them.

Elizabeth nodded at Meg to explain.

"No, my lord," the girl said, patting the thick, brightly hued table rug. "After I make the queen's sweet bags, pomanders, and tussie-mussies, Her Majesty likes me to crush the rest of the herbs and flowers to strew about. They've got to be fine as powder but with a touch of ambergris worked in so's it won't blow away right off and lingers."

As if they'd exhausted conversation, they spent the next quarter hour hunched over stones, hoping they could match a contour or pattern, turning each rock to compare its rough facets from all angles. Most of the stones were smaller than the size of the wound drawn in Cecil's sketch, and the ones that were large enough had no texture to match it.

"I thought it would be this golden stone, but it doesn't fit, either," Cecil said, examining it after the queen finally put it down in frustration.

"Ned had best not say, 'Foiled again,' " she said, wishing she could lighten her mood. Here it was, she thought, the third day of Christmas, and, evidently having opened Pandora's box, they sat about like lunatics, staring at stones.

Sighing heavily as her gaze lingered on the other sketch, she reached for it and held it up. "I had originally thought we would use this boot print only when we'd narrowed our field of suspects, but I'm getting desperate to save these holidays from further mayhem. Meg, do you have more of the dusting powder from making tussie-mussies for all my ladies?"

"Two bags of it, one even in a coffer in your bedchamber, Your Grace, so things in it will smell sweet."

"Then if you will fetch it, we shall tread another path."

As the queen stood, everyone rose. Meg darted off and was back in a trice with a cloth bag as big as an open handkerchief. The powerfully scented dust within made them all sniffle or sneeze.

"What—choo!—are you thinking, Your Grace?" Harry asked and blew his nose.

"I am thinking that no one will suspect aught is amiss if I ask my strewing herb girl to place some of this here and there on palace floors. As I recall, Meg, you spilled a goodly amount last Yule, and we all stepped in it, tracking footprints in and through it."

"Aha," Cecil said. "A good idea if Meg can pull it off."

"But how are you going to get the men we're wary of to step in it?" Harry demanded, before sneezing again.

"I'll leave that to Meg," the queen said as he sneezed yet a third time. "Oh, Harry, do go over by the window and breathe fresh air through the cracks. My lord Cecil, please make a copy for Meg of that boot print. Jenks, place the stones back in the box and—oh, Ned, that leaves you. Meg, put some of that dust on the floor, and we'll test Ned's print in it to be certain this works."

She could tell that Ned—her dear, volatile, talented Ned— wanted to protest but dare not. Meg did as she was bid, strewing a bit on the floor before his feet.

"It's like the conquering hero cometh," Meg muttered, not looking up at him. "I warrant the Earl of Sussex, Sir Simon Mac-Nair, and for sure Lord Darnley will like the idea of crushed rose petals being strewn under their feet."

"And what about Giles Chatam, if you suspect him, Your Grace?" Ned asked. "Meg can't follow him about all day, and I don't trust him not to harm her if he's at all suspect."

"Not to mention how she'll manage Vicar Bane," Cecil said, as he came to watch, holding out to Meg the copy of the sketch. "He'll think such as sweet smells at Yule is right up on the list of sins with snowballing and eating manger-shaped mince pies."

"Let's not spend our time worrying about what we can't do but what we can," the queen commanded.

"But since you are here now, my lord Cecil," Ned put in, "why don't you try your print here, as I'd best be off."

"Because I've got to talk to Jenks again about the porter's confession he left his post for a while the afternoon Hodge was killed," Cecil told him, frowning. "One of the carters Jenks questioned said he came in with barrels of fresh water and no one was at the gate. As for doing your print, man, just pretend this is the epilogue of some play, and in recognition of your talents, your boot print is being preserved for all posterity."

Clenching his jaw, Ned stepped into the small rectangle of pale powder. He expected it to be more gritty, but he hardly felt a thing except the continued undercurrent of Cecil's distrust. It had begun when the queen's wily chief secretary had questioned him, apparently nonchalantly, about why he'd left the queen's apartments the night of the fire and where he'd gone. It seemed everything Cecil said of late had a double meaning that he couldn't quite decipher but knew didn't bode well.

"Just walk away now, Ned, naturally, normally," the queen prompted. Was it his imagination that she too seemed to be watching him like a hawk? "Oh, yes," she said as he stepped out of the stuff, "that's a good one. All right, then, this may work. Meg, take what's left in that bag as well as the other you mentioned and go about your duties, appearing to strew crushed flowers but actually gathering specific prints."

"I'd best spread this near others we don't suspect, too."

"Good idea," the queen assured her. "It may be tricky, and, of course, the person who made the original may have changed footwear, but the approximate size may allow us to eliminate some from further surveillance."

"I'll sweep this up so she has enough powder," Ned said and moved toward his ghostly print.

"Stay!" the queen said, grabbing his arm. "Ned, you said your uncle admitted that Giles Chatam left the inn the afternoon Hodge was killed, supposedly to see the shops at Cheapside. Because of Giles's earlier rivalry with Hodge, he must be suspect, especially if the porter left his post for a while when Giles could have hied himself into the kitchens, confronted Hodge, and then killed him. Since you are concerned Meg not tip Giles off or get too near him, I want you to stick close to the company's new player, both openly, when possible, but also covertly."

"But I'm needed around h—that is," he tried to temper his tone, "the Earl of Leicester hasn't overseen all this before, and he expects my help."

"I know it irks you he's changed some of your plans for this evening," she said, obviously trying to soothe him, "and I'd never ask you to be skulking in shadows if it weren't necessary. By the way, I think the earl has quite a lovely evening planned for tonight."

"Right," he told her. "I've laid all the plans for that, though much of it will be raucous and impromptu."

"Ned, don't fret, for Leicester does seem to be getting things under control."

Hell's gates, Ned fumed silently, *he* was the one about to lose control again. Stalking chatty Chatam was all he needed, especially when he'd like to get rid of him—and of Leicester, illustrious Lord of Misrule—so that he could rule and reign again at royal Yuletide. And to protect his queen, of course, for Leicester had never been worth the powder to blow him up, and she was secretly besotted with the man, he was sure of it. Ned almost laughed at his own mental pun, for Leicester had long been fascinated by gunpowder and had invested heavily in its production. But he summoned up his best acting skills to appear serious and calm.

"Of course, Your Grace, anything to help, but what if Giles slips out on one of his city tours again?"

"Then, if possible, you must follow, for who knows to whom he might lead us."

Tours of London, in this damned cold! Ned wondered if she—with Cecil's complicity, of course—just wanted him out of the way. Or had that pompous peacock Leicester asked that she keep the man who knew exactly how to arrange the holiday entertainments out of his hair?

"Meg," the queen was saying, "after you've managed to get a print, and before anyone else can scuff it out"—here, Ned thought, Her Majesty glanced back at him again—"you must compare the print to Cecil's drawing. You are to try to make impressions from the Earl of Sussex, Lord Darnley, Simon Mac-Nair, Vicar Bane, and my chief cook—just to eliminate the possibility the latter stepped in the cumin accidentally. All of you may go to your duties now, and my thanks as ever."

When Ned saw that Jenks dawdled, he went out with Meg and followed her down the servants' narrow back stairs. He'd often used the anteroom just off the last turn before the ground floor for quick liaisons. Hoping no one else was there this early in the morning, he snagged Meg's elbow, opened the door, and pulled her in after him.

"Hey-ho, what's this?" she cried as he closed the door behind them.

Fortunately, he thought, the room was deserted, but it was quite dark. Someone had left a single fat tallow candle on the table, nearly gutted out. Backing a few steps away from him, Meg stood with the sack of sachet dust held before her breasts like a shield.

"I just need to talk to you," Ned said. "I need your help."

"My help? What's the matter, then?"

"Meg, we're old friends. Those months you were not in the queen's good graces, exiled from court, I always believed you'd done no wrong—believed in you."

"Let's hear it, then, and never mind the buttering up. What have you done?"

"Nothing, I swear to God, that's just it. But because I just happened to leave the palace the afternoon Hodge died and because I was in a fit of anger that Her Grace had put Leicester in my place as Lord of Misrule . . ." Amazed his voice caught and cracked, he raked his fingers through his hair. "And," he added, more quietly, "because I had to use the jakes the other night when the boathouse burned, I think she's vexed at me."

"Don't blame me for mentioning you stepped out."

"I don't blame you for anything. But I can't believe Her Grace would suspect me of doing something so horrid to try to ruin her and Leicester's Yule—"

"There was a murder, Ned. A man's dead."

"I know, I know, but Cecil's been acting strange toward me, and you know how she heeds him. Meg, I'm telling you the truth," he said as he stepped forward and placed his hands over hers on top of her sack. Suddenly, the flowery scent was almost overpowering, yet strangely seductive in this little room. His pulse pounded, and his knees were like custard, when he'd never had any sort of stage fright, let alone quailed before a woman. And this was only Meg.

Her lips slightly parted, she stared up into his eyes. How could they look so luminous in this dim chamber? He'd long known he had sensual power over this woman and hadn't really cared. She'd been to him the younger sister he never had, one to tease and take out his temper on. He might be proud of her accomplishments, but he'd never say so. Yet now an alluring woman stood here, one of flesh and blood, and she wasn't like a little sister anymore.

"Help you how?" she asked so breathily he nearly had to read her lips. "Put in a good word for you with Cecil or Her Grace?"

"No! No, you mustn't let on that I'm suspicious that they're suspicious. But you must let me know if you hear anything, even if it's from Jenks, about their moving against me."

"Your footprint back there—the two of them set you up to make a print?"

"I fear so."

"I vow, I didn't know."

"Of course you didn't."

"But I can't betray the queen, Cecil either, certainly not Jenks, even to help you."

"I'm not asking you to betray anyone, my Meg, really."

She almost swayed on her feet. He moved his hands to steady her at the elbows. It was as if he embraced her, for the small, sweet sack was the only barrier between them.

"You didn't—do anything—did you?" she asked.

"Kill Hodge?" he exploded, loosing her and stepping back. "Hell's gates, it pains me sore you'd even have to ask!"

"Ned, I'll think on it and try to do what I can, but I cannot risk angering the queen again. And Jenks loves me, so don't ask—"

"So don't ask if there's anyone else but Jenks who loves you?" He stepped closer again and lifted three fingers gently to her trembling lips. She either pouted or lightly kissed his fingertips. It made him almost tilt into her like a magnet to true north.

"I must be off now," she said as she took two steps back. "You heard I have much to do."

"I too, sticking to that new playacting Adonis like a burr. Meg, please just think on what I've said, and I beg you not to betray my confidence, that is, both my fears and my utter confidence in you."

"My lips are sealed," she said, but they were still parted in the most becoming way. "Have a care, then, Ned."

"I will, I do," he whispered. He opened the door and stood back so that she could dart out before him.

At the feast of St. John the Evangelist that evening, Elizabeth found her deep-buried love for Robin Dudley, Earl of Leicester, Lord of Misrule, bubbling to the surface again. Perhaps it was simply the glow of the holiday season, but he was a charming host, regaling everyone with memories of Yuletides past.

He had people laughing as he conducted a lottery with prizes for small token gifts, blindfolding the queen before she picked out slips of paper with names from his fancy, feathered hat. Nor did Robin flinch when his archenemy, the Earl of Sussex, drew the lot to present the boar's head to the queen later this evening, a singular honor. Robin cajoled lords and ladies to be in their best voices for the later singing of the traditional carols. And, after an hour of dancing where he led the queen out onto the floor to stately pavanes and gay galliards, he announced that all would sit in a circle before the burning Yule log and share their best memories of Christmas.

"A delightful evening so far, Robin," Elizabeth told him as he sat her in the center seat before the hearth and took the big footstool at her feet, while others of the realm were given full-size chairs or stood in two rows behind. "So restful, and I needed that," she whispered and squeezed his hand.

"I heard," he whispered back, "you are having the preparation of your food guarded. And I shall protect you with my life, love, and honor—always."

Things were looking up, she thought, for who could ask for a better Yuletide gift than that?

Robin gestured for the ewers of mulled cider to be passed among them, but he poured his and the queen's from an embossed flagon he kept at his feet. Kat, at the queen's request, was the first to recall her memories; however forgetful Kat was these days, the past seemed ever present to the old woman. "But this Christmas is almost as fine as those of old," she concluded as Elizabeth blinked back tears. Through them, she smiled at Robin again and mouthed, "Thank you from Kat and me."

"Your Grace, will you grace us with a graceful memory of

your own?" Robin asked, and everyone chuckled at the way he'd put that. As the room grew hushed again, the crackle of the flames and hiss of sap from the huge log whispered to them all.

Elizabeth cleared her throat. Thank God, Christmas was *not* ruined this year. The good times were still within reach, and she felt protected here, despite the fact that in this friendly company could be the one who wanted to do her and Yuletide dreadful harm.

"I treasure the memory of the time my father went in a sleigh with my brother—Prince Edward—and me at Greenwich," she said. She hesitated, surprised that the long-buried memory had just lain in wait for Robin's invitation. She must have been barely six or seven then, Edward even younger. "The sleigh was a gift from the ambassador from Muscovy, where they have feet and feet of snow, my father said, and we laughed and sang, and then got out and made snowballs, but Edward and I knew better than to hit him hard with one."

Everyone laughed at that, the warm memory of a father merging with the reality of the huge, tempestuous king they recalled. But Elizabeth caught Vicar Bane's baleful gaze as he stood by the screen in the corner of the vast hall. The other day he'd claimed throwing snowballs was near sacrilege, so she glared back. "Someone else's turn," she said, her nostalgic mood now marred. "My lord envoy from your queen in Scotland," she went on, turning to Simon MacNair, seated at the end of the row, "will not you favor us with a memory of Christmas?"

"I shall be honored," Sir Simon said and stood, though no one else had done so. "Just last year," he began, "at Holyrood Palace in Edinburgh, it was, actually on Twelfth Night. One of Her

Majesty's maids of honor, Mary Fleming, found the bean in the Twelfth Night cake and so was declared 'Queen of the Bean.' Her Majesty ordered Mary decked out in a gown of silver and jewels, while the queen herself was appareled in mere white and black with not a ring or necklace or pin, so humble is our queen, so confident in any comparison with others. And how dearly her lowest servants love her for it—that is all of my memory."

As he dipped a little bow in Elizabeth's direction and sat again, she felt her dander rise. The man was subtly criticizing her for her elaborate dress. And did he imply that her own servants did not love her? 'S blood, how she hated all the mincing and maneuvering of court life when she would like to just have this jackanapes banished, along with anyone else who might wish her and her people harm.

"Thank you for that picture of your humble Scottish queen," she replied sweetly. "Rosie," she went on, turning to Lady Radcliffe, sitting two chairs down the other way, "pray tell us your story of how you came to court."

"I was a Yule gift fit for a queen," Rosie said, "the most lovely, gracious, and grand queen in all the world. My uncle, the earl," she went on with a nod and smile at Sussex, "said I should serve our new young queen and plucked me from my parents to meet the monarch—and here I am and likely to remain so, for who, high or low, would not be loyal to our queen?"

"I could not do without you. But tell, then," Elizabeth prompted, "the story of your parents, a great love story, and Christmas is the best time for those, both the sacred and profane."

Blushing now, Rosie began, "During the reign of Her Majesty's father, King Henry, the Earl of Sussex—the previous earl, this was—rode out of London to take part in a tournament.

As the cavalcade passed the little village of Kensington, people hurried to windows to see the parade. A beautiful merchant's daughter, Isabella Harvey, leaned out so far she dropped a glove just as Sir Humphrey Radcliffe, younger son of the earl, rode by. Sir Humphrey dipped his lance, picked up the glove, and returned it to Isabella most gallantly, so who dares say chivalry is dead in these modern times?"

"The Radcliffes yet cherish chivalry and loyalty," Sussex put in as if he'd been given leave to speak. "Well, continue, niece."

"The entourage rode on," she said, her eyes alight, "but Isabella had entranced Sir Humphrey. He doubled back and, calling himself a squire of the earl, made himself so agreeable that he was invited by Isabella's father to supper."

"I knew we'd get to food," Robin put in with a hearty laugh. "After all that dancing, let's have some pastries here—and suckets," he called to the hovering servers. "Marchpane and comfits! Go on, then, Lady Rosie."

"The friendship between Sir Humphrey, alias Squire Humphrey, and the maid Isabella, daughter of a mere merchant, grew to love. She came to marriage well dowered, but indeed they were wed for weeks before Sir Humphrey told her who he truly was, that her husband was the son, not the servant, of the Earl of Sussex, once Lord High Chamberlain of England. And I am their first child."

The courtiers applauded the charming tale. The queen noted even Simon NacNair looked pleased. But to everyone's surprise, Kat cried out, "It just goes to show you can't trust men!"

"What?" Robin said, looking half annoyed and half amused. "All present company, no doubt, excluded."

"To carry on like some player on a stage," Kat went on, "to

mislead Rosie's mother so! For a Radcliffe, brother of our earl, to pretend to be something he was not is—"

"Is not something we shall discuss this night," the queen concluded for her, rising.

"Time indeed for the bringing in of the boar's head," Robin added. "And yet," he whispered for Elizabeth's ears only, "Lady Ashley probably only spoke what she's heard you say more than once in private."

"Perhaps she only spoke the truth," the queen countered with a tight-lipped smile. She raised her voice to the crowd. "Let us all move back to the table, where the Earl of Sussex, surely a man to be trusted, has the honor of the presentation of the boar's head."

"Because I allowed him to do so," Robin groused.

Evidently, Sussex heard that as he walked on the queen's other side. "Don't you know?" he muttered to Robin behind her back, "that, ah, the point of lotteries is that the Lord God can actually choose who wins or loses, Leicester? In a lottery no man is rigging the results, though I suppose you'd like to try."

"Rigging?" Robin replied. "Rigging like that which tries to hold in the big-bellied sail of a ship, a ship which should take you right back to Ireland so you can cool your heels in the bogs there—"

"Leave off your slurs!" Sussex demanded. "Your vile temper is like the gunpowder you produce and then charge all of us outrageous prices for to match your sense of inflated importance, and—"

"Enough!" the queen commanded. She jerked Robin's arm and glared at Sussex. "Perhaps Kat was right about men being like actors in a drama. They may seem charming and chivalrous, but underneath they carp and cavil and can ruin more than my mood or even Christmas!"

A pall of unease hung over the company as everyone was seated. The queen took a deep breath to steady herself. To the blast of trumpets, in came four tall pages bedecked in red and gold taffeta, carrying the heavy platter with the silver cover over the traditional boar's head. For the first time, Elizabeth was aware Ned Topside was here, for his voice rang out to start the familiar song:

> Tidings I bring you for to tell
> What in wild forest me befell,
> When I in with a wild beast fell,
> With a boar so fierce . . .

Elizabeth smiled, though she felt on edge from Robin's and Sussex's arguing—and from Vicar Bane still staring from the corner as if branding them all pagans in need of strict Puritan salvation. Margaret Stewart, pippin red with anger, evidently that she had not been asked for a Yuletide memory, was whispering to her frowning son Darnley. MacNair looked maddeningly smug after his flaunting of Queen Mary. But at least, thank the Lord God, it had escaped Kat that she'd caused a row, and she looked happy.

> The boar's head in hand bear I
> Bedecked with bays and rosemary.
> I pray you all now, high to low,
> Be merry, be merry, be merry.

When the dish was set before the queen, the Earl of Sussex stepped forward to do the honors of uncovering the boar's head.

With a smirk sent Robin's way, the earl swept the cover from the platter with a flourish.

Kat screamed. Robin cursed. The queen stared agape not at the head of a boar with an apple in its mouth but at the decapitated head of a red fox with its snout adorned in gold foil.

Chapter the Eighth

Suckets

Take curds, the paring of lemons, oranges, pome-citrons, or indeed any half-ripe fruit, and boil them in sweet wort till they be tender; then make a syrup in this sort: Take 3 pounds of sugar, and the whites of 4 eggs, and a gallon of water, then swing and beat the water and eggs together, then put in your sugar, and set it on an easy fire, and so let it boil, then strain it through a cloth, and let it seethe again till it fall from the spoon, then put it into the rinds of fruits. One of the queen's favorite delights, especially the orange, all the year round, but for their hue, use limes at Yule.

"I THANK GOD NOTHING DIRE HAPPENED ON HOLY Innocents Day," Elizabeth told Cecil as she paced in her presence chamber two days later. She was eating orange suckets as she walked, for they seemed to give her the physical strength she desperately needed. "At least there was an entire normal day after the shock of that fox's head on the platter."

"If you call it normal," Cecil said as he stood at the window, sometimes glancing out, sometimes at her. "The upheaval of searching the kitchens and questioning the staff about how the switch from boar's head to fox's head had been made, and coming up with naught—"

"Naught but the discarded boar's head in Hodge's old work area," she said as she tossed her fruit and spoon back on the silver tray with a clatter. She stopped to look out the window, too. A swirling snowstorm had blanketed London with a good half foot of huge, heavy flakes yesterday. "You know," she went on, her voice calm at last, "Ned suggested that nothing happened yesterday because the culprit lives outside the palace and was snowbound, but I don't think so."

"I'm afraid I don't either."

"Even Vicar Bane has a chamber here when he wishes it," she went on, reasoning aloud, "and he's been here more than he's been with the bishop lately. The fact that nothing happened yesterday could be because our tormentor is matching his wretched surprises to each day. The human peacock was killed and displayed just before the presentation of the peacock on Christmas Eve, the box of stones came on St. Stephen's Day because the saint was stoned to death, the fox after our fox hunt . . . 'S blood, I don't know, Cecil," she cried, banging her fist on the windowsill. "If that's the pattern, can we predict what's coming next?"

"I thought the fox's head might be as if to say, 'The fox may be traditionally freed on the Yuletide hunt, but I killed him, because I'm breaking or damning all your traditions.' "

"Yes, but more than that, I think. Death, past or present, is suggested by each outrage, but what about the threat of a future death? It worries me that the fox is redheaded. Remember when we tried to solve the poison plot, a dead red fox was left in my bed with the note 'The red-haired fox is next,' meaning me? At least I am taking even more care than usual not to eat or drink anything that isn't guarded from start to finish or tasted first."

"That is wise, Your Grace, but you don't think there's a threat of poison here? The culprit seems obsessed with food as symbols, not as weapons."

"Oh, Cecil," she cried, covering her eyes with both palms, "I said I don't know what I think anymore. Perhaps nothing happened yesterday, even on a day that commemorates the biblical slaughter of young children by King Herod, because the name of the day is Holy Innocents. Because we have no babes at the court to harm, our tormentor gives us the day off, so to speak. But tonight—the Feast of Fools—I'm fearing something more bizarre than what we've yet seen."

"You could cancel everything."

"For what reason?" she demanded, smacking her skirts and starting to pace again. She took another sucket off the tray, a lime one. "Shall I announce to my court and city—so to all of Europe—that some specter, some phantom, stalks our court, and the queen is sore afraid and too stupid to stop it?"

She talked with her mouth half full as fear and anger—and sugar—bolstered her passion to solve this plot to kill Christmas. "Should I arrest all those we suspect, and on what grounds?" she railed. "Shall I send the powerful Earl of Sussex, my military commander from Ireland, to the Tower? Lord Darnley, whom I intend to send to tempt Queen Mary? Should I put some poor, possibly innocent itinerant actor on the rack? Imprison Vicar Bane, of my Church of England, however much I'd like to have his scowling face out of my sight? I won't have him and Bishop Grindal preaching that our traditional ways and my Christmas decrees are cursed. The river's frozen over, and the building of booths for the Frost Fair I've promised has begun, so I can hardly halt the holidays at the court or in the city!" In utter frustration, she heaved the half-eaten sucket and spoon at the tray. Both missed, and the sucket spun away on the floor.

"It's like a snowball rolling down a hill," Cecil muttered calmly, staring at her discarded lime. She saw he was so used to her outbursts he hardly flinched anymore. "But, Your Grace, we shall find who is behind it all, I know we shall."

"It's taken Meg too long to get some of the prints, though I realize she can't admit what she's doing. And worst of all, I'm worried about Ned. I can't bear the idea he's involved somehow, not Ned, a Privy Plot Council member, no less."

Her yeomen guards knocked on the door; Jenks was admitted, out of breath. "You sent for me, Your Majesty?"

"I did," she said as he straightened from his bow. "I'm afraid we must backtrack to find our villain. I'm sorry to send you out in this deep snow, Jenks, but I want you to ride back to Greenwich to question my steward and gamekeepers there. It's possible they saw someone poaching or hunting or some signs of the fox kill can be found."

Turning his cap in his big hands, Jenks nodded; despite her frenzy, she was touched he was ever willing to serve her. "With the new snow," he said, "finding tracks or blood will be hard, but maybe the men saw something. I can ask around more about where the lad that brought the box of stones could live. I'll ride the river, since the Earl of Leicester has ordered the blacksmiths to put studded shoes on the horses. But first, I want to tell you Meg's gone."

"Gone? Missing?"

"Not that kind of gone."

"Gone where?"

"Don't exactly know, spur of the minute, I guess." He pulled a piece of folded paper from his leather jerkin and extended it to her. "She left me this in our secret place we pass notes—private notes—out by the stables, so guess she went toward the city."

She didn't ask what it said, but opened it. "It's just the sketch Lord Cecil made of the boot print," she said until Jenks pointed to the back of it. Written small, around the edges, in a hasty scrawl were the words *E. of S.'s foot fit. He went out, I've gone after. M.*

The queen sighed and handed Cecil the note. "If Sussex's foot fit," he said, "it's not much, but it's a place to start. Yet I can't believe it of him."

"I can't believe it of anyone we suspect," she admitted, crossing her arms as she felt a sudden chill. "But then again, to what place is the Earl of Sussex heading in the snow this cold morning when he should be staying in with his wife and anticipating the festivities this evening? Jenks, do you know if Meg got all the other prints yet?"

"She was going to report to you this morning, but guess I'd best tell, then. Lord Darnley's boot print was narrow and too long, so's it's probably not him stepped in Hodge's seasonings."

"All right. Darnley's rather slight to be hoisting Hodge up into a noose anyway, though I still trust Darnley as far as *I* can throw him. Say on."

"Chief cook's feet are far too big, so he didn't step in the stuff by accident, sending us on a wild goose chase. That reminds me, the Earl of Leicester stepped in Meg's powder, too, and smeared out the first one she'd done of Sussex 'fore she could study it, and was she vexed at him!"

"I can imagine," Elizabeth said. "The man does have a way of tramping on the best-laid plans. But she obviously managed to redo Sussex's print?"

"She's clever, my Meg. She used the fresh snow to get prints from Vicar Bane when he left this morning, same for that new actor Ned doesn't like."

"But how did she know Sussex's boot print fit, as her note says?"

"He too went out somewhere's, I'd guess, since she followed him but managed to write this note on the way and stuff it in our spot—out by the stables, like I said."

"Yes, heading for the city. But you must hie yourself to Greenwich, my man."

"We're still clutching at straws in this," Cecil said wearily after Jenks left to fetch his horse and get more bundled up to face the weather. "Flower dust is frail, and snow prints melt."

"It's more than what we've had. My lord, let's go down to see the river and watch Jenks set out. I'm feeling cooped up in here. Besides, I want to see how a stud-shoe horse does on the river ice. I may be a fine horsewoman, but this may be something different. When I ride out to see the Frost Fair, I'll not have my horse go down to its knees, nor," she added, emphasizing each word, "but for praying for divine help, shall I go to my knees in this chaos of Christmas!"

Meg had to hustle to keep the Earl of Sussex in sight. He was on foot and alone, not even a servant or guard with him. If he'd been ahorse, she'd have lost him sure, for banked snowdrifts on one side of the narrow streets made for rough going. Some well-trod spots were slippery, and each breath of cold air bit deep inside her. At least the city seemed not as crowded as usual, since many folks had gone down to walk on the frozen Thames.

If she'd known Sussex would take off like this, she would have donned a better cloak than this thin one. She had no gloves and only the stout shoes she wore about the palace instead of the fine Spanish leather boots the queen had given her last New Year's Eve. Now Meg's stockings were wet, and her toes tingled.

But Sussex's foot fit Cecil's sketch so well she just had to take this chance. It was not at all like him to be leaving the comfort of the court, not after all he said he'd suffered in the chill bogs of Ireland, which had given him the ague. Unlike some courtiers, he doted on his lady wife, so Meg didn't think he was stepping out for a tryst. The proud, stern Earl of Sussex was in love with his family name and honor and possessive of his closeness to the queen.

Down the Strand, past her parents' old apothecary shop she'd finally sold after she was widowed, through Temple Bar, Meg kept the tall, thin earl in view. As she crossed the slippery humped bridge over the frozen River Fleet and trudged through Ludgate, St. Paul's Cathedral loomed straight ahead, and she wondered if he was going there. After all, many people did for many reasons.

Although religious services were held on a regular basis in the choir before the high altar, the vast outer nave of St. Paul's had become a marketplace. So much traffic moved past the many trading stalls set up around the cathedral's tombs and font that the covered nave had become known as St. Paul's Walk, an extension of nearby Cheapside Market. Lawyers received clients there, and horse fairs were held, though probably not at Yule. "See you at St. Paul's" was a common cry. But why was the Earl of Sussex, who had servants to do his bidding, evidently headed there?

As she neared the cathedral, looking up, Meg again felt awed by the magnificence of this sentinel of the city, though, after the fire, the roof had been rebuilt without the spire. The massive morning shadow of this largest building in all England swallowed Sussex and then her, and that chilled her even more.

Yes, Sussex was indeed heading into the precincts of the cathedral. She hurried past St. Paul's Cross, where speakers of any ilk were permitted to give sermons of their choice, as long as they did not slander church or queen. Cloaked with snow, it stood alone in the cold. The Bishop of London's house was a stone's throw away, and she wondered if Sussex had come to see Bishop Grindal. But Vicar Bane was always around the palace, so the earl could simply have done business with him.

Sussex, slowing his strides, passed the bishop's house and went directly in the great west door of the cathedral. So as not to lose him in the crowds, pressing her hand to the stitch in her side, Meg hurried even faster.

The queen and Cecil donned warm cloaks and hats and went down the privy staircase to face the buffeting winter wind on the frozen river. "It feels good," the queen insisted as her cloak flapped like raven's wings. "Cecil, I've been praying to God for a clue to save Christmas."

"A clue like a star in the sky hanging over the culprit, or angels singing to point the way to his next outrage?"

"I am still not in the mood for jesting. Tonight, as Lord of Misrule overseeing a raucous mumming, Leicester will do enough of that."

Squinting into the wind, she looked upriver to the charred

ruins of the boathouse. It would be rebuilt when the weather turned warmer, but she knew she should soon order the clearing of the debris and ashes. Her eyes watered and her cheeks stung, but it was a bracing cold. Out on the ice the wind had swept clear of snow, men were cobbling together crude booths for the Frost Fair. Children and adults alike were sliding and falling and laughing on the solid white river as if they had not a care in the world.

"There he is, my lord," she said, pointing to Jenks as he rode out onto the ice and headed east. "The horse looks a bit nervous, but they're managing."

"And with you as our queen, so shall we all," he said.

As they turned to go back in, she glanced after Jenks again, half wishing she could stay outside on some adventure and not be closed in with her thoughts and fears, waiting for the other shoe—or boot print—to fall. Her gaze caught the rough stone foundation of the palace, rising from the frozen riverbanks just before the brick facade began, now all etched with driven snow. Had God indeed answered her prayer?

"Cecil, look, there," she said, pointing again.

"He's almost disappeared into the growing crowd on the ice."

"No, look at the very foundations of the palace. Down that way, toward where the boathouse stood—that rough hole in the lower wall that's pockmarked and has caught the snow. I want to look closer at it, for I swear it wasn't there before."

They crunched through the carpet of snow toward the spot. On the corner of the foundation, almost directly under the royal apartments, someone had hewn out pieces of gray stone—twelve of them.

. . .

Meg had been right about no horse fair today, but, despite the lure of the frozen Thames for the first time in years, many Londoners were in the nave of St. Paul's. Hawkers screeched to buyers, selling everything from books to plateware to expensive sugar, which was imported on Venetian galleys when they could navigate the river. She heard cries for roasted pig's trotters, gingerbread, even lemon suckets. Like the queen, Meg loved those, but she hadn't brought a farthing with her and could snitch all she wanted off the queen's trays anyway.

She watched Sussex make his way toward a vendor of pewter and silver goods. "Oh, no," she whispered to herself in the echoing hubbub under the vast roof.

Her spirits fell. She'd braved the cold and got her hopes up she was onto something in this search for a murderer, and this powerful peer of the realm had merely come to buy a gift for his lady wife or even the queen? Though the wind didn't blow through here, she shuddered. Now she'd have to head back all the way to the palace to tell Her Grace she'd come up with nothing but a numb nose and toes.

She stayed to the side of the nave, keeping one of the elaborate tombs between her and Sussex. Yes, he was looking at what appeared to be a fine pair of silver filigreed flagons with a raised design. She bet those cost a pretty penny. On a crude plank cupboard behind the vendor were displayed tankards and ewers, pitchers, flagons, and rows of plates all flaunting designs in relief. She sighed. Though she and Jenks would share a room in the servants' wing of the queen's palaces over the coming years, would she ever own something as fine as those?

She gasped. Standing at the side of the cupboard as if waiting for Sussex stood that new actor, Giles Chatam. And if he was here, could Ned, who'd been told to keep on his tail, be far behind?

Ned almost shouted for joy. Now he could report to the queen that Sussex, who hated Leicester, was here whispering to Giles when, if his business had been on the up-and-up, he could simply have spoken to him in the palace. Ned's mind raced through all the possibilities: He could suggest to Her Grace that, although Sussex would not dirty his own hands to disgrace Leicester or ruin the festivities over which the peacock presided as Lord of Misrule, he could have hired Giles to murder Hodge and ruin Christmas. And Giles could have wanted to get rid of his old rival Hodge, so Sussex could have told him about making him look like the peacock . . .

But no, Ned realized, he'd never convince the brilliant queen that those men had by chance found each other early enough to connive to kill Hodge. Still, anything to muddy the water to take her and Cecil's scrutiny off himself.

Then, to his surprise, he saw Meg Milligrew, peeking around the corner of one of the tall, ornate tombs, looking the part of a skulking grave robber. Had he taught her nothing about trying to blend in with the surrounding cast of characters? She looked flushed, disheveled, and windblown, but it was somehow beguiling.

Ned scanned the crowd around her and then the booth where Sussex was paying coin for something he'd bought, which had now been placed in a velvet drawstring bag. The pewterer had taken off his cap to reveal such a bright red head that he looked more Irish than English. Carefully, being sure Giles didn't spot him, though the young man was craning his neck to look up at the lofty ceiling like some rustic cowherd who'd never seen a big building, Ned worked his way over to Meg and came around the tomb behind her.

"If you came to meet a lover," he said low, "I hope it's me."

"Oh, Ned!" she said, spinning toward him. "You scared me near to death, even though I was looking for you. When I saw Giles here waiting for Sussex, I thought you might be near."

"If there wasn't a connection between the two of them before Hodge was killed, there is now. I think we can make some hay with that."

"But can we get close enough to overhear what they say?"

"In this noise? Best just keep an eye on them. Look," he said as he took her elbow and propelled her around the next tomb with its stone figure of a knight staring eternally upward, "Sussex is not one whit surprised to see him and is giving him a slip of paper."

"With his new orders on it, I wonder?"

"Be sure to tell the queen that's what it looked like to you."

"And now he's paying Giles!" she cried as Sussex extended coins to the handsome young man, just as he had to the redheaded pewterer before.

"Seeing is believing."

"And so, I'll stay with the earl and you stick to Giles, but not together."

Her cheeks were roses, and the excitement of the chase seemed to make her usually pale beauty bloom, even in this big barn of a place.

"Why not together?" he challenged and squeezed her waist. "We'll be careful."

But their quarries separated, and Meg went her way, probably back to the palace, behind the Earl of Sussex. With Ned shadowing him, Giles walked out of the cathedral and strolled down the bitterly cold, broad and windy Cheapside, gazing at the ornate swinging signs of goldsmiths' shops as if it were the mildest June day. Giles had told his fellows in the actors' company that he wanted to walk the city whatever the weather, and that seemed to be the truth. Hell's gates, but Ned had no intention of gawking at this man while he gawked at London. He was heading home.

But as he strode back through the nave, then out into the wind again, as if it were a sign from heaven that he'd been ignoring Meg too long, there she was again, huddled behind the big gray hulk of St. Paul's Cross.

"What are you doing here?" he asked, making her jump again. He took off his cloak and wrapped it around her shoulders, however much he was trembling, maybe not only from the cold, but the closeness to her again.

"You won't believe it," she said, pulling him behind the cross, "but Sussex went inside to see Bishop Grindal, and that croaking raven Vicar Bane met him at the door to let him in. I've never seen Bane as much as smile, but he out-and-out grinned, and they started whispering right away!"

"The plot thickens," Ned said, "and plotting they must be."

Chapter the Ninth

A Christmas Fool

The curdled custard called "fool" is an excellent dish for all the year, but with the dates and caraway comfits, fit for a special Yule dinner for young or old, poor or rich or royal: Take a pint of the sweetest, thickest cream, and set it on the fire in a clean scoured skillet, and put into it sugar, cinnamon, and a nutmeg cut into 4 quarters, and so boil it well. Take the yolks of 4 hen's eggs, and beat them well with a little sweet cream, then take the nutmeg out of the cream, then put in the eggs, and stir it exceedingly, till it be thick. Then take fine white manchet bread and cut it into thin pieces, as much as will cover a dish bottom. Pour half the cream into the dish, then lay your bread over it, then cover the bread with the rest of the cream, and so let stand till it be cold. Then strew it over with caraway comfits, and prick up some cinnamon comfits, and some sliced dates, and so serve it up.

"I'VE BROUGHT YOU A STURDY MARE WITH STUDDED shoes for the river ice," Robin told Elizabeth as he bowed before her in her presence chamber early that afternoon. "I know, consummate horsewoman that you are, you would appreciate a grander mount, but this one's closer to the ground, and I'm sure you don't want your usual horse chancing a fall and broken leg."

"His or mine? Well, Robin, as you are Lord of Misrule by my

own hand this season, I had best ride out with you to see how my people are doing. I believe it will do me good."

Yet she felt torn as she went into her privy chamber to don warm boots, cloak, and hat. She wanted to stay here until Jenks reported from Greenwich and Meg returned from following Sussex. Cecil was down on the riverbank with her guard Clifford, ascertaining that the twelve stones were indeed hewn from the foundation of her palace. Kat was napping while everyone else went hither and yon, preparing gifts for the New Year's exchange or arranging their fantastical costumes for the mumming this evening.

But the queen refused to be kept prisoner in her own palace, and she did want to be out with her people and with Robin. She was taking no chances she would be made to look the fool or put herself in danger. She rode out between Robin and Harry with Rosie and three other ladies in her wake. Four yeomen guards were mounted, and ten others walked the ice, keeping their distance but also keeping her in their sight.

The cold and the thrill of riding on the river invigorated her. After yesterday's storm, the sky was a shattering blue, and the sunlight off the expanse of ice was almost blinding.

"It's like another world," she told Robin as they slowly walked their horses straight out from the palace. Her sometimes sooty, dirty city seemed to sparkle, as if she rode the gold, gem-studded streets of heaven. When the Thames was water, she thought, it never looked as wide as this. From the palace to the broad bend that hid distant London Bridge, she could see her people as busy as ants, working to build their Frost Fair. However cold, they looked happy and so festive that her oppressive mood lifted even more.

"Needless to say," Robin told her, "the closer you get to the city proper, the more activity there is. Oh, by the way, with your gracious permission, my queen, I thought I'd plan something special for New Year's Eve. I've ordered my men to explode small bits of gunpowder on the ice—much noise and flash to bring in the new year. We'll save the rockets and firewheels for Twelfth Night."

"As Lord of Misrule, you are in charge of all that."

The wind whipped their words away in puffs of breath. "Good day to you," she called to a group of men hammering to erect a stall. Amazed it was their queen, they cheered and huzzahed, which made others come running and sliding. Elizabeth saw that some citizens had built bonfires on the ice and were cooking food; one enterprising lad had cut a hole through and was fishing.

"Robin, look at that plug of ice he's pulled out. The river has frozen to at least a foot thick here! I don't think even your gunpowder blasts could break that ice."

Their gazes caught and held. Robin sucked in a deep breath, and his nostrils flared. He was, she mused, like the powerful gunpowder he believed was the future of warfare. Like her, he was of volatile temperament; together they were match to saltpeter in a blast of heat and light. But gunpowder could blow everything apart.

Not wanting to be seen lurking outside the bishop's house, Meg and Ned hied themselves back toward Whitehall, rehearsing all they had to tell the queen. Meg was so excited to be with Ned she almost forgot to breathe. It had been so long since just the two of them had worked together.

"At least we've discovered something to pursue," Ned said.

"It will be your best defense if you think Her Grace and Cecil believe you could have been involved," Meg tried to encourage him. "Dreadful how being part of the Privy Plot Council soon has you suspecting everyone. Next, we'll be thinking poor Kat's in on this, and then I'll know we've taken leave of our senses."

"Let's stop off at this tavern to get warm," he urged and steered her toward the Rose and Crown.

Despite how she was enjoying her time with him, she almost panicked. This was hardly like old times when Ned taught her to carry herself like the queen, to talk properly, and to read in those heady days she came to care for him. So much had changed.

"But we're almost back," she protested.

"Just for a few moments. To warm up."

"I should return this cloak you so sweetly—generously," she amended, "loaned me. I can't be walking into Whitehall in it anyway."

"Jenks would understand."

"He wouldn't understand us spending time in a tavern, now would he?"

"But this is the very place my uncle's troupe played for a day or two, so I thought we'd best ask a few questions here, to be able to report to Her Majesty how Giles behaved then. Actually, if we weren't so chilled, we ought to visit the inn where I found them and inquire there, too. Meg, this won't take long," he wheedled. "Jenks will understand, as he's always devoted at any cost to Her Majesty's best interests."

Despite her better judgment, she went.

Shading her eyes in the blaze of sun on ice, Elizabeth turned her horse reluctantly toward the palace. Cecil and Clifford were no longer outside by the palace's foundations. Rather, a mounted man who looked familiar was there on the snowy bank.

"Robin," she said, pointing, "that man ahorse near the palace directly under my apartment windows. Is that not Simon Mac-Nair?"

"I believe it is, my queen, for I recognize his Scottish border mare. He wanted studded shoes on it and on another fine beast he said belonged to Duncan Forbes, his messenger to the Scots queen."

Elizabeth turned to look Robin full in the face. "Have you ever sent notes to *that* queen by MacNair's messenger?"

"Never, I swear it," he vowed, hastily crossing his heart like a fond lad.

"You did not entrust to him a privy letter saying Queen Mary should not consider you for her husband?"

His cheeks colored, more than they had in the wind. "No, I sent my own man with that."

"I don't believe the Lord of Misrule must tell the truth," she said, looking away from him, "but then neither do most men believe it is a necessity."

"Your Grace, you wound me sore to imply such. I knew Kat was parroting your words the night before last when we told our stories and she denounced men."

"You like to tell stories, I warrant," she shot back. "I've not forgotten MacNair's mention of that large portrait of Queen Mary in your privy rooms, my Earl of Leicester. Come on, then," she cried, and urged her mount forward, "but I shall speak with Sir Simon alone."

Though he looked as if he'd argue more, Robin kept her entourage back as Elizabeth, still mounted, approached MacNair.

"There is great excitement in the air, Your Majesty!" the Scot called jauntily to her and swept off his feathered cap in a grand gesture.

She did not move her horse onto the bank itself but stayed at the edge of the ice. Staring hard at him, she replied, "Since the view is so lovely out here, Sir Simon, why are you studying this ragged hole in the wall?"

"I would never have noted it, but I saw Secretary Cecil trying to rebuild it, or, shall I say, fitting stones into these holes. Is he also head of your building repair office, Your Grace?"

"You were there the day of the hunt," she said, deciding to challenge this man instead of jest with him or put him in his place for his subtle impudence. "You saw someone sent me a box of stones, and, amazingly, they came from there. I must say, someone has a sick sense of humor—a fool's sense of humor, and here we are now on the Feast of Fools day."

She studied him closely, for she had positioned herself so that he must stare into the afternoon sun to face her. Not a flicker of guilt or even further interest crossed his broad countenance at that sally. She'd best try again.

"Where is your messenger whose horse you asked to be shod with studs?" she asked.

"I don't rightly know, Your Grace, as Forbes headed north the day before yesterday with a letter to Her Majesty in Edinburgh. Sad to say he probably was caught in the snowstorm, but he'll fight his way on northward. We Scots are a hardy lot, you know."

"I do know. And what did you report to your queen?"

"That I wished her the heartiest and healthiest New Year, and told her I would soon send her a fine gift. By the way, some Scots call New Year's Eve Hogmanay, you know, Your Majesty."

"A strange name and not, I warrant, because you have many roasted hogs on that day?"

"It's spelled Hog-m-a-n-a-y, Your Grace, though most north of the border can't spell worth a groat."

"Are you implying that since I misspelled it, I would make a good Scot?"

"But you could only be a queen, Your Majesty, and then we would have one queen too many in fair Scotland."

"When I became queen there in place of my cousin Mary, I would dub the day Queenmanay and order both roasted hogs and Christmas fool custards for all my loyal Scots subjects. I shall see you at the feast this Feast of Fools, will I not, my Scottish lord?"

He gave a hearty laugh at her wordplay, and at the moment she rather liked the man. "You will see me but not recognize me," he said, "for I will be with the group of mumming men performing for Your Most Gracious Majesty. And I hear we are not allowed to talk but only sing—or laugh."

Their gazes met and held. Apparently open and honest, seemingly bluff and good-natured, Sir Simon MacNair appeared to be a hail-fellow-well-met. But the queen knew better: Like all political creatures—actually, like all men—he bore watching. She'd known that from the first Christmas she could recall, when her father had called her his little dearest on one day and named her bastard of a whore the next.

Once Ned convinced Meg to go into the Rose and Crown with him, he felt very nervous, and that wasn't like him. Was it suddenly because it seemed as if he were courting her, or because he had so much at stake convincing the queen to believe Giles was not to be trusted? Whether or not Giles was guilty, Ned needed him to look guilty. Not that he'd want the pretty boy to be arrested, of course, for if it began to look bad for him, he'd tip Giles off and suggest he flee London and never return.

"You're frowning something dreadful," Meg said as he seated her on a bench in the back corner of the common room near the hearth. Unlike the other day, the place was nearly deserted.

"Just thinking too much," he told her, squeezing her shoulder. "Shall I buy you ale or beer?"

"Mulled cider, if they have it. Hot!"

"I intend to bring back the tapman I talked to the other day about Giles."

He walked through the smoky common room with its mingled smells of wet wool, burning firewood, and four chickens sizzling on a single spit over the flames. His stomach growled in anticipation of the feast tonight with its roast suckling pig. It was not half as crowded here as it had been the other day, and he spotted the tapman easily at the counter amidst the few customers. The fat, jolly man went by the sobriquet of "Duke" since in his youth he'd been footman for the Duke of Northumberland.

Ned ordered two mulled ciders and tipped Duke extravagantly before the man realized who he was.

"Eh, you again, then? Still looking for your actor friends?"

"Looking for some information, if you've got the time," Ned told the nearly bald man. Duke had such a bull neck it looked as if his head were set directly on his huge, rounded shoulders. Every time he nodded it seemed to be in danger of rolling off.

"Why not?" Duke said and left his fellows to follow Ned. "If a man can't take a whit of a respite at holiday time, however much debt he has or problems, too, what's the point of things?" Duke guffawed as if he'd said something hilarious. "This your wench, then?" he asked as he saw Meg waiting on the bench. "Red-haired like the queen herself, eh?"

"Meg's a close friend of mine," Ned told him, and Meg nodded vigorously. "And we're here," he went on as the three of them huddled on the bench, Meg squeezed in the middle, "to inquire if you can give us any information about the handsome, young blond actor who was with the players."

"Wet behind the ears, he was, I could tell, but smooth."

Hell's gates, Ned thought, that wasn't much help and seemed slightly contradictory.

"Clever like," Duke tried to explain, rubbing his bearded chin, "and real int'rested in everything 'bout Londontown, that's what he called the city."

"Yes, I've seen he was interested in everything."

"Good 'nough actor, I warrant, but kept running out and 'bout between the short plays they did, used this hearth right here for a stage, they did."

"But how was Giles clever?" Ned pursued.

"Tried to make a good impression, least 'bout one thing. Boasted he was going to see Whitehall Palace soon, not only from the outside but inside, too. Had a friend who could get him in, leastways far's the kitchens."

Ned and Meg gave each other a pointed look. "Did he say who his friend was?" Meg spoke up before Ned could.

"No, and wasn't like to be the queen, was it? Why, I could of thrown the Duke of Northumberland's name at him—see, I was once his footman, missy," he said to Meg, "looked fine in liv'ry, too, 'specially new liv'ry at Yule, I did."

"Yes, I'm sure you did," Meg told him.

"But I was too busy that day, not like now," he added with a nod at the sparsely populated common room. " 'Sides, I been in a few fancy kitchens myself. Naw, just give me the small hearth here with the spit aturning at Yule, my wife in our warm room upstairs, and I'm content, no more court life or fetching and scraping for my betters in a rabbit warren o' rooms, e'en castle or palace, not me."

Duke leaned contentedly back against the wall behind the bench and belched as if to punctuate his thoughts. This time, Ned's gaze snagged Meg's and held. He wondered if she was thinking what he was, that there was some lure to the life this man described, even so crudely.

"We'd best get back," Meg mouthed.

Ned nodded. They finished their cider and thanked the man; Ned donned his own cloak this time, and they started out. But in the small entry hall, before they stepped into the cold world again, Ned blocked her in against the closed door.

"I've got a sprig of mistletoe in my jerkin," he said, amazed his voice was so rough.

"You already got what you came for," she countered, "more goods on Giles. Are you the one who's been taking the mistletoe off the kissing boughs I put up?"

"Not I—just this one. Do I need to get it out? I can't be seen giving you a Christmas kiss back at Whitehall if I don't want Jenks's fist in my face, peace on earth and goodwill to men this time of year, or not."

"No, we can't have that," she said with a sigh.

He moved quickly before she changed her mind. It was just a way of thanking her for sticking with him in this, he told himself. Just a cheery, holiday, one-time thing . . . a sort of good-bye since she was to marry Jenks, and the queen sometimes talked about having a wedding for them soon. It was just . . .

Meg gave a little moan and seemed to sink into him. His hand left the door latch to tighten around her waist; his other hand steadied her chin. They melded together, for much longer than he'd intended or expected. And yet it seemed to go so fast, the deepening kiss and the way they clung to each other, mindless of the place or time or who they were.

It was another loud guffaw from Duke, talking to someone in the common room, that brought Ned back to reality. He lifted his head, and Meg stepped quickly away from his embrace. Though no one was so much as looking at them, another man laughed at something Duke had said, and "That's a good one!" floated to them.

Quickly, Ned hustled Meg out the door. The queen would not think it one bit humorous if they didn't get back soon.

"My lord Harry," Elizabeth said to Baron Hunsdon the moment she'd heard all Ned and Meg had to tell, "please find the Earl of Sussex and escort him to my presence forthwith!"

She felt somewhat relieved that Giles Chatam's suspicious activities might help exonerate Ned, but her principal actor still bore watching. It seemed to her he was trying too hard to make Giles look bad. Meanwhile, the Privy Plot Council members still sat around the table in the queen's privy chamber. Cecil had reported that the twelve stones had indeed come from the palace's foundation, Jenks had said he'd turned up no sign or word of a fox killed at Greenwich, and Meg and Ned had come back brimming with news from their joint investigation.

"But what about Giles?" Ned asked now. "I thought, that is, Meg and I thought—"

"I will look into his actions, too, I assure you," Elizabeth interrupted, "though I don't think a frontal assault is the way to deal with him. On the other hand, Sussex understands the old saying, 'Might makes right.'"

"Sussex may head a powerful court faction," Cecil said, "but he dare not defy his queen."

"Let us hope," she muttered.

"Perhaps," Ned put in, "just removing Giles Chatam from among the mummers tonight and sending him away from court—"

"Ned, enough!" Elizabeth commanded and sat in the chair at the end of the long table so fast her skirt whooshed air. She intentionally did not bid the others to sit again. "And," she added, pointing at him, "don't be confronting Giles Chatam on your own until we at least arrange for someone to overhear what he may say."

"But I would report back faithfully what he said and—and I ask your permission to take my leave now," he added hastily, no doubt, she thought, when he saw the look on her face.

"All of you but Cecil may leave," she said, "but remember to keep a good eye out at the Feast of Fools for anything untoward. And if I manage to shake any confessions out of Thomas Radcliffe, Earl of Sussex, I will let you know."

When everyone did as bidden, Cecil said, "I note you didn't tell them you've secreted Clifford and Jenks in the kitchen for this evening. Do you still mistrust Ned?"

"I cannot afford to trust anyone—present company excepted, my lord—until we find and stop this Christmas-plot culprit. I cannot believe Ned would stoop to murder, though he is entirely capable of the cleverness of the assault on our traditions. He was livid when I named Leicester Lord of Misrule. Perhaps in passing through the kitchens that day he happened upon Hodge, they argued or there was an accident—and then he's been forced to hide what he's done ever since. In my heart I cannot fathom Ned a killer, even accidentally, but as queen I must be ruled by my head."

Instead of tempestuous Ned, she pictured her volatile Robin again, so handsome, so intense. She wearied of holding him at arm's length. She cherished the ride on the frozen river with him today, even though they'd argued. Sometimes she thought that if only she had a husband to help bear her burdens—but if she had a husband, then England had a king, and kings had a way of ruling over queens, too, so . . .

A sharp knock on the door shattered her musings.

"The Earl of Sussex awaits," Harry announced, sticking only his head and shoulders in. "And," he added, whispering now, "he's just returned to the palace."

Sussex had obviously come in great haste. When he swept off his cap to bow, Elizabeth saw that his boots—those boots that were the exact size of the probable murderer's—were mottled with melted snow. His hair was still mussed, and he nervously smoothed it more than once. His gloves were yet stuck in his belt, and his cheeks were burnished like two autumn pippins.

"Your Majesty, ah, what is the cause, and what may I do to help?" he inquired as he rose from his bow.

"Perhaps much. I have it on good authority you have been abroad this day, and as I've been no farther than the river, I'd like to hear all you've seen and done in my city."

"Ah, all I've seen and done in the city."

"Cecil, is there an echo in here?" she asked. Sussex shot Cecil a sideways glance. 'S blood, the queen fumed, but Sussex looked guilty of something, like the boy who stuck his thumb in a pie and pulled out a plum. But whether Sussex was a good boy or not remained to be seen.

"Someone saw me, I take it," he said, shifting from one foot to the other.

"Perhaps a little bird told me," she said, glaring at him.

"And you want to know if people are in a festive mood, or the condition of the snowy streets, or—"

She smacked the arms of her chair with her fists and jumped to her feet. Sussex stepped back so fast he nearly tripped. "Don't fence with me, my lord," she commanded, pointing her finger at him. "I may be a woman, unskilled in the military maneuvers you have practiced and perfected, but I am your queen. And I want to know why you went out today to meet someone you could well have spoken to in the warmth of this palace!"

"Ah—Vicar Bane? I stopped to wish good Yuletide cheer to Bishop Grindal, and Bane happened to be there, that's all. Is Bane back already—and, ah, mayhap mentioned he spoke with me?"

"Yuletide cheer was it? You stopped to wish Bishop Grindal good Yuletide cheer? I suppose you were simply shopping for New Year's gifts at St. Paul's Walk, too?"

"I—yes. You had me followed, Your Majesty? But what have I done to deserve—"

"I am asking the questions, Sussex, though you are doing a pitiful job with the answers."

His ruddy glow went white as bleached linen. Damn, but she'd be distraught if a powerful peer of the realm had caused this upheaval at court, let alone committed or ordered a murder. And all because he so hated his rival Leicester, his promotion and position?

"Did you see anyone else I would know on your goodwill jaunt, Sussex?" she went on. If he lied about seeing Giles Chatam and passing him a note and money, she must have Sussex more thoroughly questioned.

"Ah, yes, I saw someone else, but it's a private affair."

"Shall I tell your lady Frances of that? A private affair?"

He blanched again. "Not that sort of thing, Your Majesty, I swear it."

"And I swear to you that this is serious business to me and I must know it all."

"I saw the new actor, Giles Chatam," he blurted.

"Aha. A private affair. Meaning?"

"It's a sort of Yuletide secret, Your Majesty."

"Cecil, this is a man who can command an army but cannot command himself in my presence!" she cried, looking to her chief secretary and then back at the shaken but defiant Sussex. "I cannot afford secrets, man! Why did you meet and bribe and pass orders to an itinerant young actor you surely could not even have known before a few days ago?"

At last, Sussex looked shocked. "Is—is something wrong with him? I overheard he was going to be at St. Paul's. Ah, he loves to wander the city, Your Grace, and I said he should look me up."

"Obviously! Because?"

"I had a poem for him to recite to someone special on New Year's Eve, a poem I wrote myself, for, as you know, speaking is not my *forte*. I can fetch you the rough copy of it from my chamber where I have it hidden. A gift for my lady wife, as were the finely wrought flagons I bought from a vendor who was highly recommended to me."

Elizabeth sank into her chair again. The anger ebbed from her; she felt deflated. All that could be true, of course. She wanted to believe him. Still, he could have handed the poem and money to Giles Chatam here at court. And since when was he in so tight with Bishop Grindal, or was it Bane he really went to see where they would not be seen talking—perhaps plotting—together? She supposed neither of the churchmen could stomach Leicester's growing power any more than Sussex could.

"Shall I fetch you the poem for proof, then, Your Majesty?"

"My lord, as you know, there is someone skulking about our court, mocking our attempts to have a happy and holy holiday. The only proof I want from you is that you keep your well-honed eyes for enemies wide open and report to me should you note anything amiss."

"You—you suspected me?" he asked, aghast.

"I suspect anyone who acts suspiciously, my lord. Frankly, your foot fit the print of the one we believed murdered Hodge in the kitchens."

"M-murder? But—boots are made in such general sizes by so few boot makers and imported. These were," he said, frowning down at them.

"I realize all that."

"Who took my print, or did someone just eye my size? But why would I kill your privy dresser in the kitchen?"

"Never mind all that, Sussex, but heed my words to be watchful. I will not have another bizarre affront on me or our holidays here. And I charge you to keep this quiet."

"Because I detest Leicester, is that it?" he asked, evidently not knowing when to leave well enough alone, but the man's family pride was meat and drink to him. "And the corpse decked in peacock feathers mocked him? Ah—you asked me earlier, Your Grace, by what sobriquets he was known at court. But he has many enemies beyond me, I assure you, and some not so vocal about it who might sneak around to do something vile and sordid, which I would not."

"You may go, my lord, but I do thank you for your testimonial about how many others hate him and about your innocence in the matter of murder or general mayhem."

He looked as if he would argue more, but he bowed and left.

"I've done something I don't usually do, my lord," she told Cecil when the door closed.

"Anger an important courtier?"

"No, I've actually confronted two of the possible culprits today, three if you count Ned, and tried to put the fear of God—or of queen—in them. But MacNair and Sussex have both stood up well."

"So you're discounting them?"

"If I'm not discounting my dear Ned, I'm discounting no one. Keep a good eye out tonight, my lord, for at the Feast of Fools everyone will be disguised, not only the man we must unmask."

Despite being strung tight as a lute string, Elizabeth enjoyed the evening. The roast suckling pig was good—the first solid meat that had appealed to her in days—and naught appeared under silver serving lids on platters that should not be there. She had a double helping of the rich date-and-cinnamon Yule fool, the music pleased her, and everyone seemed happy to be wearing splendid costumes, Kat especially. Vicar Bane was the only one not so attired, though he did deign to don a plain half mask with huge eyeholes, the better to spy on everyone, she thought. But evidently the fun and gaiety were too much for him, for she saw him rip his mask off and depart in a huff after dinner.

She soon began to breathe even easier. At Robin's sign, while the ladies waited, the men who would return as the mummers slipped out to prepare their grand entrance. For some reason, the audience waited for an inordinate amount of time. She supposed she should have kept Ned as Lord of Misrule, for Robin was surely a novice at all this.

But everyone oohed and aahed when the men piled into the room helter-skelter, laughing and singing about "Good King Wenceslas," though the second time through they changed the chorus to "Good Queen Elizabeth." Along with everyone else, she tried to pick out who was who, but the mummers wore matching armored breastplates and helmets with their visors down. Identical bouncing white plumes made them look like knights ready for joust or battle. Yet everyone was soon laughing that their singing, echoing strangely, came from inside those domes of steel.

"I should think they would all go breathless and deaf in those!" Rosie cried, holding her sides she was laughing so hard.

Occasionally, two or more of the mummers would stage a willy-nilly sword fight between songs, or open a visor just enough to gulp down more ale or mulled cider. Cecil, nervous as a cat, came up to stand beside her chair.

"Ordinarily, they'd all be in the Tower for so much as drawing a sword in the monarch's presence," he groused.

"My dear Cecil, it's Fools day," she chided gently, "and the Lord of Misrule is in charge tonight, not me. Besides, my yeomen guards stand at the ready all around the room should someone step out of line."

Even though she was tempted to give a sign to Robin to stop the swordplay, she couldn't be sure which knight he was. Their tall helmets and feathers made them look the same height, the same build, and they all wore black hose and shoes. She supposed that was why her father finally halted the mumming years ago. Men got away with drunken or raucous deeds and were completely disguised. But she could tell the mummers were running out of strength and breath in those hot shells. Soon they would lift their visors and be done with this tomfoolery.

She was wrong, though, for they were leaving, being herded out by someone, though that knight didn't carry himself like Robin. Nor like Ned. Perhaps Ned's uncle or even Giles Chatam was taking charge of the scattershot exit.

But as all but one cleared the door, that man pulled out two small stuffed dolls from inside his breastplate. Everyone grew silent to see what was coming next. One doll had red hair and a wire crown; the other was a male doll with peacock feathers sprouting from his bum.

The queen gasped. Had Robin arranged to make light of his own nickname, or of what had happened to poor Hodge? It all happened so fast, in a blur.

The lone mummer held the dolls tight face-to-face, rubbing them together as if they were kissing—or performing a more lewd act. If that was Robin, she would kill him for this. Lord of Misrule or not, he had greatly overstepped.

Her ladies and the few men scattered throughout the audience remained silent but for a smothered snicker or two far behind her.

"Enough," Elizabeth declared, rising, "whether those poor

puppets stand under the kissing bough or not!" Appalled, she fought to keep from blushing. She didn't care whether Robin would plead Misrule's rights or Fools night or the end of the world, she was going to have his head on a platter, either for doing this or allowing this.

"Cecil," she whispered, "see that my guards detain that man, I don't care if it is Leicester."

"Yes, Your Grace," he said and disappeared into the crowd as her ladies prepared to follow their queen from the room. But when she glanced again at the door, it was empty, for the lone knight had disappeared behind the others.

Elizabeth went directly to her rooms and dismissed her entourage, saying Kat and Rosie would help her undress for bed. But the moment the back hall cleared, she asked Rosie to look after Kat and, with only her yeoman Clifford with her, headed for Robin's rooms. Good rooms, she fumed, warm rooms, she'd given him. Whether drunk with liquor or with power, he had gone too far.

Nearing his chamber, she came face-to-face with Ned, Jenks, and Meg, coming her way in a rush down the corridor, so she sent Clifford back to his post.

"What happened?" Ned cried.

"Were you among the mummers?" she asked him, not breaking her stride. They wheeled about to follow her.

"Yes, but I only heard something happened at the end I didn't see. Who did what?"

"I saw," Meg said. "I went to see how Jenks was doing guarding the kitchens, but I saw it. Jenks and I just met Ned in the hall."

"Wait here," Elizabeth said and pounded her fist on Robin's door. If he was not back, she'd post Jenks here to bring him right away when he returned. His title of Lord of Misrule was going back to Ned forthwith, and Robin was being banished from court.

"Guess he's not back yet," Meg said.

"If he has one bit of brain left, he'll just keep going, clear to Scotland or to hell!" Elizabeth declared. "I trust him to keep a lid on things, and he makes it all worse."

But as she turned to march back to her apartments, she heard a muffled sound. Had she knocked on the door so hard that she'd pushed it partway open? Had it not been closed or latched?

She gave the door a little shove, and it swung easily inward.

Trussed with a web of ropes, Robin lay belly down, stark naked on a table, with his lower legs bent up behind him. His blue face contrasted with the red apple jammed in his mouth. He was desperately trying to keep his ankles close to his head, for if he let them straighten, the noose around his neck cut off his air like a garrote. Stuck within the ropes were two crudely lettered parchment signs, which partly hid his nakedness. One read YULE FOOL and the other ROAST SUCKING-UP BORE.

Chapter the Tenth

Roast Suckling Pig

To roast a pig curiously, first tie the legs back. You shall not scald it but draw it with the hair on, then, having washed it, spit it and lay it to the fire so that it may not scorch, then, being a quarter roasted, and the skin blistered from the flesh, with your hand pull away the hair and skin, and leave all the fat and flesh perfectly bare; then with your knife scotch all the flesh down to the bones, then baste it exceedingly with sweet butter and cream, being no more but warm; then dredge it with fine bread crumbs, currants, sugar, and salt mixed together, and thus apply dredging upon basting until you have covered all the flesh a full inch deep; then, the meat being fully roasted, draw it and serve it up whole. Place an apple in its mouth and surround it on the platter with baked apples and onions, also sprigs of rosemary and bay.

"HELP HIM!" ELIZABETH CRIED, BUT SHE TOO RAN TO Robin. Ned held his legs to ease the strain on the noose as Jenks cut his cords. Forgotten for now, the two bizarre messages sailed away and were trodden underfoot. The queen loosened the rope around his neck as Meg seized his shirt from the floor and covered him.

"Jenks," Elizabeth said, "carefully cut the apple in half so we can get it out of his mouth. Robin, you're all right now, you're safe," she told him, plucking the fruit out in two pieces. While he heaved in huge breaths that shook his big frame, she grasped his shoulder, then rubbed his bare back as if she were comforting a child.

"He would have died for sure if we'd not come!" Jenks said as he finished cutting and tearing the ropes away.

Attempted murder! Elizabeth thought. What if she had lost Robin? Brushing tears from her cheeks, she felt flushed, but her skin was gooseflesh. To think that she'd blamed him for that rude affront downstairs when he was fighting for his life up here.

"You must have been tied before the mummers entered the hall tonight," she told him as Jenks pulled a sheet off the nearby bed to wrap him. "And the demon who did this could have taken your place among them."

With their help, Robin sat up slowly. "Would you prefer a chair or bed, my lord?" she asked. He nodded toward the bed Jenks had just ripped apart, and they helped him to it. However, he sat up in it, leaning back against the carved headboard, his face now livid, his neck red and welted where the noose had chafed him.

The queen fetched wine and held it to his lips. Weakly, he lifted one hand to hold her wrist. Though no doubt still shaken and shamed, he lifted his gaze to hers at last.

"I thought I would die," he whispered, "and never see you again. My last thoughts—of you."

"Meg, go fetch one of my physicians," the queen commanded.

"No!" Robin whispered, gripping her wrist. "No doctor. I do not want this all over the court and country. Please tell no one, my queen."

"Yes, all right. The three of you, wait just outside the door," she ordered, "and leave it ajar. I will speak with my lord alone a moment to hear what happened."

The three of them did as bidden; she could hear them whispering in the corridor. She lifted the heavily embossed flagon of wine so Robin could sip again and stroked his wayward tresses off his forehead, wet with sweat. Carefully, she sat on the edge of his bed, her hip next to his knee.

"I should have heeded your words of warning," he said. "Because of all we mean to each other, the love I bear you, someone wants to humiliate and kill me. I desperately need your help and protection, my queen."

"God as my judge, you shall have my help!"

"And your love, too? Just a bit?"

"You know I do—I have and do," she stammered. "But to keep you—all of us—safe, I must discover who did this."

He frowned and lifted both hands to his head. Rope marks marred each wrist. "Splitting head pain," he whispered. "I can't recall much. After the feast, I was in a flurry, getting the mummers ready. I realized I'd left my speech upstairs ... here, in my chamber. My servants were downstairs, helping everyone into armor, so I ran up here to fetch it, up the back servants' staircase."

"So you weren't with the mummers," she repeated, feeling greatly relieved. "You were no part of what they did. But did you see anyone with two dolls?"

"Dolls? There were no dolls."

The sheet slid off one muscular shoulder, and she hastily reached to rewrap him. Now that her panic had ebbed, cold clarity and common sense set in: the Virgin Queen of England was alone with her so-called favorite on his bed, and he was naked under that sheet. It terrified her how much she wanted to stretch out beside him to comfort and be comforted. But she must plan her next move, though that was rather like playing chess with a phantom.

As for keeping this attempted murder quiet, she agreed with Robin. She did not want him privily or publicly mocked by his enemies. Such ridicule must be the motive behind Hodge's death and now this. But these were also affronts against her. She had no doubt Queen Mary of Scots would laugh herself silly if she knew the illustrious Earl of Leicester had been displayed as a boar, a pig. Those rag dolls so lewdly tumbled together were bad enough—but this . . .

"Meg, Jenks, Ned," she called as she stood, "enter!"

"Yes, Your Majesty?" Ned asked, as if he were spokesman for the group.

"First of all, I hold the three of you accountable to keep what happened here a secret. If our Christmas culprit wants to cause more chaos, he must fail at least in having this noised abroad, or if someone gossips of it, we shall trace the source and have our man. Meg and Jenks, stay here while I question my lord Leicester. It is obvious he may have beheld our murderer, though the horrid experience has made it hard for him to recall."

"The blow to my head," Robin explained, his voice much stronger.

Elizabeth set down the flagon of wine and stooped to look closer at his head. "You didn't say that before. Hodge was hit on his head, too, yet I see no blood on you. Will it hurt if I touch it?"

"Never. Not your touch," he whispered for her ears only.

Perhaps the real Robin was back now, she thought. He looked almost smug. She felt through his thick, glossy hair, her fingertips skimming his scalp. He flinched. "There," he said. "I was hit there with something from behind, that's all I know. I can't remember anything else until I heard your voice at the door and tried to call for help."

Elizabeth realized she did not want Ned to hear all this lest she had to question him later. "Ned," she said, turning toward him, her hands still on Robin's head. "Oh—I didn't see you take those insulting messages out with you," she noted when she saw the parchments in his hands. "Leave them here, and go make a list of all those who were among the mummers tonight. Then I will have you as well as Lord Leicester and his servants peruse the list and mark off which men they are certain were in armor, and perhaps which one came late to be costumed and was the last one from the room with those damned dolls."

"What's all this about dolls?" Robin asked.

"I'll explain later."

"So by process of elimination, you hope to discover who hit me and arranged this part of tonight's performance—ow!" he cried, jerking from her touch on his head. "That must be the very spot I took the blow."

Strange, she thought, but unlike poor Hodge, not a bit of blood, scab, nor so much as a bump marred Robin's pate. The tender spot she'd just touched was inches from the first place that had caused him to flinch. But the man was hardheaded in more ways than one; a lump would no doubt rise like a goose egg on the morrow.

"So the last thing you recall," Elizabeth prompted after Ned left, looking much dismayed, and Meg and Jenks stayed by the door, "is running up the back servants' stairs. Those twist and turn so someone could be close to you yet remain out of your sight, even if you turned around to look back down."

"Which I didn't," he said, then added, "at least I don't think so."

"And, pardon, Your Grace," Meg put in from across the room, "but there's a small room off those stairs someone could have popped out of."

"Yes, that's true," Robin said, frowning. "I regret to say that I'm going to be about as much help in this as poor Hodge was."

"Jenks," Elizabeth said, "take a torch and search the entire length of those stairs to see if something was dropped. Look in the anteroom Meg mentioned, too."

"Yes, Your Grace. Shall I take these two signs, then? Mayhap we can match handwriting like we tried to do with the murderer's boot pr—" he got out before he evidently recalled that Leicester knew nothing of their investigation.

'S blood, Elizabeth thought, perhaps he knew now, so she might as well tell him everything. "Yes, when you go, Jenks, put those signs in my rooms. They are clues indeed."

"Wait!" Robin said. "Your Grace, I didn't see the signs you speak of, though I have suspected that you were privily looking into what seems to have gone so awry this holiday. Let me see those, man," he ordered.

Elizabeth gestured for Jenks to show Robin the stiff parchments with the heavy slashes of dark lettering. "It's someone clever with words," Robin said, frowning at one message and then the other. "He's clever but so evil that he's actually enjoying this, making a game of it all. And he hates me with a passion."

"And therefore hates and defies me," Elizabeth added. "All right, then, Meg, remain with me, and Jenks, be off with you."

"Sit again, please," Robin pleaded, patting the bed.

Instead, she shoved the nearest chair close and sat, leaning forward to hold his hand. "I assure you, I have a list of those who could want to shame or harm you, Robin. Sussex at the top, for obvious reasons."

"I'd wager my entire fortune on that."

"But he is so obvious, we must not jump to judgment. The wily Scot MacNair obviously resents your slighting, and therefore insulting, his queen. Lord Darnley and his mother detest you, since they want Darnley to wed Mary and probably think you're simply playing hard-to-catch with her, though I have reason to believe Darnley did not harm Hodge. Some suspicion for Hodge's demise has been thrown on that new blond player, Giles Chatam, but I can't fathom he'd dare all this. Oh, and have you had harsh words of late with Vicar Bane or his master Bishop Grindal?"

"I have indeed. A fortnight ago Bane warned me in no uncertain terms to steer completely clear of you but for council business. He believes I'm a bad influence, of course, a libertine who draws you even farther from the stern Protestant faith."

"*His* version of it," she amended. "Cecil and his wife have Puritan leanings, yet they are hardly harbingers croaking doom for such things as snowballs and a little fun at Yule."

"Exactly. At any rate, I saw Bane huddled with Sussex, so he may have put Bane up to warning me off. As Bane snidely put it, our relationship, yours and mine, my queen, might look morally compromising if I had the queen's ear—and perhaps had even more of her than that."

"He said that? The weasel! Then he is to be watched even more than I thought. And I saw him throw down his mumming mask tonight as if it were a gauntlet and stalk out early. Pray God he didn't do this to you and then don armor to try to shame me with that crude mummery of the dolls. My father was right to outlaw mummery however much everyone loves the tradition."

"Speaking of the mummery tonight," he said, "pray tell me about those dolls."

"All right. The last mummer to leave the hall pressed together two small figures which mimicked us in a most lewd way."

"Or in a loving way?" he countered. "Lucky dolls."

Though his grin was more of a grimace, she at least knew she had her Robin back. But things were different now. She would allow him to help her in the investigation. Cecil might balk, but she could use the extra help, and Robin must now be protected at all costs.

"I don't want to leave you alone," she told him. "Why haven't your servants returned?"

"I gave them leave to watch the festivities in the hall, then take their leisure with the kitchen workers tonight," he explained, scooting down in the bed as if he'd take a nap, "but it's not of my servants I must speak." He squinted toward Meg, then added, even more quietly, "You see, now I do recall seeing a single person on that staircase tonight."

"Meg?" the queen whispered.

"No, Ned Topside."

The next day, December 30, was Bringing in the Boar Day, originally a time to replace the domestic hogs supposedly eaten so far during the holidays with fresh meat. But, despite wanting to cling to tradition, the queen canceled the hunt, claiming cold weather. The truth was she could not face some other dreadful occurrence.

She still was not sleeping well, for the same horrid dream had disturbed her more than once.

In it, she and Robin walked the riverbank after their wedding. The marriage was not the nightmare of it, for she rather relished that, at least until the horrid part began. Down they went, holding hands, their feet and legs, then bodies, sucked into the bog along the banks. And all around them, as river water rushed in to drown them, stood a pack of dogs howling at the skies and baying for their blood.

Even now, she shook her head to clear it. She must ignore such sick fancies and solve what crimes had already been committed. She must stop whatever dreadful deed her tormentor planned for New Year's Eve and the first day of 1565, the seventh year of her reign.

"You wanted to see me, Your Majesty?" Ned's voice carried from the door of her privy apartments. She had told her yeomen guards to let him in where she and Cecil sat catching up on writs and decrees that could not wait for the new year.

"We did," she said, gesturing him in. She could tell that he was not happy to see Cecil and that he took note when her favorite yeoman guard, Clifford, stepped into the room instead of simply closing the door behind him.

"Ah," Ned said, "Secretary Cecil here, too. I heard there was a Privy Plot Council meeting earlier this morning without me, so I assume you want to catch me up on everything now. Your Grace, must I really stick so tight to Giles Chatam? He's starting to think I favor him, when I want him out the door when the players head for the shires again."

"Would you like to sit, Ned?" she asked.

"If it please you," he said and sat across the table from her and Cecil.

"Anything else to report on Giles?" she asked.

"He's got the heart of a rustic but the brain of a courtier, I fear. Sad to say, if he can't win me over—which he cannot—he'd probably just as soon knock me on the head to get my post."

"Knock you on the head? An interesting turn of phrase. Are you hinting that he might have knocked the earl out and wants to do the same to you?"

"I would not go that far—yet," he said.

"Then how far would you go?" Cecil demanded.

Ned had seldom been afraid, but he was now. Surely Her Grace could not believe, after all they'd been through together, that he was guilty of heinous acts. Ned knew how she still cared for Robert Dudley, her damned precious Robin. Why, if Dudley hadn't been suspected of murdering his wife several years ago, he'd probably be in Elizabeth's lap in more ways than one, and Ned would give anything to counter that.

But now he was starting to be terrified he wouldn't be around to keep that from happening. A few years back when the queen had discovered Meg had defied and lied to her, there'd been hell to pay, and that wasn't even a question of murder. However much she cared for Meg and valued her skills, the queen had banished her from court.

"How far would I go?" Ned threw back at Cecil, knowing he was about to play one of the most important scenes of his life. "I'd go to hell and back to help Her Grace."

"Then tell us," Cecil went on as if he'd suddenly become the queen's inquisitor, "why the Earl of Leicester saw you on that staircase where he was struck and from which he was, no doubt, carried or dragged to his room to be trussed like a dead boar. Ned, you really should have volunteered that you saw him rushing up that back staircase, to help jog his memory."

Ned's insides cartwheeled, but he fought to remain calm. "I thought it best to let the earl tell his tale while things were fresh in his mind, and then the queen ordered me away. The plain facts are that I saw him run out of the mumming preparations last night and thought he might need help, so I followed him. Of course, I would have brought all this up later in a Privy Plot meeting—if I'd been invited to the meeting."

"You say you thought you'd be of help to the earl, but you haven't been, have you?" Cecil parried, folding his arms over his chest. "To him or us?"

Ned didn't like the staging here, sitting across a table facing both queen and Cecil, but too late to change that now. He'd have to carry this off with commanding eye contact. "I called to him," he explained, speaking slowly, "but he was a ways ahead of me on that twisting staircase. When I caught up to him, he said I should head back down and keep an eye on things. If he doesn't recall all that, I would attribute it to his head blow, which must have been delivered by someone else when I left him. I immediately did as he said, went back downstairs, got into my armor—"

"On your own?" Cecil interrupted. "It seems no one recalls helping you don your armor, and most remarked they needed aid with it."

"Yes, on my own, my lord," he said, trying to keep his rising dread in check. Cecil had just given away the fact that they'd been questioning others besides Leicester. "After all, I've been in and out of stage armor half my life, and that's what that was, most of it," Ned plunged on. "The weather was too cold to send someone to the Tower to fetch pieces from the royal armory, so some of it was the property of my uncle's troupe."

"Yes, we heard. But back to the topic at hand."

Ned swallowed hard. Cecil was too wily to give things away without intending to, so he must mean to make him sweat a bit. Now he'd let on they were asking the Queen's Country Players about his behavior. Ned had not tried to change the subject just now, and curse Cecil for implying that in front of Her Grace. He prayed they hadn't questioned Meg about his trying to get her to vouch for him, because she'd said she wouldn't lie to the queen or even to Cecil.

"Ned," Her Majesty put in, "several of the mummers say you planned the activities for last night, though I take it the speech Leicester left in his chamber was his own. People have said that you planned the similar armor that made everyone look so alike. Furthermore, I recall that in a jesting way you mentioned to me both a peacock and roast boar shortly before Hodge Thatcher and the Earl of Leicester were attacked and horribly displayed as such."

He shifted his gaze, carefully, not dartingly, from Cecil's hard stare to the queen's worried countenance. Desperately he hoped she, at least, could be convinced to be on his side.

"Mere circumstance, Your Grace. As for the earl being named Lord of Misrule, frankly, it's been entertaining to help him. I'm happy to do it, for all the detailed planning is really not his strength, you know." He managed a slight smile and little shrug.

"What is his strength, then?" Cecil pursued, leaning over his clasped hands on the table. "Leicester seems to think you, like several others at court, might resent Her Grace's friendship with him."

"I'm just an actor, my lord, a servant, and not some peer of the realm to be dabbling in political or personal matters."

"Can you deny," Cecil said, narrowing his eyes, "you were especially annoyed that Her Grace named the earl Lord of Misrule in your place, when, indeed, so much of the work and planning for the Twelve Days has been yours in the past—let alone how all your preliminary work this year was simply assumed by him?"

Yours *in the past*—the words seemed to echo in Ned's stunned mind. What if the queen dismissed him and his career at court was in the past? What if he was forced to go on the road again, or worse, if she kept the handsome Giles to replace him? God forbid, what if she had him arrested for further questioning?

It was then that he made a gut-wrenching decision. All life was a gamble, wasn't it? He opted for being insubordinate and defiant rather than proper and cowering.

"Your Majesty and Secretary Cecil," he said in such a clarion voice that they both blinked and sat back a bit, "I see no reason such insinuations and slights should be aimed at one who has served Her Majesty well and would give his very life for her, indeed, for both of you. If you think I've done aught amiss, or am behind the dreadful deeds which I have been proud and vigilant to help you probe, say so and let me deny it plain. God's truth, but I am guilty of naught but perhaps pride and a bit of bombast here and there, a necessity in my calling. And as for not favoring the Earl of Leicester, I believe you yourself, my lord Cecil, have had harsh words with him and even harsher feelings for him over the years. Am I dismissed or worse, Your Most Gracious Majesty?"

"A pretty speech, but—" Cecil began, his usually controlled voice aquiver with anger.

"You are dismissed," the queen cut in, "only from the Privy Plot Council for now, Ned, because I want you to keep a closer watch on Giles."

"I see," he said, not budging immediately. Actually, he did see. How like the brilliant queen he'd adored and studied for over six years. She would keep her true motives close to her chest, but she would also keep him close. Time and again he'd seen her do that with those she suspected of deceit or treachery before she cut them down.

"I suppose I should be grateful you are even willing to see me," Margaret Stewart, Countess of Lennox, told Elizabeth that afternoon. The countess gave her usual disdainful sniff as the queen walked the Waterside Gallery for exercise with her ladies trailing behind. You might know, Elizabeth thought, in this Yuletide season, when most wore merry colors, Margaret was cloaked in black velvet and satin. As they turned back along the vast array of windows overlooking the frozen Thames, Margaret sniffed yet again.

"Have you a cold or the ague, Margaret?"

"No, I have what goes beyond a physical complaint, Your Majesty, and I thought it best I tell you."

"Please do. I much favor honesty. And so I will tell you that when the northern roads clear, Lord Darnley may visit his father in Scotland and, of course, personally deliver my best wishes to Queen Mary."

"But you have said so before and changed your mind."

"What is that they say?" Elizabeth countered. "Ah, 'Do not look a gift horse in the mouth,' I believe. Consider it my New Year's gift to both of you. And what is it vexes you so sore, Margaret?"

"This holiday especially you have treated me as if I am of inferior or no rank, Your Majesty. Kat Ashley is not of royal blood nor of the peerage, and you favor her more than you ever have me, worrying whether she enjoyed this or did she see that. Best queens should heed rank if they want theirs heeded. You did not ask me to tell a tale of my memories of Christmas the other night, but Kat told hers. And do you know what my Yuletide memory would have been?"

"I believe you will tell me," Elizabeth murmured as they turned and walked back again. Through the windows, she kept her eyes on activities on the Thames rather than on Margaret's sour face. It looked so cold out there, but she preferred it to the chill she'd always felt with this distant relative who had been so cruel to her in her youth when she desperately needed friends at court. Besides, Elizabeth was in a wretched mood today and didn't need Margaret's carping. She had a meeting with Vicar Martin Bane soon, and the mere thought of that was ruining the whole day.

"I recall," Margaret plunged on, "the Christmases when I was treated as one of the Tudor family, which I am. I recall the times I

was esteemed and honored, harkened to, and trusted for counsel—"

"Times before you sent your son to woo Mary of Scots in
France, perhaps, in direct opposition to my royal wishes?" the
queen interrupted, keeping her voice low and sweet. "Times
before, once she returned to Scotland, you parlayed behind my
back with the Scots lords, perhaps times before there were Christmases when someone tried to ruin things with a dead kitchen
worker, a box of stones, and a fox's head in place of a boar's head
on a platter." Elizabeth wanted to throw the outrage about Leicester in her face, too, so she could read her reaction, but she bit her
tongue. Perhaps whoever was responsible would make some sort
of slipup on that.

"Well," Margaret declared huffily, "I have no notion of why
you're fussing about all that to me!"

"Good. Let us keep it that way by not talking about this anymore, or talking at all. You see, I have a Christmas memory of
when I was ten and you intentionally ruined my gown with gravy
and told me I was skinny and whey-faced and had freckles bad as
pox marks and that your ties to the Tudors would always elevate
you over a king's bastard, so that I must walk at least two steps
behind you. But Margaret," she added, taking a breath and ignoring the woman's shocked stare, "thanks to my good graces, here
you are in step with me—perhaps even several steps ahead."

Abruptly, the queen stopped walking. Margaret swished past
before she could turn back, but Elizabeth had already headed for
the corridor to return to the royal apartments where Kat was waiting.

"You know," Kat whispered when Elizabeth told her what

Margaret had said, "the countess was in a foul mood last night, too. Even though her son was to be among the mummers, she left the hall before they came in. She was probably upset she wasn't the center of attention or given some special honor."

"Kat, you never cease to amaze me," Elizabeth said and gave her a hearty hug. "Do you remember when you used to help the Privy Plot Council solve crimes, and you'd keep an eye on people for me?"

"I do, but I'm glad it's not those dreadful days again, even if we are having an old-time Christmas."

Elizabeth smiled grimly as she left her ladies to go alone into her bedchamber to use the close stool. There she startled Rosie Radcliffe, bending over the table, rifling through the stack of court documents she had yet to sign.

"Oh, Your Grace!"

"Rosie, whatever are you doing? Why aren't you with the others?"

"I—I was, but I seem to have lost a piece of your jewelry—a bracelet, the one with rubies and emeralds you favor at Yule—and thought it could have come unclasped or snagged in these while you and Secretary Cecil were working earlier today."

Rosie went red as a rose indeed; the queen knew the bracelet was missing, but she had thought she'd lost it on Feast of Fools night. Could Rosie, who cared for the jewelry cases now that Kat no longer could, have hidden it to give herself an excuse to snoop?

The queen's stomach knotted, and her head began to hurt again. Surely Rosie had not been sent by her uncle Sussex to discover how much the queen knew of his plotting against Leicester.

Lest that be true, Elizabeth knew she must keep an eye on her too. It was a sorry state of affairs, the queen fumed, that at this joyous season, she couldn't trust dear friends much more than she could her enemies.

Chapter the Eleventh

Christmas Candles

At Christmastide only, much delight of the season can be added to candles, and not only through dipping them to additional thickness. As ever, for making fine beeswax candles use linen rags to wax and roll, but with links or torches use coarse hemp. For the holidays, the wax can be scented with scents such as lavender, rosemary, or lemon verbena. Dye the molten wax red or green, expensive though it may be. Red hues can be achieved by adding ground imported sandalwood or brazilwood from East India, imported by galleys on the Thames and purchased from a booth on St. Paul's Walk. If used at court, a rich Tudor green can be made by adding juice of spinach or crushed green wheat. Of course, such are the colorings used to make puddings, sauces, and gravies bright at table the year round.

"STATELY AND LOVELY AS THE STURDY FIR, SO STANDS our queen, who may bend to help her people but shall never break. And should cold winds of foreign discord buffet her, she shall shed her cares like melting snow and be our guide and sign of green and sunny springtide days and years to come . . ."

Elizabeth heard the flattering words echo off the hammerbeam ceiling of the Great Hall. From behind the decorative screen that kept drafts from creeping down corridors, she stood listening to the Queen's Country Players rehearse their new drama.

She knew they were planning a play that Ned had written but

Robin had carefully overseen lest other disasters befall. People were yet whispering of the dead privy dresser and the severed fox's head. Cecil had said rumors were rampant that the insults were aimed not only at Leicester but at her for championing him. Vile gossips were insinuating that a queen who could not control a court Christmas could hardly command a kingdom.

Now she and Robin were determined that all other entertainments planned for this holiday season must throw favorable light on the queen, for well they knew that stagecraft could be statecraft. Beyond that, how she hoped that her once trustworthy Ned did indeed believe those flattering words of praise he had written for this play.

With Lady Rosie and Lady Anne Carey with her, Elizabeth stepped from behind the screen into the hall near the dais the players were using for a stage. She surveyed their scenery. A wooden ladder poked above the canvas backdrop of painted snow and frozen Thames.

The first to see her, Ned's uncle Wat, gestured for the rehearsal to halt. She was both annoyed and alarmed that Ned was not among his fellow players. She had expected to see him here and perhaps spot Jenks off in the corner, for she'd told him to keep an eye on Ned and Giles, even if Ned did catch on. Should Ned question Jenks, he was simply to say that the queen had put a second watch on Giles.

"Welcome, Your Majesty! We are most delighted to have you visit our humble efforts," Wat Thompson told her with a grand bow immediately aped by the other actors, including the two boys dressed and bewigged to play women's parts. The handsomer of the two was attired as richly as a queen; indeed, he sported a red wig and a crown. The curly-haired lad wore a Tudor green gown with white puffs of satin on his shoulders and atop his hat and very bushy skirts. Then Elizabeth realized he *was* a bush——a fir tree, at least.

"What is the plot of this play?" she asked, though she'd meant to inquire first where Ned had gone.

"Ah, Your Majesty, you are puzzled by the two lads' parts," Wat said and gestured the boys forward. "Rob is the personification of you, the beloved monarch of our realm, as the sturdy fir——though graceful, too. Look graceful, lad," Wat muttered *sotto voce.* "And Clinton, more slender and prettier of face, is to represent you at the end of the drama, Your Majesty, as eternal queen triumphant."

"I've been symbolized by a great oak once, but never by a fir."

Even as Wat opened his mouth to reply, Giles Chatam stepped from behind him and spoke. "The fir is ever green, Your Most Gracious Majesty, ever young, strong, and supple despite the burdens of snow, wind, or cold——"

"Or," she put in, noting a stuffed nightingale stuck on Rob's shoulder, "despite birds in her branches. I am certain it is a lovely play. Shall I lend you a tiara in place of that tin-looking one?" she asked, gesturing toward Clinton's head. She frowned at the sight of it. The thing reminded her of the wire one the mummer's doll had worn last night.

"We would be most honored, *most* honored," Wat declared, stepping in front of Giles in turn, "and will guard it most closely. The performance is for January the third, Evergreen Day, Your Gracious Majesty."

"Then it makes even more sense than I thought," she told them. "And what part do the others play?"

"Of course," Wat said, glaring at Giles as he sidestepped again to be in the queen's line of sight, "you perhaps heard my voice as narrator of it all. Randall portrays our mighty England, and Giles is the new year with all its blessings and bounty to come, later to be draped in garlands of apples and walnuts, *et cetera*."

"And Ned?"

"The old year which passes," Giles put in before Wat could respond. "Being much older in appearance and outlook than I, he'll be weighed down by a garland of regrets, I don't doubt."

It was the first time the queen had disliked the handsome man. The slur against Ned had been subtle but sly. "But do we not all have regrets?" she asked, staring at Giles. "Do you have none, even recent rueings of mistakes or sins, Master Chatam?"

"I, Your Most Gracious Majesty? I rue that I did not come to see my old playfellow Hodge Thatcher before his untimely death, of course. And that I cannot continue to live in Londontown, however much I admire this company of players and enjoy the countryside of fair England. Frankly, I rue that Ned Topside has a place in your court and in your regard I would die for."

She almost asked the brazen boy if he would kill for it, too. Surely he had not somehow set up Ned to look guilty of something he himself had done. All the mummers from last night, including Giles, Wat, and Randall, had sworn to Baron Hunsdon that they did not leave the presence of the other players and had no notion of which disguised man had produced the two dolls at the end.

Unfortunately, Elizabeth thought, Ned's own actions kept testifying against him. Today he'd disobeyed her by leaving his post here, as he had several other times recently. "Where is Ned, then?" she inquired, as if it were an afterthought. "I believe the old year is just as essential as the new one in this rehearsal."

"Don't know why," Wat said, "but he had business outside on the riverbank and said he'd be back in a trice."

"But a trice has come and passed," Giles said.

However angry she was at Ned, the queen came to mistrust Giles then and silently scolded herself for being taken in by his fine face and form ere this. A long shot he might be in this search for the Christmas killer, but he bore watching, and that tricky Ned was not here to do it. This time she wasn't sending Jenks or anyone else to look for him but was going herself.

Trailing Rosie and Anne, the queen hurried to her apartments to don her boots and hooded, fur-lined cloak. Kat sat alone in the early afternoon sun slanting through the windows. But that was not what seized the queen's attention; she stopped dead still where she stood.

Earlier this morning she, Cecil, and Harry had been minutely examining the two parchment signs Robin's attacker had bound to him. They had left them on the window ledges here. Now, with sunlight streaming in, something they had missed stood out starkly.

The two large sheets of stiff parchment, which were obviously of fine grade, not only showed the slashing strokes of dark letters and words but, beneath that, revealed even more.

" 'S blood and bones!" Elizabeth cried, stomping over to the windows.

"What is it, lovey?" Kat asked from where she'd apparently been contemplating sunbeams.

"Rosie," Elizabeth said, turning to her startled ladies-in-waiting, "please take Kat for a slow stroll in the gallery, and I'll rejoin you here later."

"But I can stay here with you, if there's a problem," Rosie said, nervously plucking at the folds of her skirts.

"I'm not leaving if anything's amiss!" Kat cried.

"Neither of you is to worry," Elizabeth insisted. "Lady Anne will be quite enough company for now." When Rosie looked as if she'd balk, the queen began to panic that perhaps Sussex *had* told his niece to keep an eye on her queen. "Rosie, perhaps you can look for my lost bracelet while you are walking in the gallery," she added pointedly.

At that, Rosie hustled Kat out while Anne remained. "Whatever is it, Your Grace?" she asked.

"I want you to go fetch both your lord husband and Cecil for me, quickly," Elizabeth told her as she pounced on one piece of parchment and held it up close to her eyes in the sun.

When Anne hastened to obey, Elizabeth seized the second sign, then darted to her table, where a pile of documents still went unread. She scrabbled through her papers until she came to what she wanted. When Cecil and Harry came in with Anne, the queen had three pieces of parchment, the two large ones with big, bold lettering and a smaller one with regular script, set on the windowsills.

"A clue right under our noses we missed!" she said by way of greeting and pointed at the parchments.

"You are brilliant as always, Your Grace," Cecil clipped out as he hurried to the windows and stooped to get on eye level with each parchment in turn. "How could we have missed this? Sometimes it's the tiniest, most everyday thing that escapes us."

"It is indeed, my lords, but I've learned the hard way that is the important thing about solving crimes. Do you remember the old adage 'For want of a nail, the shoe was lost, for want of the shoe, the horse was lost, for want of the horse, the rider was lost'?"

" 'For want of the rider,' " Cecil added, " 'the battle was lost, and for want of the battle the war was lost.' "

"But you have not gone far enough, Cecil," she added, "and that's what worries me. 'For want of the war, the kingdom was lost,' and I'll not have that here!"

"But the clue you're speaking of here still escapes me," Harry said, shaking his head. "What in heaven's name are you two talking about? We already went over all that writing, but it was too big and crude to try matching to any of our possible villains' regular hand script."

"The watermarks in the papers," Elizabeth said.

"They all match," Cecil muttered, nodding.

"But those indicate only the place the parchment was made or purchased," Harry protested, though he too bent to look at the ghostly watermarks on the three parchments. "I've seen it done, Your Grace. A wire in a shape to identify the parchment's maker or seller is pressed into each piece of wet rag before it's dried."

"Harry," the queen said as Anne came up behind her husband to also peruse the papers in the sun, "some watermarks indeed identify the prospective buyer, if he or she is of great wealth or power—or of righteous reputation . . ."

"But what, exactly, does this watermark depict?" Cecil asked, turning the smallest parchment upside down. "I just hope we can trace its dagger-like shape."

Almost giddy with excitement to be getting somewhere in this labyrinth of leads—and to be outthinking Cecil—Elizabeth could not help but smile. "The watermarks are not dagger-like shapes, Cecil, but the now burned spire of St. Paul's."

"Aha," Harry said, sounding pleased to be following at last.

"Which," the queen went on, "was not replaced after the fire, because I would not allot the Bishop of London and Vicar Bane the money they wanted for it. As you recall, the city needed additions to St. Bartholomew's Hospital. Bane dunned me hard for the funds, but I have a duty to my treasury, to Parliament, and to my people. So I did not give in to building the steeple rather than helping the hospital when I had already donated much toward the rebuilding of the cathedral's roof."

"And revenge for tying the purse strings, which made Grindal and Bane look bad, could be a secondary motive," Harry declared. "Your Grace, perhaps your declaration of a festive Christmas is only rubbing salt in their already open wounds."

"Exactly," she said, hitting her fist in her palm. "Now look closely, my lords and Anne, at the small parchment which matches the others. That is an epistle charging me to 'clean up Christmas' which Vicar Bane sent me just yesterday."

"Aha!" Harry repeated. "But would an educated man like that be so stupid as to tie signs to Leicester with the bishop's watermark on them?"

"We didn't think to look for watermarks at first," Elizabeth argued while Cecil put the small epistle close to his face and sniffed at it.

"Remember, Your Grace," he said, "when my sketches of the boot print and of Hodge's head wound took on the scent of that flowery *pot pourri* of Mistress Milligrew's?"

"You mean you smell that there, too?"

"No, I smell smoke, as if the very pores of the paper have

soaked it in. Smoke and the faintest whiff of—something sweet, I think it is."

He extended it to her, and she sniffed at it. "I warrant you are on the mark, my lord," she told him.

"But those very scents could have come from this room," Anne put in. "Smoke from the hearth here, sweet scents from the strewing herbs or even the queen's fine-scented clothes."

"No," Elizabeth said, shaking her head so hard her pearl drop earrings rattled. "Unlike these larger pieces of parchment, this letter from Vicar Bane has been somewhere unique. He's hardly one to have sweet scents on his person, so perhaps it's a question of where he wrote this letter or kept the paper. Now where could this have been stored or written that these other, larger parchments were not?" She took up both of the mocking signs, sniffed at them, then passed them to the others.

"No," Cecil concluded, "it's only the epistle from Vicar Bane that reeks of that strange smell, not these two signs. So does that mean Bane did or didn't knock Leicester unconscious and truss him like a roast boar—or bore, as this sign says?"

"I believe," the queen said, "I shall now look forward a bit more to my meeting with Vicar Bane today, to discuss," she added, taking his letter and reading from it, " '*that signs from heaven are wreaking havoc on our pagan, impure court and city Christmas which could soon spread to all the kingdom.*' You know," she added, looking at each of her cohorts in turn, "the smoke of this letter reminds me of the burning of the boathouse. Cecil, I'd appreciate it if you could spare a man to keep an eye on Vicar Bane for me, after I speak with him—unless he gives himself away and I have him arrested."

"I've just the man."

"Harry and Anne, I was about to take a walk outside to find

Ned Topside, and I just had a thought that I may know where to look."

"Where's that?" Harry asked.

"Either where the stones were taken from this building's very foundation or, more likely, the place where Cecil, Jenks, and I were almost baked alive."

In the biting air on the riverbank, Ned Topside had no idea what he was looking for, but he knew he had to find it. The idea had occurred to him when he'd looked out the window of the Great Hall. He'd climbed to the top of a ladder from which two pillowcases of cut lace would be dumped, sending snowflakes from heaven onto their makeshift stage during their little drama on Evergreen Day. From the ladder, he could gaze out the high windows at the riverbank, where he'd seen four workmen raking up the rubble of the burned boathouse.

Being forced to leave off watching Giles and taking a chance on disobeying the queen's orders, Ned had made excuses and set out.

"Find anything unusual in this mess?" he'd asked the workmen, hoping the queen hadn't given them those very orders. He should have come out here ere this to look for evidence left behind.

"Metal oarlocks," the big-shouldered one told him as they raked through the ruins, which had finally stopped smoldering. "Fire started underneath and went up, so's not much wasn't charred real good."

"Charred bad," his loutish-looking fellow worker corrected him, as if they were tutors about to give a lecture on good grammar. " 'Course things that was dragged out, like the royal barge, was saved."

Starting to feel cold instead of warm in his excitement, Ned nodded as he gazed at the big barge, wrapped with layers of protective hemp like a massive mummy.

"Where did they get that much hemp?" he asked the workers. "I could use some of that for a court entertainment I have coming up."

"Don't know," the big-shouldered one said to him.

"I do," muttered the lout, who suddenly wasn't looking so loutish after all. "The boatmen good as robbed the chandlery of it, and there was a real fuss, 'cause hemp's needed to make extra torches for the holidays. You know, like the one I saw way over here," he added and shuffled to the very edge of the charred pile to lift the remains of a short torch called a link.

"Was that found in the charred remains?" Ned asked, walking through snow and ash to look closer at it. What was left of its wax showed it had been dyed red for Yule, so it must be a current one. "But why didn't it burn up, too?" he added.

" 'Cause it was over here a ways!" the man told him, vaguely pointing in the direction of the Bishop of London's Lambeth Palace. "It didn't come direct from this burnt pile," he added as if Ned were a dunce.

Ned knew link torches were made by pieces of hemp being dipped in precious beeswax and rolled together, then attached to a short pole, though little was left of this one but a red stub of waxed hemp and the shaft. The point was, Ned thought, as his pulse quickened, it was an expensive link only someone of wealth or position would use. And it had been evidently heaved out of the way of the burning building, or perhaps dropped when someone fled.

He'd take it to the chandlery in the back buildings of the palace and see if one was missing or if someone had asked for an extra, especially just before the boathouse burned. After all, individual types of lights were doled out by rank, and these colored Yuletide ones might be carefully counted. Most of the men the queen suspected could probably lay their hands on a fancy link like this, though Ned was around the palace enough to get his hands on one, too.

Sadly, this evidence did not bode well for him to throw suspicion on Giles Chatam: Besides the fact that a man of his station would not have access to such a link unless he stole it, Chatam had not been staying at Whitehall when the boathouse burned or when Hodge was killed. Although Giles might have burned his own parents alive in their house, Ned finally faced the fact his own goose was cooked unless he could link this link to someone else the queen suspected.

Holding it gingerly, Ned spun to hurry back into the palace. Standing in his path, Jenks waited not ten feet away, legs apart and arms crossed over his chest. But worse, slightly behind him stood Baron Hunsdon and the queen herself.

"I—I believe I've found a clue," Ned blurted, looking straight at Elizabeth as he rose from his shaky bow and held the link out toward her.

"Of . . . ?" she said, not budging. He thought she looked livid; surely the wind could not have polished her usually pale cheeks that red.

"A link . . . that is, a torch, no doubt a fairly recent one from the palace that appears to have been heaved aside in haste—from over there," he added, gesturing toward the general direction of Lambeth Palace. It was then, as rattled as he was, inspiration hit him. "The Thames was fairly well frozen that night of the fire," he plunged on, "so someone could have slipped across the ice from that direction, from Lambeth." Though his arm was shaking, he pointed directly at the Bishop of London's property and prayed the wily queen took his bait.

"But you just said it appears to be a torch from my palace," the queen countered, narrowing her eyes in the wind—or at him.

"Yes, but Bishop Grindal's emissary Vicar Bane is in and out of the palace like a specter day and night!" he insisted.

"Let me see that," she said, and Ned hastened to hand it to her.

"What if," Baron Hunsdon said, "its scent matches that of Bane's epistle and the stench of this burned boathouse? It's all circumstantial evidence, but it's starting to add up."

"Bane's epistle?" Ned declared. "I hope not more condemnations and threats against the queen's Christmas?"

"Let's not get off the subject of your behavior, Master of the Queen's Revels," Elizabeth said, her voice as cold as he felt. "I asked you to remain with Giles Chatam, and yet here you are out by the boathouse. It reminds me of the night of the fire when I commanded you remain with Meg in my apartments and yet you left her and went out who knows where."

"My stomach was indisposed. Yes, I stepped outside for a breath of fresh air. I—I simply wasn't myself that night."

Ned knew he was talking too fast. He hadn't dressed warmly enough; he was shaking, and his teeth were chattering. Jenks and Baron Hunsdon seemed to block him in now, as they all stood facing the queen. He hoped Jenks didn't know he'd been trifling with Meg, but both men would do anything for Her Majesty, even, no doubt, turn on one of their fellows of the Privy Plot Council. Her Grace had looked only worried when she'd questioned him before, but now she looked outright angry.

"You weren't yourself—so you said. You didn't come out here that night to torch the boathouse in your anger at me for naming Leicester as Lord of Misrule, did you?" the queen demanded.

"How can you even ask such of me, Your Grace?"

"Stow your flippant rejoinders for now, Ned! I'm not suggesting you thought I was in the boathouse at the time, so it could have been mere coincidence that you burned it in a sort of protest and now came out to destroy the link you pilfered—"

"No!" he shouted and stepped back only to bump into the solid strength of Jenks, who had somehow shifted behind him. To Ned's utter horror, he heard Baron Hunsdon scrape his sword from its scabbard.

"I want to believe you, Ned," the queen said, "but I cannot take that chance right now. You tried to sneak the two lettered signs from the Earl of Leicester's room last night, didn't you?"

"What? No! As for this torch—I was going to check in the chandlery to see if anyone had taken an extra. Since the stubs are collected and remelted, I thought I could tell, especially with one colored for Christmas, as surely they keep close track of those— this, I mean."

He was losing control of himself in this nightmare. How long had it been since he hadn't commanded a performance, hadn't known all his lines and just where to stand and move?

"The chandlery! Of course," she said, nodding at Hunsdon. "That could be the source of the combination of scents on the epistle. Ned, you are relieved of your duties for now. I am sending you to stay at Greenwich for a while because—"

"But no one's at Greenwich! Just a skeleton staff! No one's coming to Greenwich for the Twelve Days!"

He knew at the moment of his outburst that he should never have interrupted her. Worse, he should never have tried to cover his tracks or conceal his resentment and anger at her. He fought to get hold of himself, to stand up straighter, to keep his voice in check.

"You're exiling me to Greenwich for the holidays, Your Grace?"

"Yes, we shall put it that way. And when people ask where you are, I shall say—like that night I went to the kitchens and then the boathouse—you are indisposed."

"I was only trying to help, always," he said, his voice suddenly sounding very small.

"We shall see. I'm afraid," the queen was saying to Baron Hunsdon and his wife, Lady Anne, "that locking up everyone I suspect of not dealing straight with me may be the answer, but then there would be so few left for the New Year. Jenks, see that Ned gets inside, and then have my yeoman Clifford escort him downriver."

Accompanied by Baron Hunsdon and Lady Anne and carrying the burned red link, Her Majesty headed back toward the palace. Ned saw her sniff at the link again as if it were a bouquet of flowers some fond, departing lover had given her.

He stumbled as he turned away with the grim, stoic Jenks walking behind him, now not a companion but his guard. He craned his head to look back at Elizabeth of England, suddenly fearful he'd never be summoned or scolded and smiled upon, mayhap never see her again. He prayed that his years with her would not soon be mere memories. What if he would never again make her laugh, or trade puns with her, or help her privily to ferret out someone who would harm her people or her person? However could this Christmas and New Year, his favorite season of the year, have gone so dreadfully, deadly wrong?

Edward Thompson, alias Ned Topside, once called the queen's fool, Master of Revels and Lord of Misrule, only realized he was crying when his tears iced on his cheeks.

Chapter the Twelfth

THE QUEEN'S FIRST THOUGHT WAS THAT THE PLACE THAT made lights for her palace looked very dim indeed.

But for the kitchens, structures that employed open fires were set apart for safety, so the chandlery huddled among the back buildings near the smokehouse and laundry. The large room with its vent hole in the ceiling and pots of molten wax simmering over wood fires was one place at Whitehall she had never visited. It smelled of the soot that encrusted the walls and ceiling, but——her heart beat harder——there was also the faint hint of floral scents.

"All here within," Harry's voice boomed out from the door set ajar, "your queen is paying you a holiday visit!"

His voice echoed in the domed room; the three women stopped stirring and gaped. The only man in sight, bent over his desk writing, exploded to his feet and bobbed a bow while the workers, still holding wooden paddles dripping red or green wax, curtsied. Their full-length canvas aprons, stiff with wax, crackled.

As Elizabeth's eyes adjusted, she saw that ropes strung with different-size candles, links, and torches draped the stone walls. Great loops of woven wicks, ready to be cut to proper lengths, hung like wreaths on hooks; rolls of hemp and linen and stacks of torch poles were piled around the room.

"I can see you are all hard at work," she told them and threw back her hood in the warmth, though she kept her cloak wrapped tight to avoid splatters. "You are the master of my chandlery?" she inquired, regretful she did not know the man when she could rattle off the offices, titles, and names of so many in her service.

"Aye, Firk Bell, Most Gracious Majesty," the small, thin man replied. He looked as jumpy as if his feet were being held to a fire under the vats. "Ah, something wrong with that link, then?"

She handed him the stubby light. "I am wondering how much you can tell me about this and the person to whom it might have been allotted. It is from this chandlery?"

"Aye, made just a few weeks ago," he told her, squinting at it. "Melted us a new batch of the same Surrey beeswax Penny's been astirring, much demand for colored, scented lights for the rest of the Twelve Days."

"I can't tell if that link is scented."

He sniffed at it. "If 'tis, the odor's light, but with real good candles they only give out scent when they're burned, Majesty. As to who could have had it—pardon if I look in my books," he said as he scuttled over to his table, walking backward so he wouldn't turn away from her. "Hm," he said, then louder to his staff, "all of you, back to work or the vats will crust over. You know that, and I shouldn't have to tell you—pardon, Majesty.

"Links this length," he went on, bobbing up from his desk again, "shorter than the torches for your chambers and the Great Hall, go to many nobles and advisors, but I'm trying to recall who got the red and who the green, 'cause we didn't mix them, but I'm not sure we had a method, that is, we have a method and I keep good books, but not with colors, 'cept for Vicar Bane, of course."

At that, Elizabeth could have fallen into a vat of wax. She glared at Harry and shook her head to warn him from blurting something out. She'd been intending to work up to mentioning Bane.

"Except for Vicar Bane?" she said. "And why is that?"

"When he's here at Whitehall, a great deal lately, must say, won't accept scented candles—smacks of popish incense, he says, told us that several weeks ago."

"So you make special unscented and plain candles for Vicar Bane?"

"Unscented, of a certain, Majesty, but he wants red ones, picks them up himself, the color of martyr's blood, he says."

"Although lights are always allotted and then delivered to everyone's rooms, he comes here to pick them up himself, Master Bell?"

"Oh, aye, likes it here better than anyplace else in the fancy palace, he says, 'cause it 'minds him of where the scribes and Phar'sees of the day are headed, you know, to Hades, to burn forever, preached me quite a sermon on it 'bout a fortnight ago, said fancies and fripperies at Christmas was the devil's work. And sat here just a few days ago at my writing table to wait for his allotment of candles and links, working on his 'spondence."

She fought to remain calm while her heart nearly beat out of her chest. It must be Bane behind all this. "You mean his correspondence?" she asked.

"Aye, that's it. So other than the red and unscented—which this one might be," he added, sniffing again at the link in question, "not sure who got scented red ones."

She would burn it herself to discover if it was scented, the queen thought, as she took the link back from Firk Bell. And then she would await her once dreaded interview with Vicar Martin Bane today with great relish. He was all too obviously a creature of darkness, who was working hard to provide hell on earth for the peacock Leicester and his fancy Christmas queen.

"What do you mean you can't find him?" Elizabeth cried when Harry, Jenks, and her yeoman guard Clifford returned empty-handed. When Vicar Bane had not kept his appointment with her, she'd sent them to bring him here. Now, at her outburst, all three of them looked mute.

"Well?" she went on, jumping up from the table on which the unscented red candle still sat smoldering. Both Robin and Lady Anne were with her. Once again, Elizabeth had sent Rosie out with Kat, then had summoned Robin to explain to him all their efforts to discover who was behind the bizarre insults and crimes.

It was Robin who spoke before the others could. "You heard the queen, men. Clifford, did you look in the chapel as well as in

Bane's chamber? Jenks, has he taken a horse from the stables? He's not the sort to enjoy the Frost Fair, but for all we know, he's gone out to chastise those having a good time out there. Best we send guards, armed if need be, to both Lambeth Palace and the bishop's house at St. Paul's, should he be visiting his lord and master, Bishop Grindal!"

"We will keep searching, Your Grace," Harry said simply, in effect ignoring Robin's commands. He gestured to the two men to follow him out.

"Clifford, stay a moment!" Elizabeth called, and the tall yeoman came back in and closed the door.

"Robin," the queen said quietly so Clifford wouldn't hear, "I've found it best to treat all in my Privy Plot Council kindly and keep my temper on a low simmer so as not to insult or scare off assistance."

She hoped she hadn't made a mistake bringing Robin in on all this, but, after all, he had borne the brunt of the attacks and had a right to help defend himself. When she'd told Cecil that the Earl of Leicester was *pro tem* on their Privy Plot Council, he'd nearly had steam hissing from his ears.

"It's only," Robin muttered, "that no one but us seems to be able to think for themselves."

"Unfortunately, the Christmas killer seems to," she whispered. "Clifford, a question before you go," she said, speaking louder and gesturing for him to approach. "You delivered Ned Topside safely to Greenwich and put a watch on his door?"

"Just like you told me to afore you accused him down on the riverbank, Your Majesty. It's a decent-sized room on the second floor, that east wing overlooking the river, and I asked for some wood for the hearth there, like you said. The skeletal kitchen staff will be sure he gets enough to eat, though it'll be plain fare compared to here. And I told the visiting players he's indisposed."

"At least, in a riverside room, he can watch the activities on the ice," she mused aloud, strangely angry with herself that she regretted sending Ned away. A pox on the bombastic meddler and prevaricator—or worse, but she missed him already.

"There's nothing much on the ice outside of Greenwich," Clifford said. "The Frost Fair doings are mostly 'tween here and the bridge. No, he's looking out at not much but snow and your herds of Greenwich deer been wandering out on the river."

Poor Ned, alone with only deer to oversee at Yule. At least if the phantom struck again while she had him locked up, she would know he was not to blame and could release him. Despite her frustration and anger at her principal player and former Lord of Misrule, that was her hope.

"That will be all, then, Clifford, and my thanks."

"No thanks from you ever needed, Your Majesty. It's enough—the best New Year's gift of all—I can serve and help protect you. We'll find the vicar soon and have him back here for questioning."

"See that you do," Robin piped up, reminding the queen again of one reason she abstained from matrimony. Never would she entrust the power she now wielded or the care she bore her beloved England to a husband, especially one who not only thought he was, but truly was, king of his castle.

> Wassail, wassail, all over the town,
> The cup it is white; the ale it is brown . . .

New Year's Eve had always been Elizabeth Tudor's favorite part of Christmas. Not only the continuation of wassail caroling but the gift giving, the sumptuous array of food, the first foot custom, and the fireworks . . .

> The cup it is made of the apple tree,
> And so is the ale of the good barley.

But tonight she felt tied in knots so tight she could scream. Cecil was standing stiffly by, frowning despite the merriment. Meg had red eyes from crying about Ned, Jenks was testy, and Rosie was sulking over the queen's continually sending her on distant errands. At the head table elevated on the dais, only Kat seemed to be oblivious to twisted tensions.

So much in the queen's view annoyed her, but then, she must admit, she was easily annoyed of late. Among her courtiers and guests seated below the elevated dais, Simon MacNair was all smiles and smooth manners as he chatted with Margaret, Countess Lennox, while her son Lord Darnley amused himself by leaning against the wall near the wassailers and ogling Giles Chatam.

The hall was ablaze with red and green torches sweetly perfuming the air, so Vicar Bane, who was still missing, hardly had a shadow to lurk in, should he appear. The pompous prig had now become first on her list of culprits, though she still had devised a way to test Sussex tonight. He was vexing her this evening by whispering to almost everyone he met, all while glancing askance at his queen—or perhaps at Robin at her side.

Meanwhile, Robin was sticking too tight, with his hand on his ornate sword, whether to protect himself or her from the next onslaught, she was not sure. Worse, though the Lord of Misrule was expected to give commands for the festive evening, he seemed to think he could also order her about.

Robin rose to his feet and cued the royal trumpeters to herald his words. When their clarion tones died away, the hubbub in the vast hall, stuffed cheek by jowl with peers, nobles, advisors, ambassadors, senior household officials, and servants, slowly quieted.

"By my decree, the order of events this eve," Robin announced grandly, "shall be the banquet, gift giving, and then the first foot custom, followed by fireworks on the Thames—one of my gifts to you, Your Majesty—which we shall all view from the Waterside Gallery. Your Lord of Misrule commands you to eat, drink, and be merry!"

"Did you have to put it that way?" Elizabeth groused, though she forced a smile as he sat back down beside her. "You do know the next line of that, don't you?"

"We shall not die but live and love, my queen," he told her and reached under the tablecloth to squeeze her hands clenched in her lap. His heavy touch there jolted her, but she managed not to show it.

"Rest assured of your safety," he promised, "for I have ordered all dishes not only to be tasted but to be brought in uncovered to-night, even if we eat cold food. There will be no surprises this night but in the opening of gifts."

"And in that, I pray there will be no more shocks such as that box of stones with its note that said they were for murdering martyrs. Which reminds me," she said, tugging her hands free and folding them on the table, "that Vicar Bane told my master of the chandlery he wanted red candles because red represents the blood of martyrs."

"Then it must be Bane behind all this."

"If so, he's taken leave of his senses, though perhaps he at first simply ordered Hodge Thatcher not to gild the peacock—a frivolity, of course—and Hodge refused," she rushed on, thinking aloud. "They may have argued, and it went awry. If Bane can wander into the chandlery, he could certainly drop in on Hodge through that back door to the kitchens. Bane must fear I have ferreted out his crimes—his sins—and so he's fled."

"Then we are safe this night and can enjoy ourselves," he tried again to cajole her. "And if it's Bane, I should have insisted I be the first footer instead of Sussex, but you were so sure putting him on the other side of that door would prove something."

"I knew he would be in a like position to you the other night when you were attacked, that is, alone for a moment. If he goes unbothered, it means something. Besides, I'm giving him a second opportunity to bring in a strange item under that cover I must open, and if something is amiss there," she said, glancing at Sussex, "I can at least accuse him of complicity against us and have him further examined."

"And if the first foot custom goes awry, will that mean everyone will believe we face a dreadful new year?" Robin demanded, though his tone remained light and teasing.

"I know it's a risk, but I can't help that. We may not even reach the new year if I can't stop these outrages now!"

"My queen, cannot we have some joy of this day? To cheer you, I must tell you what one of your gifts is. I took to heart, as I do all things you say, your Christmas memory you shared the other day."

She felt her panic mute, her fears momentarily soften. "The sleigh ride with my brother and father?" she asked.

"I've had metal runners put on a small wagon bed and lined it with soft furs and pillows. Tomorrow I shall take you for a ride on the river with it, clear to Greenwich, if you'd like, to see the Frost Fair and greet your people, who love you dearly—but never as much as I."

Tears wet her lashes, and she longed to hug him. "Robin, I thank you. That is so thoughtful and so dear. But if someone's out to harm you or me, we must take precautions for our safety."

"Jenks, Clifford, others can ride along. Somehow, with this jackanapes who has been bothering us, I think the farther from Yule food and your royal kitchens we can get, the better off we will be." He threw back his head and shouted a laugh that made her wonder if he'd been into the wassail.

Though deeply moved by his thoughtfulness, she couldn't help but fret that Robin could joke about what had happened to him and call it mere bother when he had nearly died. And *jackanapes* was nearly a term of endearment, something you called a naughty, saucy child. It hinted at capering and jesting, when their enemy was a foul plotter and killer. She was probably just too on edge, she thought, but Robin's mood reminded her of that bump on his head. Neither was quite right.

Ned judged it to be nearly midnight, but he couldn't sleep. Unless those ghostly hounds on the isle across the river—and he wasn't superstitious—were yet baying over the legendary watery deaths of their master and mistress, the queen's hunt dogs should be silenced. He stopped pacing and looking out.

The full moon in the clear wintry sky shed silver dust on the scene out his second-story prison window. He was being held in a chamber usually assigned to the staff of important visitors in the east wing, which had a view of the forest and, if one looked far sideways, the river flowing in from London. Moonlight etched the skeletons of trees, ice weighed down the river, and snow blanketed the Isle of Dogs, the entire view as heavy and cold as his heart.

"Hell's gates!" he cracked out to the empty bedchamber they'd locked him in.

He began to pace as he had all day since he'd been left here to rot. At least the queen hadn't sent him to the Fleet, Bridewell, or some other prison, he thought, trying to buck himself up. He wasn't of lofty enough rank to be put in the dreaded Tower, but if he'd been any sort of lord instead of her Master of Revels, she probably would have sent him there. He fancied that, if he pressed his forehead to the frosty windowpanes and craned his neck to look to the left, he could see its cold gray stones.

As he passed his tray of bread and cheese and cold sliced duck, he kicked at the table it was on. The single fat candle shuddered but burned on. He could full well picture what queen and court were feasting on tonight under a hundred blazing lights. He could hear the raucous noise, the rollicking music, the jests, of which he was master. Her Grace would be accepting expensive, unique gift after gift and giving her friends and advisors sacks of coins or silver plate in return.

And for her closest servants—well, she'd given them all fine Spanish leather riding boots last year. How rich the creaking, pliant leather had smelled, how very opulent it had been, so what was she giving out, perhaps even right now?

Though his eyes teared up, he sniffed hard to keep from crying. He forced himself back to the window to survey the frozen world outside. Down below, on the ice, he was certain he saw someone move. And not the deer he'd noted earlier, nosing about for water on the banks before settling for eating snow. Was that not a man on a horse, way down here, far from the Frost Fair?

He prayed it could be Jenks or Clifford come back for him, but he knew better. That was the only New Year's gift he longed for, to have Her Grace forgive his lies and anger and all they had wrought and call him back. But why would someone sent for him dismount out there in the cold and dark?

When he looked again, he saw naught amiss.

He stared out, wide-eyed but no longer seeing. He did want something else besides Her Grace's forgiveness. He wanted Meg's smile, Meg's approval and trust, Meg in his arms again, opening her mouth to his, Meg in his bed.

"Hell's gates!" he repeated as if cursing would cure his pain. He thumped his fist against the window, then saw something else move outside.

Another rider—or the same—had come up into the trees, but he seemed to have dismounted, to be hunched over. Perhaps a messenger had become ill, or decided to walk the rest of his way in, or his mount had gone lame. Whatever could the man be doing while his horse stomped impatiently, a horse evidently fitted with studded shoes to traverse the ice? It was a little too late to be ripping mistletoe off those huge oaks.

Ned scrubbed at the mist his breath had made on the thick pane, blinked, and stared yet again. No, he must have been totally mistaken, for now no one was there at all.

Chapter the Thirteenth

Figgy Pudding

Chop ½ pound imported, dried figs, and mix with ¼ cup bread crumbs. White manchet bread, preferred by those of wealth or rank, is best, but a lesser bread such as yellowish cheat is fine. Do not serve, at least at holiday time, the coarser breads of black rye or especially oats, favored in rude or rural places. Lightly brown 1 cup of autumn-gathered walnuts and mix with other elements including 1 cup brown sugar, 3 tablespoons melted butter, 4 beaten hen's eggs, and spices: ½ teaspoon precious cinnamon and ¼ teaspoon nutmeg. To make special for Yuletide tables of rank and honor, add ¾ cup of sugared citrus peels, perhaps left from the making of suckets. Bake for at least 1 hour and serve with cream or hardsauce; the latter made from Madeira or malmsey is best.

ELIZABETH WISHED SHE COULD ENJOY ALL THIS AS MUCH as Robin seemed to. She noted that the marks on his neck and wrists had faded fast, as perhaps the terrible memory of his assault and attempted murder had, too. That was what made him so merry tonight, to have back his life, which could have been tragically cut short, she thought.

"It's most generous of you not only to give me the sleigh ride but to foot the bill for tonight's fireworks," she told him. "But then you have always adored gunpowder and explosions of all sorts."

"Especially the sort we could have between the two of us," he murmured, leaning close with his big, brown hand on the table beside hers. "Around you, I am but a burning match, my queen, waiting to ignite your—"

"Favorite fireworks on the river. Ah, the first course!" she declared, nodding at Master Cook Roger Stout as he made his appearance at the head of the parade of platters.

The queen tried to smile, to nod and even applaud with the others when a particularly spectacular dish came in. She took a hearty swig of wassail, hoping that would help to lighten her heart. But she still kept envisioning a bizarre peacock, a fox's head with a gold snout, and Robin trussed like a roast boar instead of the fineries of the feast that were set before the queen.

If the uncovered banquet food came cold, fine, Elizabeth thought, for cold food was the first of the ten traditional courses; the second was hot, the third sweet, and onward through a great array. The red gravies, blue custards, and yellow sauces looked especially festive against the layers of white linens covering the table, which glittered with silver plates and glass goblets. Huge saltcellars in elaborate shapes adorned each table. All the guests soon fell to with their personal knives and spoons.

Accompanied by the wail and beat of music from the elevated musicians' gallery, sallets came first, some boiled, some compound, followed by a flow of fricassees, boiled meats, stewed broths, and sundry boiled fowls. Then all sorts of roast meats, everything from capons to woodcocks. Wild fowl, land fowl, and hot baked meats such as marrow-bone pie arrived to make the table groan. Next came cold baked meats of wild deer, hare pie, gammon of bacon pie, then shellfish, though not so many dishes of that since the rivers were solid ice.

Among the sweets came candied flower petals, fat green figs from Portugal, dates, suckets, tarts, gingerbread, florentines, and spiced cakes, and the queen's childhood favorite, figgy pudding, though she merely picked at it now. At last came the annual massive marchpane masterpiece, rolled in on a cart. People stood at their places or even on benches to see a miniature frozen Thames with tiny booths upon it and a replica of Whitehall Palace on its bank side. All of this was washed down with a selection of malmsey, Gascon or Rhenish wines, beer, or ale.

As the tables were cleared and her courtiers lined up for the exchange of gifts with their queen, Elizabeth's spirits began to sink even more. This was the point at which Ned had always stepped forward to amuse and amaze her guests with quips, jests, or riddles. What a riddle these Christmas crimes had become, she agonized. She could not bear to believe Ned was a deceiver and a killer, and yet a parade of evidence suggested that very thing. On the morrow she intended to send guards out looking for Vicar Bane, but now a whispering Sussex, an ever watchful Simon Mac-Nair, and a gloating Robin were driving her to distraction and—

She almost choked on the last bite of figgy pudding. She had just put her dear Robin in the list of possible villains when she knew he could not possibly be guilty. No, the attacks had been aimed *at* him, and he'd suffered greatly, being mocked and molested.

Putting down her golden spoon and nodding that her place could be cleared, she noted a smiling Simon MacNair working his way through the press of people to stand before her.

"Some happy news, I hope," she told him by way of greeting as she stood and was escorted to her throne under the scarlet cloth of state.

MacNair hurried behind her, chattering. "Although I have gifts for you from myself and from your royal cousin, the Queen of Scotland, Your Most Gracious Majesty, I wanted to give you another sort of gift, if you would allow it."

"What sort of gift?" she asked warily.

"Sleight-of-hand tomfooleries, Your Majesty. Queen Mary adores them between courses or entertainments, and I thought you might, too."

"I'm not in the mood for surprises, nor is our court like Queen Mary's."

"Of course not, Your Grace," he said, still smiling up at her most pleasantly. "I swear to you there will be no silly dolls or boxes of stones. I offer naught but blessings for the beautiful Queen of England at this start to the new year," he declared with a flourish as he produced a gold crown coin from midair, one with her likeness on it.

Elizabeth laughed as other crowns seemed to drop into his flying fingers from his nose, his earlobes, and then—with her permission—her chin. Ohs and aahs followed, until quite a crowd had gathered, watching raptly. Soon her lap was full of coins, and she was delighted at their bounty. Was this, she wondered, the gift from him or his queen? Cecil shuffled forward, and Robin leaned in with his hand still on the hilt of his sword, but this clever display seemed harmless enough to her.

"Sir Simon MacNair, you are a man of surprises and hidden talents," she told him, loudly enough for all to hear. "Imagine, tricks with crowns—and my very image—disappearing and then appearing."

He only laughed as he seemed to lift a coin from Robin's pouting lower lip. "And now," MacNair added as he flapped open a large linen handkerchief, "will not Your Grace wager these coins by allowing me to wrap them in this cloth?"

"Will I get them back with interest?" she demanded, as it seemed everyone in the room leaned forward, breathless to see what the Scot would do next.

"I do promise you it will be interesting."

All this made her miss Ned dreadfully. Even though voices in the crowd called out such things as "Never trust a Scot!" and "You've heard how tight they are with coins—and tight with their Scots whiskey, Your Majesty!" she put the crowns into his handkerchief.

Everyone, even the musicians in the balcony, went silent as MacNair knotted the handkerchief, then, holding the ties, swung the bundle once, twice, thrice over his head.

"And so!" he cried and untied it with a flourish. "See, Your Majesty, it still has crowns within!"

The queen saw the coins were gone, every last one of them. But within lay two gold-framed miniatures, each of a woman wearing a crown—herself and Queen Mary, only Mary was smiling and Elizabeth looked sober as a Puritan.

Everyone huzzahed and cheered and clapped as MacNair plucked them out and held them up for the crowd, turning so all could see. Elizabeth wasn't sure whether it was a slight or the miniaturist's failure that Mary looked far better, but she intended to pin MacNair down about it later. Yes, she was certain Mary's was more flattering.

"And so I ask Your Majesty's forgiveness for giving my gifts before those of loftier rank, but I could not contain myself," MacNair said with a deep bow as he produced a purse of coins from up his sleeve and offered them to her too. "I fear, Your

Grace," he added, his voice more intimate now, "that Ambassador Melville would have my head, my position at least, for this, but as he is not here, and it is holiday time . . ."

"When the cat's away, the mouse will play, my lord?" she countered, also keeping her voice low. "Do you find it difficult to answer to one who is not here to see the lay of the land, yet to whom you are responsible?"

"How logical and perceptive you are, Your Majesty. I fear that being at best the *aide-de-camp* to those greater than I is my lot in life, however high I rise. I began as the youngest of eight children and so must of necessity make my own way in life. I am envoy for an exacting master and an even more volatile mistress."

"My cousin Queen Mary?" she asked, fascinated. "And is she volatile, while you call me logical and perceptive? I give you leave to speak freely on this and would count it as a favor if you do so."

"Your cousin Mary Stuart, Your Grace, is sensitive and sensual, a creature of feelings and emotion. You, I have observed, may feel deeply, too, but your head commands your heart, for your intellect is most impressive."

Again, she found herself liking this man, though she could ill afford to. "I hope, though you are away from your people at this time of year," she told him, "that you will enjoy yourself among us. Is there aught else you would say before I proceed with the other gifts? For back in the array of them is a fine silver plate for you. And when your messenger Forbes returns from Edinburgh, I shall send him north yet again with a New Year's gift for my cousin and sister queen."

"You are ever gracious, and I am grateful," he said, shifting slightly so that he seemed to block Robin out for a few moments, though her Lord of Misrule was now giving orders for the exchange of gifts. "Just one more thing, Your Grace," MacNair said, whispering. "As the earl—" here he darted a look at Robin, then back to her—"proved he was not to be trusted by my queen, perhaps he should not be trusted by any queen, even one ruled by her head more than her heart, as queens indeed must be."

If he meant to say more, it was too late, for Robin turned back and clapped his hands to signal the highest-ranking peers to step forward first. By then Simon MacNair had melted back into the crowd.

As in every year since she'd been on the throne, New Year's gifts had been showered on the queen, including jewels, uncut or mounted in rings, pendants, or earrings. She received finely wrought saltcellars, ink pots of Venetian glass, and the traditional gifts of garments: ivory-ribbed fans, veils, sets of sleeves, bejeweled stomachers, embroidered smocks, cloaks, ermine muffs trailing silken ribbons, collars, and the new-style wider, stiffer ruffs. Lengths of russet and garnet satin, red grosgrain and taffeta, damask and camlet. Scissors, pinchers, penknives, fragrant filigreed or porcelain pomanders, bodkins, ear pickers, tooth pickers, hair crispers, and ornate seals. In turn, according to rank or service, for each presentation, Elizabeth's Lord Treasurer gave the giver the appropriate weight of coin or plate.

Many crowded even closer to see what the Earl of Leicester's gift would be. He held his presentation for last, a set of twelve gold forks imported from Italy.

"What are those?" Kat asked, leaning close.

"Ah, tiny pitchforks," Sussex put in, "to prick all of us when we misbehave."

Elizabeth looked up straight into Sussex's pale blue eyes. "And have you been misbehaving, my lord?" It was so unlike the man to jest that she took it for a clever if circumspect criticism.

"They are all the rage for spearing food," Robin said, his stance rigid and his tone taut as he and Sussex seemed to square off again. "However, they are so civilized that Ireland, where you've been, Sussex, or Scotland, for that matter, will never have them."

MacNair, political creature that he was, merely frowned from afar at that, and Elizabeth silently blessed him for not jumping into the coming fray. She put her hand on Robin's arm and smoothly poked him in the ribs so no one could see, while she said quietly to Sussex, "I believe it's nearly time for the first foot custom, so best you'd go before you put your foot in your mouth instead of over the threshold, my lord."

Swallowing his stubborn pride, Sussex went out the side entrance behind the screen. He would walk around to the front doors, which had been barred all day, and enter from there.

Cecil edged closer to the queen; by tradition, at ten minutes until midnight, he took out his timepiece and signaled the musicians. They began to play a fanfare. Heads turned toward the main doors. Although the queen felt the first foot custom was mere superstition, it was one many still clung to and one Kat dearly recalled.

The honored "guest" came in precisely at the stroke of twelve, carrying a large silver salver on which sat—under a cover—something traditionally green and growing, such as a potted plant, to symbolize the new year. At court, the first footer was admitted by the monarch, since he or she must accept the gift. Supposedly, all sorts of bad luck could befall if the first footer should hesitate or trip. Many English households followed the same custom, but word always spread throughout the kingdom of what had happened at the palace.

Now, in a way, Elizabeth thought as she rose to walk toward the doors, Sussex had become an actor in her play. She had set a possible trap for the molester and the murderer who terrorized her court and ruined her Christmas. She did not mean to make Sussex either scapegoat or sacrificial ram, but she hoped the villain might take advantage of this coming moment: Sussex stood alone with a covered tray. If he were assaulted—and surely, as a military man, he was on his guard—or if something insulting or shocking appeared on his salver, she would go on from there to link it to him or someone else she suspected.

And, but for Vicar Martin Bane, she knew exactly where all her possible candidates for the Christmas culprit were right now. Margaret and MacNair were in her line of sight, as was that damned Darnley, who was hanging drunkenly on an annoyed Giles Chatam, while Ned was safely stowed at Greenwich.

In the hush of the crowd as the new year approached, Elizabeth started toward the doors to open them. The crowd of courtiers parted for her as the Red Sea had for Moses when he was fleeing Pharaoh's murderous hordes. Though her yeomen guards lined the room, and Robin, Jenks, and Harry came behind, hands on swords, she clutched a fork she had seized at the last moment. Inspired by MacNair, she had it hidden up her sleeve, a personal if paltry defense against what might await her on the other side of those closed double doors. She was certain the villain would do something new on New Year Eve's.

. . .

During the gift giving, while the dishes had been cleared from the banquet tables and whisked by in the corridor between the Great Hall and the kitchens, Meg had easily lifted the remnants of figgy pudding off a passing tray. Morosely, she had shuffled into the kitchen and sat alone on the hearth and picked the figs out. She was expected to be in the Great Hall for the first footing, but no one would miss her in that crowd, and it wasn't Ned at the center of attention this year. He was as good as the queen's prisoner, sent to exile from court and Christmas, and Meg was both furious and fearful about that.

"You not going out for the ceremony, then, Mistress Meg?" Roger Stout asked her as he hurried past. "I'm going up to watch from the back of the musicians' gallery. It's in less than five minutes, I'd wager."

"Oh, yes, I'm coming," she lied and didn't budge, though she figured she was probably getting her lemon yellow best skirts smudged, perched on the bricks like this. But the silvery embers gave off a steady warmth that felt good. Since Jenks had told her Ned was taken away, she'd been as cold as ice, and she and Jenks had had an argument over that.

So she wasn't just moping over Ned's predicament but over her own. Meg felt half of her had been ripped away, and she'd never felt like that before, not even when Jenks disappeared into plague London earlier this year. He was always kind and sweet to her, which Ned seldom was, so why didn't she feel the same sweeping way for Jenks as she did for Ned? What in heaven's name was wrong with her?

One of the sturdy-legged dogs that ran in cages to turn the hearth spits somehow got back inside from the small kennel out back and slumped at Meg's feet.

"You too, eh?" she muttered and fed it sopped pieces of bread she fished out of the pudding. Though apparently exhausted, the dog devoured each morsel. "Least you're not one of those howling dogs the queen's been having nightmares about."

"Want a meat tart?" the sergeant of the pastry, who used to ogle her, asked. She figured he couldn't see the dog at her feet as he rushed by, so he must mean it was for her. "I've got some leftover fancies here much better than those cold puddings, sweetling," he said with a wink.

"I'd count it a high favor," she said listlessly. "Just leave it there on the table." The man picked one off a shelf in the shadows, left it where she'd said, and darted out, probably to see the first footing, too.

The thing was, Meg thought, as angry as she was with Her Majesty for sending Ned to Greenwich when Meg was sure he was innocent of any part of the attack on the queen's Christmas, she did know one way to maybe help him out. If she did, though, she'd probably get the queen vexed at her, and she didn't need that, especially if she had to plead with her to keep Ned on. And the Earl of Leicester would have her head, too, if she told the queen what she knew about him.

Sighing heavily, Meg got up and took the meat tart off the table. When she bent down to give it to the spit dog, he leaped up so fast she nearly tripped over him and had to grab the edge of the table to keep from falling. As the dog devoured it, Meg went out to watch Her Majesty open the Great Hall doors to the first footer.

In the sudden hush in the Great Hall, the single knock echoed. At least it sounded, Elizabeth thought, relieved, as if Sussex was not only present but right on time. She opened the doors herself, and there he stood, safe and alone, holding the covered silver salver. Though Sussex was sure of foot and in fine physical form, Elizabeth held her breath as he stepped into the hall itself without hesitation, or stubbing his toe, or falling.

Amidst the swelling cheers and corporate sigh of relief, he went down on one knee and delivered his little speech. "Ah— a New Year's gift for—Your Majesty, though the Lord of Misrule—asked me not to, ah, gaze upon it."

Elizabeth could only be grateful his stumbling words did not count as a curse for first footers.

"Robin?" she said, turning to him. "Is something special on that salver?"

"Very," he said only.

Yet after Sussex's presentation of the cutoff fox's head the other night, she was fearful of what lay beneath. As she reached for the handle of the cover, she could see, distorted and bizarre, her reflection in its polished dome. Holding her breath, she lifted it to reveal a fresh sprig of mistletoe. And before she knew Robin would move—or before she could give him the permission he did not ask for—he kissed her in front of them all.

Silence stretched out at first, then cheers and laughter bubbled up, no doubt from Robin's supporters, while Sussex—and Rosie, standing beside him now—looked quite vexed. The queen felt she was two women, the one who had long loved this irrepressible man and the queen who could afford to love and trust no man.

"And now," Robin hurried on, perhaps fearful of which woman would speak, "your Lord of Misrule commands you all on to the Waterside Galley for the fireworks."

"Seen a few of those here already!" a male voice in the crowd called out as, once again, her courtiers parted for her to pass through to lead the way. With a tight smile on her lips, which still tingled from Robin's kiss, she ignored his proffered arm and walked back into the heart of the hall alone.

Her usual retinue swiftly fell into step behind her; the others surged forward. But as she passed her now empty throne, she saw a wooden box upon it.

"What is that?" she whispered as her gaze swept past Robin and sought Cecil. Where were Harry and Jenks when she needed them? The box greatly resembled the one that had held the stones.

"And who leaves a gift without waiting to receive one in turn?" the queen asked, her voice ringing out to quiet everyone.

"Does no one come forward to claim this gift?" Cecil asked, blessedly stepping from the press of people to help her. "Did anyone see who placed this here during the first footing?" No one spoke up; hardly anyone, she noted, so much as moved. "Then," Cecil said, "we shall take it with us, and you may open it later, Your Grace." He picked it up before Robin could get to it.

At the top of the great staircase as she led her shifting, swelling entourage upstairs, Cecil appeared at her elbow, carrying the box.

"Is it heavy?" she asked, turning her head toward him, for Robin walked on her other side and Sussex with Rosie and Kat behind.

"Not quite as heavy as stones. I'll take it into your apartment and look lest it be something that would harm y——"

"I'm going, too," she cut him off. "Lady Anne," she called to her, "you and the Lord of Misrule may escort everyone to the windows in the gallery, where I will join you shortly. I bid you, Robin, stay your signal for the fireworks until I arrive. Rosie, as ever, keep near Lady Ashley."

Taking only Harry with them, then admitting Jenks, who came

and knocked on the door, the queen and Cecil placed the box on the table in her presence chamber.

"Now that I see it closer and in better light," Elizabeth said, "I fear it is a very similar box to the one which held the stones."

"A box we erroneously thought held a murder weapon," Harry added.

"Stand back, Your Grace," Cecil urged, "and I will open it."

Harry stepped forward to block her from it as if it might explode. Cecil lifted the lid.

"Well?" she demanded, stepping out from behind Harry. "What?"

"Perhaps we've been too on edge," Cecil observed. "It looks to be just another normal New Year's gift."

"But no one claimed it," she noted, peering down at six heavily molded and embossed flagons resting in nests of red velvet. "Oh, a lovely set, though rather heavy and masculine."

"Perhaps a man picked them out," Cecil surmised.

"Best I lift them out for you," Harry said, and Elizabeth let him, touched by the concern they all showed her.

"All made from the same mold, I'd wager," Cecil said. "Expensive, too. Someone must have forgotten his gift or been tardy with it, then stepped out after the first footing and didn't hear you ask who had left these."

"Ha," Harry put in. "A gift this fine, someone will want to take credit for it."

Elizabeth picked up the first of the flagons and examined it closely, including the maker's hallmark on the bottom, a *V* set in the middle of a *W*, so it almost resembled one of those imported Eurasian flowers called tulips. The molded design on the exterior of the deep cups did not look like something recognizable but more like a swirling river current. The design was vaguely familiar, but after handling all the gifts tonight, she could not recall where she'd seen such.

"Ugh, this one's not been washed," Harry said. "Dried grape juice or red wine on one entire side of it."

"Wait," she said, still staring at the design. "Clean or dirty, I've seen this pattern before."

As Harry set each flagon on the table, others took them, turned them, tipped them, and peered inside. Elizabeth put hers down and seized the encrusted one.

"Maybe it's like a set you already have," Harry said when all six flagons were out and he had searched beneath the velvet on which they rested to find nothing else.

"No," she said. "I think we're looking at the pattern Cecil drew, the pattern of the crushing blow to Hodge Thatcher's skull."

"One of these is a murder weapon?" Cecil cried. "Then that dried stuff . . ."

"Hodge's blood," she said as chills swept her. "The Christmas killer is mocking us, daring us again by giving us the murder weapon we could not find nor figure out. That's his gift to me for New Year's, and I'd bet a throne he's not finished with us yet."

Chapter the Fourteenth

Winter Sallet

Indeed a good Yule sallet, fit for winter months, as it does not demand let-
tuce or spinach leaves, which may well have rotted in the cellar ere the hol-
iday season. Mix together 2 ounces each of blanched almonds (with your
shredding knife cut grossly), raisins of the sun, thinly sliced figs, capers,
and currants. Dress them with 6 tablespoons olive oil, 2 tablespoons wine
vinegar, 2 ounces of sugar, and a few leaves of sage in a deep dish. Cover
the mixture with slices of 1 orange and 1 lemon, peeled and sliced cross-
ways and laid in a circle. Put a thin layer of red cabbage leaves on top in
a circle, then olives, all arranged in circles. Excellent sundry forms of such
sallet may also include parsley, sage, garlic, leek, borage, mint, fennel, and
rue, but be sure they be washed and picked clean.

"YOUR UNCLE, THE EARL OF SUSSEX, SAYS THAT WIND'S
howling like a banshee out there, Lady Rosie," Meg
said as she entered the queen's presence chamber with
fresh strewing herbs the next day. At least, Elizabeth
thought, Meg's eyes weren't red this morning, and she was evidently no longer avoiding her.

Elizabeth looked up from her card game of primero with Kat,
Anne, and Rosie, annoyed that Meg had come up with a word she
did not know. But since Sussex had said *banshee*, she'd best pursue
the comment.

"That must be Irish Gaelic," she told Meg. "What did he understand it to mean?"

"Overheard Lord Cecil ask him the same, Your Grace," Meg replied, coming closer, "but the earl claimed the word is Scots."

Anne discarded and said, "Funny that your military man sent to Ireland comes back with Scottish words."

Elizabeth frowned, wondering if Sussex, like Robin and, of course, MacNair, had been in communication with the Scottish court. "Perhaps Sussex heard it from Simon MacNair," she said, glaring at Rosie, who had yet neither found the missing bracelet nor convinced the queen she wasn't her uncle's spy. "Meg, did he say what the word means?"

"Oh, yes. It's something about a female spirit whose wailing warns a family that one of them will soon die."

"How dreadful a thought on this first day of the new year," Kat said.

"Especially with all we've been through," Elizabeth agreed and glared at Rosie to warn her not to defend her uncle. Could Sussex be intending that as a warning he was planning another murder, the queen agonized, or was it mere chance he said such?

Elizabeth frowned down at her hand of two queens—hearts and diamonds—and her lower-count cards. She would surely lose this hand. Worse, she'd tossed and turned all night and felt exhausted, so it was just as well her official visit to the Frost Fair and ride in Robin's sleigh was put off until tomorrow. The so-called banshee wind was buffeting the booths and scouring snow off rooftops to cascade it down as if it were snowing again.

At least the stiff wind had come up after the fine fireworks display Robin had presented last night, so it had gone off without a hitch. Ignited gunpowder had sent rockets, firewheels, squibs, and pikes of pleasure vaulting into the air from the frozen river. Folks at the Frost Fair had been able to enjoy it as close as the court, while others from the city crowded the banks of the Thames to cheer and clap. There had not been as many fireworks as last year, but she had not complained, for, with all that had been happening, she thought it best not to make a pompous show.

"Was there something else you wished to say, Meg?" Elizabeth asked, looking sharply up from her cards again as the girl hovered.

"I was just wondering if you have heard from Ned—I mean about him. Jenks and I are most concerned, that is."

"So am I," Elizabeth admitted, spreading her cards on the table, only to be beaten by Rosie's hand. The young woman squealed and scooped up the small pile of silver shillings as the queen rose. "Meg, come over here," Elizabeth said, and motioned for her to sit beside her on the pillows in the window seat.

"Yes, Your Grace?" She obeyed but looked poised to flee.

"There was much circumstantial evidence against Ned, and I have exiled him from court for his own good right now. If he is locked up at Greenwich and more dire events occur here, such as the box of flagons last night, then I shall know he is innocent and release him."

"Pardon, Your Grace, but what box of flagons?"

"Ones which may include the murder weapon used against Hodge."

"Oh, then you can call Ned back if they appeared last night."

"I choose to wait a bit longer to be very sure."

"No one told me about flagons," Meg said, lowering her voice. "Was it two of them in a velvet drawstring bag?"

"No—six, nestled in velvet. Why did you say two?"

Meg mouthed the words. "Because that's what Lord Sussex

bought at St. Paul's Walk that day he met with Giles Chatam. You know, when I was following Sussex, and Ned was trailing Giles."

"Ladies, I thank you for a lively game of cards," the queen said, rising, "and would be alone for a few minutes but will rejoin you soon."

"Is aught well with you?" Kat asked, rising and coming closer. "I know that look, lovey, and it means you're fretting."

"Nonsense. We've all just had too much Christmas and New Year to boot," Elizabeth teased as she hugged Kat, then shooed her women from the room. When the door closed, she said, "Meg, come over here and look at these flagons."

"Yes, much the same," she said, examining the one the queen handed her. "At least it's the general style and pattern of those displayed on the shelves of the pewterer at St. Paul's."

"And you and Ned witnessed Sussex buy two of them, then whisper to Giles?"

"These exact ones, I'm not sure. But, Your Grace, if Ned could be brought back, he could help to identify them, too, as I'm sure he got a much better look at them, so——"

"For his own good, Ned stays where he is right now, but you have indeed helped his plight. Meg, just as Kat can read my expression, I warrant I can read yours after all our years together. There is more that you would say on our investigation, is there not?"

"No, Your Majesty. I've said it all, and you have every right not to take my advice about Ned."

They stared each other down a moment, as if Meg were an equal who did not deign to drop her gaze. The queen felt they were fencing, but over precisely what, she was not certain. If only she could recall where she had seen plateware or drinking vessels with a design similar to what these flagons bore. She'd had Harry and Anne traipse down to the storage room and look through all her New Year's gifts to no avail.

"Then you are dismissed, Meg, and have Clifford fetch Sussex to me immediately."

"Ah, yes," Sussex said, turning one of the flagons in his big hands, "I've seen their like. Works of art, every one of them."

"Seen their like where?" Elizabeth asked, trying to keep both her excitement and temper reigned in.

"Fine work done by a, ah, Master Vincent Wainwright, who has a portable booth in St. Paul's Walk. Works at night, sells during the day, I've heard, and don't know where he lives."

"Are you his patron or some such that you know his name?"

"Merely a customer, Your Grace, but then so are others of your court and no doubt many in the city. Wainwright was in fact indirectly recommended to me, ah, by Leicester."

"What? Considering that you two cannot communicate without nearly coming to blows, am I to believe you were speaking civilly with Leicester, and he kindly suggested you buy from Master Wainwright?"

"No, rather, I heard him suggesting to Queen Mary of Scots's man at your court—MacNair—that he send some to her because they were fine work."

"Yes, I believe Leicester still has a soft spot for that other queen in his heart," she muttered and began to pace. After all, she fumed silently, she had not yet forgiven the wretch that he had Queen Mary's portrait closer to his bed than the one of his own queen. And who knew but that Leicester had told MacNair where to get an artist for those miniatures that made the Queen of England look sour next to the charming Scots queen.

"Giles Chatam told you, didn't he?" Sussex interrupted her agonizing. "I mean, ah, that I bought some of these flagons? But what is the import of all this, Your Grace? Yes, I bought two of them from the same pewterer—and sent them both to my heir for a New Year's gift. Those flagons greatly resemble this one of yours, but, ah, the pattern is different, God as my judge, it is."

Elizabeth sank into a chair at the head of the long table in her presence chamber. She felt she grasped at straws again when she'd thought at last she had a handhold on all this. But she still wasn't ready to have Sussex or anyone else arrested for murdering either Hodge or Christmas.

"You sent them to your heir," she asked slowly, "who is not at court, so you do not have those different ones in your possession?"

"Exactly, Your Grace."

It smacked too much to her of Sussex's earlier far-fetched claims he'd hired Giles to recite a poem he'd written. But he had told her he could produce that, at least, and she'd not made him do it.

"Describe this Vincent Wainwright for me," she said.

"Oh, easy as, ah, pie to spot in a crowd when he uncovers his head, Your Grace. His hair is brick red, real russet in the sun, brighter than your own or even that herb mistress of yours."

"But it's hardly sunny inside St. Paul's, even if he did doff his cap to you, my lord. Have you seen him elsewhere in the bright winter sun, perhaps when you bought from him some other time?"

"I have not. Sorry if my—ah, explanation didn't suit, but

smoothness of tongue is not my strength, as truth and loyalty are, Your Grace."

Elizabeth always felt safe and happy among the common folk of her realm. The next day—Snow Day, it was dubbed on the holiday calendar—dawned brisk but sunny, and the bitter wind had spent itself. At midmorning, driven by Robin in his makeshift but comfortable sleigh, and followed by her entourage of eight mounted yeomen guards, the queen went sleighing on the frozen river. She regretted only that her most trustworthy yeoman guard, Clifford, was not with them, for she'd sent him to locate and bring in the St. Paul's Walk pewterer, Vincent Wainwright, for questioning. She needed a list of the man's clients and news of anything he might have overheard. At least the ever faithful Jenks had taken Clifford's place in her retinue.

Cheers and caps thrown aloft saluted her. She smiled and waved back, called out greetings and questions, and patted the fat cheeks of babies tilted toward the sleigh by awestruck, beaming parents. Where small crowds gathered, the queen gave short speeches wishing her fellow Londoners and Englishmen a prosperous and happy new year.

Booths, which had hastily been put back shipshape after yesterday's gales, were strung out for nearly half a mile. She graciously turned down offers of drink or food but admired wares for sale. The royal sleigh stopped at some booths for her to shop; she passed purchased gewgaws and trinkets back to her guards until their saddle sacks bulged. Though her men kept close, she felt freer than she had since Christmas Eve, when all the chaos had begun.

"Look at that big fishing hole they've chopped in the ice!" she cried over the noisy chorus of huzzahs as Robin reined in the horse pulling the sleigh. Bundled up to their eyes, men and boys stood or sat fishing around a hole in the ice the size of a banquet table, through which the cold, black-green Thames lapped roughly.

"I have a confession to make," Robin said, tugging one of her gloved hands from her muff and squeezing it in his.

"What sort of confession?" she cried, turning to him on their single seat piled with pillows.

"My fireworks the other night—some were embedded too far into the ice and blasted that hole open. And, evidently, these fishing folk have kept it that way."

"But someone could fall in! The current's fierce, and that hole could weaken the strength of the ice."

"Your people, as you can see, my queen, deem it a great favor to be able to get fish for their holiday tables. Don't fret now, for the Bible says it only causes harm."

Robin, instead of Bane, she thought, quoting scripture, and about causing harm. "Of course I'm fretting," she argued, "because I don't like being so near that big hole in such a heavy vehicle. Horses especially should not get close. Drive on. Look, over there, not far, some sort of performance."

Near the site of the burned boathouse, someone was staging a drama before a makeshift set surrounded by a crowd of at least a hundred souls. As the sleigh drew closer, the queen realized the scene was the skeleton of a stable and the performance a mystery play, one depicting the Christ child's birth, for several sheep had been brought out near a manger filled with straw. The poor beasts were all having trouble standing.

"They've apparently just started, because here comes the holy couple toward Bethlehem," Elizabeth noted as Robin reined in. The lad portraying the pregnant Mary was bent over and helped along by the older man playing Joseph. When the crowd saw the queen, they whispered and elbowed each other, then parted to give her a clear path to see.

Elizabeth noted that quite a few of her courtiers had found the performance. Giles Chatam stood in the crowd with other members of the Queen's Country Players. She saw Sussex standing a bit apart with his wife, and Simon MacNair whispering to a burly-looking man.

"Who's that with MacNair?" Elizabeth asked Robin, pointing.

"Duncan Forbes, the courier he sends to Edinburgh with messages for Queen Mary and *vice versa*," he said, then looked so glum she realized he wished he hadn't answered.

"Oh, yes, the messenger you supposedly never used for your own privy letters to the Scots queen."

"As your Master of Horse, my queen, and I've seen Forbes at the stables, that is all."

"He returned from Edinburgh in all this weather rather quickly, did he not?" she asked herself as much as him.

A man wearing cleric's garb under his cape ran, then skidded, toward them on the ice. At first Elizabeth thought it might be the missing Vicar Bane, but it was someone she did not know. Robin began to draw his sword, but Jenks stopped the man a few yards from the sleigh.

"I'm in charge of this drama and honored to see Her Majesty here," the cleric called out, and she nodded for Jenks to let him pass. Trying to bow, he nearly went sprawling again.

"Though Christmas itself is past, Your Gracious Majesty," the man said, evidently so excited he forgot to give his name, "we will deliver the message of this holy season every day here and are so honored by your visit. Far more souls are in attendance than in St. Paul's Walk, where we gave it other years with no Frost Fair."

That rather pleased her. Vicar Bane had insisted that no good could come of such frivolity as a Frost Fair.

"I certainly hope," Robin said with a chortle, "you don't intend to have wise men ride in on camels, or they'll look rather foolish sliding all over." All three of them glanced at the meager herd of three sheep huddled together to keep from going down, spread-legged.

"Those sheep and a turtledove later for the feigned temple sacrifice is all, my lord," the cleric said. "You did hear the donkey Mary and Joseph should come in with slipped in that big hole at dawn and drowned 'fore we could get him out, didn't you?"

"I'm so sorry, for the animal and you," Elizabeth said and took one of MacNair's magical gold crowns out of the pocket in her muff to give him. She caught her glove on the gold fork she'd forgotten she carried there, because it had been a gift from her dear Robin and seemed a weapon easy to conceal. "You see," she told Robin, after the man hied himself back to overseeing the mystery play, "holes in the ice can be deadly!"

"They're safe enough unless one makes an ass of oneself," he said and boomed a laugh that made heads turn just as the angel appeared, straddling the peaked roof of the stable to hold up a star in one hand and a trumpet in the other.

"Robin," Elizabeth said, thoroughly angry with him now, "drive on!" He turned the horse away, and her clattering contingent followed. They had just begun to wend their way eastward on the river when the queen saw a young woman, red-haired like herself, out on the ice waving and shouting. Meg. It was Meg.

"Robin, pull over there."

"What then, Mistress Meg?" his voice boomed out as she came closer. She was hardly bundled against the cold but flapped a pair of gloves in her hand. With an obviously uneasy glance at Jenks, Meg came around the back of the sled to the queen's side, instead of reaching over Robin.

"Your new ermine-lined gloves, Your Majesty, the ones Kat gave you for New Year's," Meg said. "Those you are wearing are not half so warm."

"What the deuce, girl, stopping us for that!" Robin cried. "Her Grace has a fox-lined lap robe and me to keep her warm."

If that was a jest, no one laughed. Elizabeth frowned but saw in Meg's gaze that the gloves meant something. Yes, when she took them from her, one crinkled. She gave Meg her other pair, and, as they pulled away, she managed to extract from the new one a folded piece of paper. She thrust it into her muff with her coins and fork until she could find a chance to read it without Robin seeing, then pulled on the new pair of gloves. As she glanced back, she saw Jenks doff his cap to Meg and Meg wave at him forlornly.

As they sleighed gaily past the rest of the fair, then under London Bridge, waving up at people who spotted them, the queen tried to relax and enjoy herself. She kept her eyes on Robin's handsome face rather than the Tower, where her sister had once imprisoned her and her mother had been beheaded. After following the broad curve around St. Catherine's Dock, they were out in the country. How often in the early years of her reign she had wished to be off with her dear Robin, alone—or nearly alone—like this.

But perhaps, she mused, not so near the Isle of Dogs. In a way, she would like to visit her kennels of hunt hounds there as she had several years ago, but the ghost tales of the place Kat and Simon MacNair had told on the fox hunt had stayed with her. The two lovers, who supposedly drowned near this spot in the river while their hounds bayed, had haunted her. She shook her head to cast off her sense of deep foreboding.

As they made the next turn and spotted Greenwich Palace upon its snowy hill, her stomach cramped. Perhaps she should not have switched from suckets to eating so much sallet, hoping that would stop her ailments and her nightmares. Just as her hounds were kept in their kennels, poor Ned was prisoner in that east wing she could see emerging from the trees.

Ned could not believe his eyes, which were aching from staring out at the sunstruck snow. The queen was coming. Coming here, to Greenwich! With only a group of mounted guards—Jenks among them—in a sleigh, the Earl of Leicester at the helm.

His insides cartwheeled. Could she be coming to see him? Release him? Perhaps that lone rider he spotted the other night was sent ahead by her to make sure it was safe for her to visit during this dangerous holiday season.

Their backs against piles of pillows, Leicester sat close to the queen on the narrow length of seat. He held the reins with one hand, for his other arm rested behind Elizabeth's back as if he embraced her. They were covered to their hips by the same lap robe as if it were a blanket on the bed they shared.

Suddenly, Ned recalled something he had overheard Leicester

tell Sussex last month, something he had not told Her Grace at first because it would have made her angry, and then it had quite slipped his mind. Ned figured it was just more of Leicester's bravado, but maybe it had meant more.

Ned had eavesdropped on the earl's bragging to Sussex that Elizabeth had elevated him to the peerage and promoted him as Queen Mary's betrothed because she wanted the world to know he was good enough, not for the Scots queen, but for the English queen, to wed.

"She'll have me yet, man, you'll see!" the earl had said smugly to the irate Sussex. "She'll come around the first time something really goes wrong to shake her plans and she realizes she couldn't bear to see me hurt or to lose me. Once Kat Ashley dies, but for Cecil, I'll wager you a kingdom no one will be her confidant and mainstay—and who knows what else?—but me."

No. Oh, no! The sleigh had stopped on the river. They weren't coming up onto the lawn or to the palace. Leicester was getting out and carefully walking the ice to talk to the queen's mounted guard while Elizabeth herself bent over something in the sleigh. Was she heartbroken? Ill?

Ned shouted and beat on the thick windowpanes until his fists turned cold and bruised.

As Robin walked away to speak to her guards, the queen quickly pulled Meg's note from her muff. He had proposed taking her just a little farther down the river, without the array of men behind them. The idea had seemed both romantic and foolish to her. Actually, she told herself, she would have insisted he head back immediately to the city had she not been eager to read Meg's note and needed him to get out of the sleigh for a moment.

I should have told you yesterday, but Earl of L's foot, just like that of Earl of S's, fit the bootprint of H.'s murderer. I didn't think a thing of it earlier, since we never suspected L. of anything. But he did say someone hit him from behind while he was going up the back stairs. But to hit him from behind, the person would have had to be so tall, and the earl's already tall. Forgive me, Your Grace, to implicate one you love dearly as a friend, but I swear by all that's true, if your loyal Ned could be at fault, could not someone else close to you need watching, too?

Meg

Elizabeth crumpled the note and stuffed it in her muff as Robin started back toward the sleigh and her guards turned to ride away toward the city. She almost screamed at them to stop.

For suddenly, certain clues fell all too perfectly into place. Robin had not only been hurt but had benefited from the recent dreadful events. The bizarre display of Hodge's body obviously mocked Robin, but could he have set that up to get her sympathy? She had felt protective of him but had not drawn him into the investigation, so perhaps he'd decided to make himself look even more threatened.

They had found Robin naked, tied, mocked, and apparently almost dead, but he could have had one of his servants or grooms from the stable tie him up. Perhaps it was not truly as bad as it had looked. He'd showed no signs of the blow to the head he claimed; his welts and marks quickly healed. Then, indeed, she'd realized she loved him. 'S blood and bones, she'd nearly climbed into his bed! She'd taken him back into her heart and her protection and trust as she had not in years.

And now he was coming toward the sleigh, closer and closer while her guards wheeled about and headed away.

And the most damning clue? Although she could not picture Robin as a murderer, some still believed he had arranged for his wife, Amy, to be killed four years ago so that he could wed Elizabeth. She had banished him from her court and life, but he'd been exonerated and fought his way back into her heart.

But when she'd tried to offer him as consort to Queen Mary and was so furious with him over heading that off, perhaps he'd gotten desperate again and decided on something brazen and bizarre to make her take him back in her arms and life for good.

True, she'd named Robin Lord of Misrule, but he had begun to presume, to order her around beyond those bounds. He'd kissed her before the court, as if he were a husband who had rights over her, as if he were the king.

Damn the man! He was to be trusted about as much as her father had been! She was tempted to stab him with his own gift of gold fork.

Just as Robin lifted his leg to climb back into the sleigh, she seized the reins and flapped them on the horse's back. "Ha!" she cried and turned the sleigh to go after her guards.

"Your Grace! Elizabeth!" Robin cried.

Jenks looked back and saw her. Her men turned.

"Jameson," she called to one of her guards as she reined in and climbed out carefully, "I want your horse. I will ride back, so you will go in this sleigh with the earl. Jenks and one more man, follow me, and the rest escort the earl back, coming behind. And

Jameson, you are to stay with the earl to be certain he arrives safely back at Whitehall and remains in his chamber."

"Yes, Your Majesty," he said and dismounted. "But you usually don't ride so tall a horse, and on the ice, and never astride with this sort of big saddle . . ."

She should have been touched at his concern, but he was just another man ordering about the woman who was queen. "I can ride anything in Christendom, man," she said, "sidesaddle or astride. Just give me a boost up. Jenks, to me, and bring another guard," she called, cursing silently as she realized her skirt would make her ride sidesaddle anyway.

She ignored Robin's frustration and fury as he walked mincingly toward her on the ice. Refusing to look back, she urged the big horse up on the bank along the river path toward London. As she did, she remembered something else that could incriminate him. The flagon she'd held to Robin's lips after his ordeal had been of a similar style to the flagon that had hit Hodge.

Though she had to ride on the ice again when she approached the city, trailing her two guards, Elizabeth set a good but safe pace back toward Whitehall. She felt even sicker than she had before, for she could not bear it if Robin had made a fool of her and staged all this to force her to openly care for him again. The contingent at court who hated him would be baying for his blood this time, even if the one murdered was a kitchen worker and not his own wife of noble rank.

Elizabeth left the river along the eastern edge of the palace boundaries and rode back to the stables. No more time could be afforded to keep things secret, to coddle reputations, or to avoid hurting someone's feelings. Even if she panicked her court and word got out to the city and kingdom, she was going to question the royal stable's grooms, curriers, and smithies immediately. She must know if Robin, her Master of the Horse and former master of her heart, had been spotted anywhere the afternoon Hodge was killed. Maybe one of his men had overheard or seen something.

"Shall I take your horse back to the stables for you, then, Your Majesty?" Jenks asked as her guards came to ride abreast.

"I need to see my stables," she said curtly. "I've visited the chandlery and the kitchens lately, but not the stables."

She was surprised to see the wide stable doors closed, but it made sense with the weather. Seldom had she come back here this time of year, and never had she approached the stables from the side walls of the palace boundary. Nor had she ever noted the circle lined with benches and knee-high watering troughs between the back of the building and the walls that ran along the Strand.

"That's a training ring for spring and summer foals when they're first weaned, Your Majesty," Jenks told her when she reined in and stared at it. "Hardly ever used this time of year."

"I can see that from so few footprints in the snow. Go inside and tell all present I have come to wish them a good new year. I'll follow in a moment."

But when her other guard dismounted and stepped forward to help her alight, her horse shied away and bumped into one of the stone drinking troughs. "There, boy, there," she said and patted his neck to calm him.

As she did, she glanced down at the bench and trough beside her. Jenks was right in saying they were not used this time of year, for the seat was covered with blown snow and the thigh-high trough held not water but ice. And the ice of the one closest to her looked a strange blue-gray hue, as if it reflected the sky.

Still mounted, she brushed a bit of snow off with the toe of her boot and peered down, wondering if she would see her reflection. She gasped and nearly fell off the horse. Staring up at her was a man, wide-eyed as if in surprise, encased in solid ice as if he lay in a stone and glass sarcophagus.

She had found Vicar Bane.

Chapter the Fifteenth

Rye Pie Crust

Rye crust is best for standing dishes, which must be stored or keep their shapes, for it is thick, tough, coarse, and long lasting, mostly for show and not for digestion. Also, dough made with boiling water will hold better for shaping. This is ideal for display pastries at court, even large ones, namely those which contain live birds to delight the ladies when the pie is opened and the birds begin to sing and take wing. How many pockets full of rye measured for the crust depends upon its size. Such crusts can be baked, then slit open with care to introduce doves, blackbirds, or larger surprises. A rye pie can bring much merriment, especially during the Twelve Days of Christmas.

SO AS NOT TO ALARM THE COURT, ELIZABETH ORDERED Martin Bane's body to be hewn whole from the water trough in one large piece of ice, wrapped, and carried by her guards into the chandlery to be thawed in a vat of water over a slow fire. When she saw it would take too long to clean wax from the vats, she sent for the largest old kettle in the kitchens.

She had realized there were only two possible places to thaw out Bane's body, and she was starting to fear the palace kitchens. After she sent the chandlery staff away, only Jenks, Meg, and the queen kept watch over the fire melting the block of ice in water in the biggest iron soup kettle the men could drag in. Perhaps it had not been cleaned well, for leaves and pieces of vegetables floated to the surface, or else the particles were from fodder spilled into the horse trough and caught in the ice, too.

Her orderly world was turned upside down, Elizabeth thought, as she personally oversaw the gruesome thawing. Robin, who had authority over her stables, where the drowning must have occurred, was being detained in his bedchamber. Cecil, whom she wanted at her side, had been sent to interrogate him, while Cecil's men had been assigned to thoroughly question workers in the stables. Vicar Bane, whose realm should have been the chapel, was dead in the chandlery. Ned, who had always been able to lighten her heart, was exiled to Greenwich.

"Of course," Jenks said as they huddled near the kettle, "the vicar could have tumbled into the horse trough, hit his head, and drowned. Still," he added, obviously, Elizabeth thought, when he saw her frown, "however slippery one of those benches might be, why would he be standing on it?"

"Precisely," Elizabeth said, frowning at the debris floating in the water.

"So," Jenks went on, "the same someone as knocked Hodge and the Earl of Leicester on the head could have done this. In that case, he meant for him to drown and become a block of ice."

"He was a block of ice anyway, if you ask me," Meg put in.

"We did not ask you," Jenks replied.

The queen noted how the two of them snapped at each other lately. Usually when they'd disagreed, it had been with calm respect, not bitter bile, though Meg and Ned had often fought with passion. She sighed and thrust such personal problems away for now.

"Meg, it's bad luck," Jenks added, "to speak ill of the dead."

"Which," Elizabeth said, holding her hands out not only to halt their bickering but to be warmed by steam escaping the vat, "is why I have sent Baron Hunsdon to explain this as pure mischance to Bishop Grindal and the city coroner. Grindal has every right to know his vicar is dead, but we shall call this an accident until we prove otherwise, and we must do so soon."

"A sad way to mark the vicar off our list of possible killers," Meg said, as Cecil came in from outside and stamped snow off his boots.

"Well, my lord," Elizabeth said, striding to greet him, "did you turn up any evidence against Leicester?"

"In questioning him, I did not," he said, walking over to peer into the kettle, then moving away again to join her nearer the door while Jenks and Meg watched over Vicar Bane. "The earl seems to have an answer, such as it is," Cecil said for her ears only, "for every question or accusation. He says he is outraged that I would suggest he did anything to coerce favoritism from you, for 'Her Grace is ever mindful of me as a man and subject and her adoring servant,' or some such wild words."

She shook her head and bit her lip to fight back tears. "Have your men finished questioning Leicester's men in the stables?" she asked in a louder voice.

"According to what they have discovered so far," Cecil reported, removing his gloves and no longer whispering either, "Leicester was in and out the afternoon Hodge was killed. Unfortunately, of course, it is not far from the stables to the back kitchen entrance near Hodge's cubbyhole."

"It can't be my lord Leicester," Jenks insisted, coming closer. "I've served under the man all the years you've been queen, Your Grace. He's smooth and wily and wants his way, but—"

"That he does," Elizabeth muttered.

"—he's not a murderer. Can't be."

Can't be echoed in her mind. Can't be Robin, can't be Sussex, can't be MacNair, can't be Darnley and Margaret, or Giles Chatam. This was all becoming a hideous nightmare in which she felt she slid and slipped upon the icebound river, edging nearer a huge hole of wild, dark water, which haunted her dreams.

"Let's go over exactly what we do know about the time of Bane's death," Elizabeth said. "Vicar Bane was alive at least until last Friday, when I saw him rip off his mask and stalk out of the Feast of Fools banquet. Did any of you see him thereafter or speak to anyone who did?"

"Not I," Cecil said. "But you received that epistle from him rebuking the court's Christmas festivities on Saturday."

"No, on Friday, but I didn't show it to you until Saturday. I believe he wrote it—at least dated it—Friday. I sent men to arrest Bane on Saturday," she went on. "They say they scoured the palace and inquired at both of Bishop Grindal's homes, but Bane was at neither place nor had been recently."

"So," Cecil concluded, stroking his beard, "he must have drowned, or *was* drowned, between Friday and Saturday."

"I have independent evidence," Elizabeth told them, as each turned her way, "that it was indeed on Friday, between four in the afternoon and eight in the evening."

"Of course, the water!" Cecil said, snapping his fingers.

"What about it?" Jenks asked.

"The one question," Elizabeth explained, "I asked the grooms before you and my other guards carried Bane away from the stables was when they last filled that watering trough. Obviously, Bane fell in or was put in when it held water and not ice. When the stable lads refilled it at four that afternoon, Bane was not in there yet, but was soon after, for he lay deep in the water and it iced downward from above. The grooms were sure the trough nearest the doors was solid ice by eight that evening, but they hardly went around in the dark peering into all of them."

"Brilliant, Your Grace," Cecil muttered.

"Once I realized my horse and those of my guards had stamped through whatever footprints might have been in the snowy circle," she added, "I had to make amends—discover something."

"But how about outside the circle, then?" Cecil asked. "The murderer's prints inside it might have been obliterated by your horse's hooves or even yesterday's wind, but what if Bane were killed elsewhere and then carried or even dragged to the trough?"

"You will yet keep me humble, my lord," she admitted. "Jenks, it's getting late, but take one of the torches from the wall and carefully search about where my lord Cecil suggests. Look for footprints or drag marks, and if you find such, ask the lads in the stables if they've been pulling sacks of grain or whatever."

"All right," he said, "but one other thing, then, Your Grace. Long as I've worked in those stables, the troughs are not used in the winter, so why did the water get changed at all that afternoon? You want me to inquire about that, too?"

"It seems," she answered, trying to keep her voice steady, "that my Master of the Horse decided that the weight of that much ice might crack the stone troughs, so he ordered the water changed, though more than one lad said they had a tough time chipping all the ice out."

"Oh, no!" Meg cried. Elizabeth turned, thinking Meg would insist that proved Robin was guilty, but she was pointing into the kettle. "He's thawed, and will you look at this!"

They rushed to the kettle. Bane's head had floated to the top of the water, though he'd turned facedown with his pale hair waving like sea grass above him. One thin hand had risen to the surface, the fingers curled as if they had just released the folded piece of paper that bobbed in the water.

The queen took it out and carefully opened the sodden piece of stiff parchment. Fortunately, it was folded tightly inward, or the water might have washed off the ink of the printed words.

"Is it in the same hand as his letter cursing the queen's Christmas?" Cecil asked.

"It's in block letters, hastily formed ones, not in script, more like the mocking signs tied to Leicester when he was trussed like a roast boar," she said and read aloud:

To all who truly worship the Lord High God—forgive me for stooping so low to physically fight the sinful frivolities which degrade true Christmas. I should not have taken things so into my hands, for " 'vengeance is mine' sayeth the Lord" and not that of a mere vicar in His calling. I have sinned, but then so did the queen's privy dresser, the peacock and boar Leicester, and, most of all, the queen. "In the measure that she glorified herself and lived luxuriously, in the same measure give her torment and sorrow." Amen.

Martin Bane

"It's turned treasonous now," Cecil whispered.

The queen gawked at the note, her mind racing.

"But it's over!" Meg cried, gripping her hands together. "Bane was behind it all! Ned can come home, and it wasn't the earl to blame!"

"But," Cecil said, "who left that package of flagons on the throne New Year's Eve, then—after Bane must have died?"

"Maybe he planned for that before his death," Jenks said. "You know, as part of his confession to the crimes. A servant could have left it there for him, Your Grace. He could have decided to give up the murder weapon, then drown himself in remorse."

"To atone," Cecil whispered. "Yes, the guilt could have eaten away at him as it did Judas Iscariot when he rushed out and killed himself. Your Majesty, are you quite well?" he asked and touched her elbow to steady her, for he must have noticed how hard she was shaking.

"I think," she said, her voice trembling, too, "that Vicar Bane would be less likely to commit the sin of suicide than Hodge Thatcher, let alone murder another. But if he were in that desperate state of mind to drown himself, would he trust his confession note to a trough of water? Yet, it is on the paper to which he would have access."

She stooped and held the note toward the fire as if she would toast it. They saw clearly that the familiar watermark on the parchment matched the earlier ones.

"But the wording sounds like him," Cecil argued. "The quote is from the Bible."

"It's from Revelations," she said, standing. "And, however much I want to believe this nightmare is over, my revelation is that our murderer has struck again, even more cleverly so. Meg, help me lift the poor man's head just a bit. There!" she cried.

Although Bane's silvery blond hair had hidden it at first, he had been hit hard on the back of his head. They saw no blood or scab, but a livid goose egg of flesh had raised there, and the ice had preserved it perfectly.

"Just like Hodge was hit—and maybe the Earl of Leicester, too!" Meg cried.

"Nor do I think," Elizabeth said, as she and Meg let Hodge sink into the water again, "that the leaves floating in the ice with Bane are from an unscrubbed kettle or horse fodder, especially not those which are common seasonings like sage and basil."

"Why, yes," Meg whispered. "That's what herbs they are."

"Our kitchen killer," the queen went on, "is amusing himself again by presenting a murdered man—one who served me—as food. I don't care what this cleverly worded note says, I don't think the killer is Martin Bane. He's just another victim."

"And so," Cecil whispered, "it's as if the murderer has given us a cryptic recipe and forced us to make vicar soup."

"Exactly," Elizabeth exclaimed.

The next morning, Ned saw that a man—one he didn't recognize—was doing something on the ice, near where the queen and her men had been yesterday. He was quite bundled and muffled up. It must be someone from the meager winter staff at Greenwich, but why would he have ridden a horse out there when he could have just walked?

Ned reckoned he might be pounding small stakes or spikes in the ice for some sort of sliding race. Yes, that must be it, for he was laying ropes from those stakes along the ice toward this riverbank. Would it be, Ned wondered, games only for local folk of the small village nearby, or would the city or court people be coming, too? At least he'd have a fine seat.

He smiled grimly as he pictured again how the queen had

driven the sleigh away from the Earl of Leicester and forced him to ride back with a yeoman guard while, mounted, she'd left him in her dust—or scattered snow. If he had not seen that she knew to mistrust her Robin, Ned would have written a note telling her what he'd overheard between Leicester and Sussex and insisted it be delivered to Whitehall. He shook his head and sighed. It had always amazed him how the queen and Leicester fought, yet still loved each other. Now, it had come to remind him of how he felt about Meg.

All these years he'd spurned her, but he admired her deeply. She'd been only a girl who'd lost her memory and her past until the queen had given her a future. When he'd been ordered to teach Meg to walk and talk correctly so she could emulate the queen if need be, how quick she'd been to learn royal demeanor and delivery. He'd never told her that, though, told her quite the opposite. But through Meg's tough times, Elizabeth had cared for her, Jenks adored her, and Ned Topside . . .

"Hell's gates, it's just because she resembles the queen I adore, a form of the queen I can touch and possess," he gritted out, hitting his fist on the wood-paneled wall.

The thought amazed him. Could it be that loving Meg was the only way he could have a bit of the volatile, brilliant goddess Elizabeth? Or did he love Meg for being Meg?

He jumped at the knock on his door. "Stand back, then, Master Topside," his guard, Lemuel, bellowed. Ned heard the familiar latch lift and the key scrape in the lock.

"Evergreen Day on the calendar, then," Lemuel said with a broad smile as he came in. "Traditional meat pie day, my mother always said," he went on as if Ned could care about his family or his damned good mood. "Capon pie, it is, still hot, too, so's hope you'll eat better than you been so far." The big-shouldered man, one of the groundskeepers here, not even a real guard, put Ned's noontide tray down. It also bore bread, some sort of pudding, and a fresh flagon of beer.

"Hand me that chamber pot, then, so's I can dump it and bring it back," Lemuel told him, and Ned sullenly did as he was bidden.

This single guard who came and went wasn't much security, Ned mused, so Her Grace must believe he wasn't really guilty. Or she thought him such a milksop she didn't worry he'd manage an escape. If he tried disobeying her again, he was done for good with her—was guilty—that must be her thinking.

When Lemuel went out, Ned sat down and began to eat the meat pie, a good one, though all food tasted like sawdust to him here. He wondered how the large, hollow, fancy pie at court this evening would look and what would pop out of it when it was cut. He'd seen everything from doves to blackbirds to frogs jumping all over the table, making the ladies laugh or scream.

Two years ago, Ned had hidden in the pie himself and leaped out to deliver a lengthy paean to the queen. This year, if he were in charge, instead of Leicester—unless she'd replaced him, too—he'd have something inside it to tie into the play the actors were going to present to her wherein Elizabeth of England reigned ever green and fresh as a fir tree in the snow and ice.

Frowning, he rose to look out the window again. The man on the ice was gone. When Lemuel returned with that chamber pot, he'd just ask him if it was someone from this palace, Whitehall, or the Frost Fair, and what in heaven's name he was doing out there.

· · ·

"The Earl of Leicester is demanding to talk to you to convince you of his innocence," Cecil told the queen the moment he entered her apartments. "He's making quite a fuss."

"Then see that he is informed of two things. Firstly, I do not parlay with those who think they can usurp my authority. And secondly, if he does not just sit there quietly and wait until I have time to see him, he will be trussed and gagged, and I know he is quite familiar with the arrangements for that!"

"Yes, Your Grace."

"Cecil, I thank you for not gloating," she said as he turned away to deliver her command.

"Gloating?" he echoed, obviously surprised. "Whatever I think of Leicester privily, I can hardly relish that he might indeed have murdered, or ordered murdered, two men who serve you, even as I serve you with great pride and care."

She pressed both hands to her head as if to hold her wild thoughts and fears in. "Cecil, I think I'm turning lunatic. It can't be Robin behind all this any more than it can be Ned, yet I am constrained to keep them constrained, and all because some demon is amusing himself by serving up my people as Yuletide food!"

"And here we stand, as at the first, waiting for the other shoe to drop."

"No, I have had enough of that. I am not taking a defensive position but am going on the offense. It's the way Sussex says he tried to fight the wild Irish, but they kept just disappearing into their bogs and fens. But this enemy will not elude me, I swear it!"

"Other than interrogating Leicester personally and hoping Clifford returns with that pewterer to question, what do you intend?"

"Come with me, my lord. It is in the kitchens that it all began, so perhaps we can find some answers there. These events have put me off food, and I've been avoiding the place like the plague, but no more. The battle is enjoined!"

Cecil hurriedly gave a guard her order to keep Leicester quiet, then followed her—she already had Jenks with her—down the servants' staircase and through the back corridor to the Great Hall. Now empty, it had already been decked out for the play and feast tonight.

The queen noted that the painted backdrop for the allegory had been turned to the wall. She started at a good clip toward the kitchens again, then turned back so abruptly Jenks almost smacked into her.

"What is it, Your Grace?" he asked.

"I am sick to death of surprises and of someone perverting our beloved holiday traditions," she said as she hurried between set tables across the hall toward the scenery with Cecil and Jenks hustling to keep up. "Move this backdrop out, will you, Jenks? See, it's all on little wheels, Ned's idea and a good one."

"We all miss him, Your Grace," Jenks said as he complied, and Cecil helped him move the set out a bit from the wall. Again, as ever, she was touched by Jenks's loyalty, not only to her but to her Privy Plot Council members when she was certain he would like Ned out of Meg's life.

"Ugh," Cecil muttered, "the backdrop is still wet—and rather sloppily painted." He held up his hand, green as grass under his smeared cuff and sleeve.

"But that was finished three days ago, and prettily done, too," she protested and, holding her skirts tight, stepped between the wall and the backdrop to gaze up at the entire expanse of it.

Her mouth dropped open, and her pulse pounded like fireworks exploding. The scene had been hastily painted over: The fir tree symbolizing her now looked drooped and tattered and was ready to topple into a hole crudely painted in the ice. Her stomach churned, for she recalled that gaping cavity in the Thames ice with the dark current of water beneath.

" 'S blood and bones, he's struck again!" she cried.

"You don't think Giles . . ." Cecil began.

"I don't know what in Christendom to think. Jenks, see that the play is canceled and this backdrop taken down. Indeed, I may halt the rest of the Twelve Days so this marauding murderer cannot keep getting the best of me. Cecil, there is one more thing I must examine to keep chaos from tonight's feast."

"What?" he cried, then just hurried to keep up with her again.

"I'm finally learning to outthink him, I vow I am," she threw back over her shoulder as she rushed toward the kitchens. "Evergreen Day it is, and he's tried to twist the scenery of a play to mock me. It's me he's after, Cecil, not just my servants or even Leicester."

"Then you think the earl's not to bl——"

"Whoever is behind this could have help."

"From someone in the kitchens?"

"I don't know yet, but what's the other tradition of this day?" she asked, not breaking stride as the delicious mingled smells from the kitchen block assailed them.

"You mean pies?" he asked, sounding out of breath. "Especially the large one you cut open with the humorous surprises in it?"

"Exactly! Just as I lifted the platter from over the boar's head only to find a fox with a gold snout, what am I to find when I slice into that pretty pie?"

They did not have far to look for the masterpiece that the pastry chefs had cooling on a wheeled cart in the hallway by Hodge's old workroom. The outside door was ajar to cool the pie as big as a card table and perhaps also to air out the smoky kitchens. Master Cook Roger Stout, evidently told she was here, soon appeared at her side.

"And what is being placed inside the queen's pie this evening?" she asked him as he rose from his bow.

"Are you certain you want to know, Your Majesty?" the man asked, repeatedly wiping his hands on his apron. "After all, for it to be a surprise..."

"What will it be?" she shouted, only to have the man and several pastry cooks who'd followed flinch as if she'd struck them.

"Doves, Your Majesty," Stout told her. "Twelve doves to symbolize not only peace, the Earl of Leicester told me several days ago. He said it also stands for God's approval on the kingdom, even as a dove flew down to give the Lord God's holy blessings at His own Son's baptism in the River Jordan."

Her thoughts scattered, and she tried to grab them back. How sweet of Robin to have planned that. He could not be behind this. If something were amiss in this pie, would it not clear him as well as Ned?

"Your Grace," Cecil said, taking her elbow, "you are not going to faint?"

"Of course not!" she declared, turning to Roger Stout again. "When you introduce the doves into the pie, you don't need much of a hole, do you, Master Cook?"

"No, Your Majesty, as they are carefully inserted one at a time, just over here, in this large vent atop the crust."

"Which," the pastry cook closest to her added, "is then stopped up with a decorative piece of crust." She ignored the fact that the two pastry cooks were muttering something about giving all their secrets away.

"Then why," she asked, "does it look as if there is a section already cut out over there by the door, a larger piece than the vent, one which looks as if it's been fitted back in place? See there?" she demanded, pointing.

Stout rose and hurried around the pie, but the pastry cooks beat him there. "I—don't know. What happened here?" he demanded, turning on his underlings.

"So skillful, it's nearly invisible," one said.

"Someone's been tampering with the best work we've done all year!" the other protested.

Elizabeth strode to the section she had seen in slanting light from the open door. Though she intended to demand a knife to cut into it, Jenks arrived just then.

"Jenks, hand me your sword."

"Your Majesty," Cecil said, "let me do it lest something dire leap out."

"I'll be careful," she insisted, taking Jenks's proffered sword. She cut carefully into the pie along the lines already there, while Roger Stout leaned close to support that piece of pastry from falling in and the pastry cooks wrung their hands. Everyone crowded close.

"You are in my light," she told them, and all but Stout and Cecil moved back.

She peered into the pie that would soon hold the flutter of doves. Within lay the two dolls that had been used to mimic her and Robin on Feast of Fools night. This time it was not Robin who was mocked, for tied to the queen doll's wire crown was a pair of authentic ass's ears.

Chapter the Sixteenth

Pancakes

Take 2 or 3 eggs, break them into a dish, and beat them well; then add unto them a pretty quantity of fair running water; then put in cloves, mace, cinnamon, and nutmeg, and season it with salt; make it thick as you think good with fine wheat flour. Then fry the cakes thin with sweet butter, make them brown, and so serve them up with sugar strewn upon them.

THE QUEEN, WITH CECIL, HARRY, ANNE, JENKS, AND MEG in attendance, paced her presence chamber, trying to decide what to do next. She knew she must act, and not just continue to rant. On the table where she often took her meals lay the pieces of paper with the murderer's mocking missives, which, she was certain, included Bane's so-called suicide note. Cecil's sketches of the boot print and the blow to Hodge's head lay there. The box of flagons and the box of stones, gold leaf from Hodge's death scene and from the beheaded fox's snout, the stub of torch, and the dolls with the peacock feathers and ass's ears also sat upon the table as if they could tell her who had used them to ruin lives and Christmas.

"At least, I believe I know where our clever culprit got those ass's ears," the queen said as she turned to walk past her friends, who lined her path. "When Robin and I were out in the sleigh yesterday, we heard that the donkey for the Frost Fair mystery play had fallen through the ice and drowned."

"Amazing he wasn't trapped under the ice," Harry put in.

"I think not," she said with a shudder. "I have no doubt the carcass was hauled off the ice, and our murderer saw the opportunity for more mayhem." She sank into the chair at the head of the table and covered her face with her hands.

"Are you ill, Your Grace?" Cecil asked.

"Only sick to death of all of this," she said as she heard the others slip into the chairs around the littered table. "I just recalled that Leicester made a joke of it, a pun. He said something like those too near the hole in the ice—which he admitted his fireworks caused—were 'safe enough unless they made an ass of themselves.' "

She nearly cried. Although she'd seen many courtiers watching that play who could have heard about the donkey's death, Robin had also jested earlier about peacocks and boars. Yet he was being held in his room, so he must have someone else working with him who had placed the dolls and ass's ears in the pie.

But Jenks was the only one she knew upon whom Robin had relied closely and continually over the last six years. She used to think that was because she favored Jenks so, and Robin saw the man as a bond between them. Since Jenks's wit was for horses, could Robin have used him somehow to pull the wool over her eyes?

She spread her fingers to stare at Jenks. He looked brooding, but no doubt only with concern for her. Unless she had suspected Meg or Kat herself, as she had Rosie, no one was more loyal to her than Jenks, and yet it had just crossed her mind to mistrust him. Who would she turn against next? She could not—would not—live in a world where she could not trust anyone.

At that moment Elizabeth Tudor could not bear her loneliness. How could she think that those dearest to her, who had been through hell to help her get her throne and protect it, would betray her? No, she would not let the whoreson bastard who was killing Christmas kill her trust of those she valued and loved.

They all startled when a knock rattled the door. The queen nodded to Cecil, who stepped out quickly and closed the door so that no one could see the mix of persons huddled in such familiar fashion around her table.

"Your yeoman Clifford's returned, Your Grace," Cecil said as he stuck his head back in.

"I have often thought we must add him to our little council, but until then, best we keep up appearances," she said with a nod to Meg and Jenks, who rose from the table and hurried out into the next room. "And leave that door cracked so you can hear," she called after them, then nodded at Cecil to admit Clifford.

Her favorite yeoman looked worn and windblown with beard stubble shadowing his cheeks, but then he'd been looking for the pewterer Vincent Wainwright for nigh on two days.

"Did you track him down, Clifford?" she asked as he rose from his bow across the table while Cecil stayed by the door as if guarding it.

"First I tried St. Paul's," he reported, sounding out of breath, "but saw no one, then found out the tradesmen had all gone to set up booths at the Frost Fair. He wasn't there, so looked high and low near Cheapside where he was supposed to live, folks saying he'd been around, that he was here or there. But finally learned he'd gone home for a few days, to his parents' home, that is, to Southwark, so finally found him."

"And brought him back with you?"

"Wainwright's sicker than a dog, Your Grace. I know you don't want someone like that here. His mother says he just ate too many Yule sweets, but he says it's the gripes, so—"

"Did you ask him about who bought at least six flagons from him?"

"Oh, aye, Your Grace, but you won't like what you hear."

"Just tell me, man."

As he spoke, he ticked off about twenty names on his big fingers, including, "The Earl of Leicester, the Scots envoy MacNair, Lord Northumberland, Lord Knollys, Countess of Lennox— for her son, she said. Also, he said the Earl of Southampton, and several other courtiers whose names he didn't know all bought from him. Sounds as if he's caught folks' fancies for gifts this year."

" 'S blood and bones!" she cried, smacking her palms on the table. "It seems, Cecil, we are still in the same stew, though this testimony might help clear Sussex, if he only bought two flagons. Clifford, my thanks. Take what respite you can, and I shall summon you if I need to go out."

Clifford accepted that with a bow and quick retreat, but Cecil had barely closed the door before he remonstrated, "Go out where?"

"I would speak with Ned Topside and then release him."

"But we can send someone to return him here in a trice. It's but an hour before the early dusk, and it's cold out there."

"I know the hour and the weather, my lord! It's just that I do not know the answers I must have, and the walls of the palace are closing in on me as if I were inside that dark crust of pie just waiting to fly! You see, now this wretched mess has me speaking in terms of food, when even that has been ruined for me lately."

Cecil, arms crossed, still leaning against the door as if he would block it, jumped away as another knock resounded. The queen indicated he should answer it.

"It's Master Cook Stout," Cecil said, not even closing the door behind himself this time. "He's most distressed at something he's found."

Her pulse pounded in foreboding. "Megs, Jenks, stay where you are," she called to them. "Harry and Anne, remain with me. Cecil, let the man in.

"What is it, then, Master Stout?" she asked as he nearly bounded past Cecil. "Something else about the pie?"

"I've tried to keep a good kitchen!" he burst out after a haphazard bow. "But since poor Hodge's death, it's all been topsy-turvy, and now this!" he cried, waving a piece of parchment.

The queen jumped up and moved around the cluttered table to snatch it before Cecil could. She held it up to the window light. "Yes, St. Paul's steeple!" she cried, which she saw only perplexed poor Stout more.

"Bane's hardly back from the dead," Cecil muttered.

"It's a recipe," Stout said, wringing his hands as if he were washing them. "Someone's been tampering with my recipes!"

"Indeed, Master Stout," the queen said, trying to keep calm, "someone's been tampering with your recipes and all our well-laid plans. When and where did this appear?" she asked as she bent to read the small script in good light.

"Don't know exactly, but since last night. I have my book of them in my office, known by heart, for can't see taking them into the fray to get them splattered and stained. I didn't write it, and few of the cooks can write. It's a mockery, I tell you that, but not in my hand or anyone's I know!"

"But it's just about pancakes, Master Stout."

"My recipe is labeled 'Pancakes,' not 'Christmas Pancakes for the Queen.' Read it, then, just read it, Your Majesty."

"Oh, I see!"

"What is it, Your Grace?" Cecil said and came to look over her shoulder as she read in a voice that went from wary to enraged:

Christmas Pancakes for the Queen

Take eggs from a wall and give them a fall, then beat them again and again. Add fast running water, spice as you ought to, then pieces of peacock or boar in their turn. Stir in wheat flour and butter fresh-churned, then fry the cakes carefully lest the topside burn. For all the queen's horses and all the queen's men can't put Christmas or court back together again.

"I've never, never," Stout protested, "put meat in pancakes!"

"A recipe for disaster," Elizabeth cried. "It's from him."

"It's from Hodge's murderer?" Stout asked, his voice now a mere squeak. "He's tampered with our peacock, boar, pies—and now this? But what are eggs on a wall?"

"He's using that old nursery rhyme, where the eggs are people," she started to explain, then realized she had no time for that. "Go back to your kitchens and lock the doors, Master Stout," she said, still staring at the recipe, "especially the one by Hodge's workroom that is near the back door."

"And near my office where this appeared."

"Go, now. I will send guards to help you."

"But the feast tonight? Is it still on?"

"You must prepare it as if nothing had happened, even put the birds in the pie, for I vow I shall be back by then to cut it."

"You're not still going out to release Ned yourself?" Cecil asked as Harry hustled Stout from the room and Meg and Jenks ran back in.

"I've felt guilty all along that Ned was locked up at Greenwich and Robin here, though someone's been making them seem guilty," Elizabeth explained as she threw the recipe atop the other evidence upon the table and hurried toward her bedchamber door with Meg behind her.

"Your Grace, I think they've done a good enough job of that themselves," Cecil protested.

"Read that recipe again, Cecil," she ordered, turning back at the door. "Read the words *lest the topside burn.*"

"Oh, no! Oh, no!" Meg cried, and Elizabeth put a steadying hand on her arm while Jenks stood yet dumbfounded. "The killer's going after Ned!"

"I fear so," Elizabeth said. "Our clever murderer, who has not only walked on eggs at court but has broken and beaten them, has killed Hodge and my court vicar and tried to kill Robin—my servants all. The bastard no doubt lit the boathouse with me in it, unless he thought he was just attacking you and Jenks that time . . ."

The queen let her voice trail off. The killer had spoken in symbols before, so it didn't actually mean he would burn Ned, though she would make certain no harm came to him and warn her staff at Greenwich. But Meg, who had gone to school too long listening to both her sovereign and Cecil, blurted, "Your Grace, what if the killer's going to try to burn Greenwich with Ned in it?"

"We will ride there, to capture and stop him. I don't like the way the Christmas killer obviously knows the grounds of Greenwich to be able to poach a fox and leave a box of stones. Meg, stop sniveling, for I need you to help me into my man's riding garb. Jenks, fetch Clifford and saddle five horses ready to run the ice and have them brought below to my privy staircase immediately."

"I'm going, too!" Meg insisted.

"You are staying here with Cecil to play queen busy at her desk," Elizabeth commanded.

"But five horses?" Cecil said.

"Myself, Jenks, Clifford, Harry—and Leicester. Cecil, spring the earl from his room and say his queen has immediate need of him—if he can keep his mouth shut on this ride so we can catch this Christmas killer."

"But it could be a trap," Cecil insisted.

"But one he himself will be caught in this time," she vowed.

She glanced at her dear people as she turned into her room. Cecil looked both frenzied and furious; Anne hugged Harry good-bye; and Jenks looked only at the distraught Meg with tears glassing his eyes.

The queen scrambled into warm hose and trunks, wool shirt, leather jerkin, cape, and riding boots. She grabbed two of the gold forks Robin had given her and slid one inside the top of each boot. Meg, who must now don the queen's garments, hastily handed her a pair of gloves, hat, and muffler.

"You're not thinking the killer's someone in the household at Greenwich?" Meg asked, blinking back tears again. "I mean like someone who comes and goes here through the back kitchen door, perhaps bringing in fresh game for the table from the forests there? If so, Ned could have been harmed long before this!"

"He'll be free within the hour. Meg, I've been wrong about Ned."

"Mayhap we all have."

Elizabeth had no time to pursue that. She squeezed Meg's shoulder and went to open the door to the privy staircase while Meg lit a lantern.

"It's been a while since you went out like this—and never for a better cause," Meg said as she rushed down the stairs behind the queen, holding the lantern aloft to light her way.

"We need Ned back here," Elizabeth vowed as her voice cracked with emotion.

"Yes, we need him here," Meg echoed as the queen opened the door to find Jenks waiting with the others.

Jenks and Meg simply stared at each other. He helped the queen mount. God help us, Elizabeth thought, to solve not only the murders but the mess Ned, Jenks, and Meg were in.

Having exhausted himself pacing and agonizing, Ned had begun to sleep irregular hours. It made the time pass and temporarily obliterated his fears. At least Elizabeth of England had consigned him to a prison with a fireplace, food, and warm bed. He snuggled down in it now, the counterpane and covers tight around his hunched shoulders.

As he inhaled deeply and sighed, he realized the ashes on his hearth, which he'd let burn down, smelled too strong. He'd just shovel them into his chamber pot and send them out the next time Lemuel came. The friendly lout seemed only good for carting food trays and emptying chamber pots, for the man hadn't even known who that could have been, both by day and night, down on the frozen river.

Ned sniffed again, for the scent was sharper now. It bit into his nostrils and his head so bitterly that his eyes watered and his throat felt sore. If he took sick here, he'd miss Meg's healing hand for certain.

He sat up and opened his eyes. Was it dusk already? It was as if fog, thickening, settling, had permeated his chamber. He saw a gray film of smoke creeping under the door, swirling and rising.

Only silvered embers lay in the grate and had sifted through onto the hearth. Yet a fire must be nearby, and he was locked in.

"Lemuel!" he shouted and began banging on his door. "Let me out! There's fire somewhere! Fire!"

This time, unlike the other day, the queen rode astride, bundled and muffled so no one would know who she was as she passed her people's Frost Fair. Harry and the newly freed Robin rode abreast, the two guards behind. Robin had evidently decided to obey her for once, since he said naught but to whisper he would guard her with his life. Their eyes had met, she had nodded, and that seemed to be enough for him right now. The queen quickened their pace as they passed under the arches of London Bridge.

As she did, she thought of the childhood refrain Kat used to sing for her: *London Bridge is falling down, my fair lady.* But worse, the innocent nursery rhyme the Christmas killer had perverted kept taunting her: *Humpty Dumpty sat on a wall, Humpty Dumpty had a great fall, and all the king's horses and all the king's men could not put Humpty Dumpty together again.*

There was no king in England, but a queen—who must be stronger than any man to hold her throne and keep her kingdom safe. Granted, her realm was ever threatened from without, but she must not have it threatened from within. She must right things. She must.

Now that they were away from people, Elizabeth was about to address her men. She intended to order them to free Ned Topside, warn her small Greenwich staff of danger, then accompany her and Ned back to Whitehall before darkness set in. And above all, to beware of tricks and traps.

But she could be too late, for she smelled something acrid on the wind.

Smoke! Dear Lord in heaven, not smoke! Fire and smoke had prepared many a dish for the table, so would suit a murderer who had a bizarre taste for displaying his kills.

Ned was appalled when he realized that burning material of some sort had been wedged under his door. It not only smoked but began to burn the door to his room.

He splashed his remaining ale and a ewer of wash water on it, but that changed nothing. Trying to keep low for the best air, through the thickening smoke, he glanced wildly about the room for something to shove the burning debris away.

He broke his wooden food tray into long pieces and poked, almost blindly now, through burgeoning smoke and the first flames, trying to dislodge the material jammed under his door. He was hacking so hard and his eyes were stinging so—he'd never get a breath to shout for Lemuel again.

It crossed his mind that the mysterious riders he'd seen outside might have come to survey the palace and set a fire. But why? Fires in palaces were usually the result of someone careless with a hearth or candle at night, or more likely an accident in the kitchens.

He was going to have to change his tactics here, he realized as his eyes streamed tears. His solid, narrow window would probably not break, and he was on the second floor, where a drop could cripple or kill him. He'd have to try to break down the door. If it was only weakened enough by the flames by now . . . if he wasn't too weak to lift this chair to pound at it . . .

The single chair in the room seemed to have the weight of the world atop it. Dragging it toward the door, thinking how distraught Her Grace would be if she lost Greenwich, for she had been born here and loved the place . . . thinking how he loved the queen and loved Meg but could never tell Meg so and hug her hard . . .

He tried to lift the chair, but he was hacking too hard. He had to get out of here to clear his name. Tell Meg something. Hugged hard by suffocating smoke, Ned crumpled against the heavy chair and slid to the floor.

Chapter the Seventeenth

Water for Cooking and Baking

Water is not wholesome, sole by itself, for an Englishman but is cold, slow, and slack of digestion. The best water is rain-water, so it be purely taken. Next to it is running water, the which doth swiftly run upon stones or pebbles. The third water to be praised is river or brook water, the which is clear. Standing water, the which be refreshed with a spring, is commendable; but standing water and well-water to which the sun hath no reflection be not so commendable. And let every man beware of all waters which be putrefied with froth.

ACROSS FROM THE ISLE OF DOGS, ELIZABETH AND HER entourage left the river and cut up into the trees surrounding Greenwich Palace, the same area where they'd begun their fox hunt over a week ago. From here they could see that flames licked inside at least one window on the second floor of the east wing.

"I know you are angry I've been ordering you about, Your Grace," Robin said and reined his horse in to block hers, "but you cannot go near a burning building. We must leave a guard here with you and ride in to rouse the staff."

"And to fetch Ned out, I promise, Your Grace!" Jenks cried and spurred his horse toward the palace before she could give him leave.

"Yes, all right. Go, Robin, but be careful. Harry can stay with me."

They gasped as a boom filled the air. Fireworks shot skyward to sprinkle sparks into the bare-limbed forest, as if it were New Year's Eve again. Their mounts shied or reared, and the distant dogs in the royal kennel howled. Robin wheeled back toward her.

"I must tell you," he shouted, "that I have learned someone stole some of the fireworks I had stored for the New Year's celebration. There weren't half the number I'd planned. I would have told you, of course, but I didn't want to be blamed for aught else—which," he added, emphasizing each word, "I did not do!"

"But gunpowder is in those fireworks," she cried, "gunpowder for firearms which could be used in an insurrection." She thought of Sussex, her military man, but surely he would not raise arms against her, however much he hated her reliance on Robin. No, it seemed as if the gunpowder thieves were using it for fireworks— and perhaps to start the fire at Greenwich.

"Harry, take Robin's place at the palace and help Jenks fetch out Ned Topside before I go after him myself. Robin, stay with me. If you don't know who took the fireworks, at least, how were they stolen?" she demanded as Harry charged after the others.

"I swear I don't know. I had men guarding them out by the gatehouse to the Strand."

"And so not far from the back way into the kitchens," she muttered to herself.

"My men didn't realize some of the fireworks were missing until they went to set them up on the ice that evening. They swore they weren't drinking or careless. Several courtiers came out to see how the powder was put in the rockets, they said, but that's not unusual. In truth, Your Grace, some of the fireworks seem to have vanished like——like that bracelet of yours Lady Rosie's been searching high and low for."

"I fear we've found the gunpowder at least," she said as another boom ensued and the rocket called a Pike of Pleasure hissed skyward. But it looked as if, she noted, it had been launched from back *in* the forest, not into it.

"Your Grace, perhaps this will bring folk from the village beyond, maybe even from London to fight the fire. Let's move away a bit, down on the river to direct help should it come."

Her leg brushed his as they urged their skittish mounts out of the trees to the riverbank. She realized that she could yet mistrust and suspect Robin, but she thought she now knew who the culprit was in this war he was waging against all she held dear.

His name——shouted in the distance——woke Ned. Was it his father calling him to come downstairs for Christmas or New Year's morn? His uncle Wat would be there, full of good cheer and good food, home from the road for a few days, presenting scenes from great dramas. Uncle Wat would let him play a soldier and speak a few lines, maybe carry a wooden sword while half the village crowded in and clapped and clapped . . . just like the crackling sound nearby now.

"Ned! Ned, where are you? Which room?"

He'd best heed Father and get up. He'd have to go outside to milk the cow and check under the hens for eggs before festivities began. Maybe Mother would be preparing pancakes today, with rich butter and cream or honey.

"Ned! Ned Topsi-i-i-de!"

He lifted his head and began to cough again. He slitted his eyes open. Why was he sleeping on the floor?

"Ned! Fi-i-ire!"

Fire! Had he nodded off in a fire?

"Here! Here!" he thought he shouted, but he was hacking so hard he wasn't sure he'd told his father where he was at all.

A rattling sound, a scrape. A bang and a whoosh of air. He tried to lift his head again but just wanted to sleep. His stage voice, that deep instrument that had served him so well, came out a croak, a wheeze.

More noise and someone's hands on him, lifting him. He tried to embrace his mother, shaking him to get up. Or was it Meg come to creep into his bed?

"Meg?" he whispered. "Meg, I love you."

"Jenks," a rough voice said, one hacking, too. "It's Jenks."

"Robin, you must do something for me," Elizabeth said.

"Anything, my queen."

"I'm certain those fireworks are coming from back in the trees and not being shot from afar into them. Can you ride back in to see who is setting them, get behind him, perhaps snare the wretch? It may be the killer—"

"My would-be killer. They told me about Bane's death, and to think it could have been me. Yes, I'll go, I'll get the whoreson murderer, if you'll swear to stay right here."

"I will, and send others who might come."

"I'll be back with the culprit who took my fireworks, at least!" he vowed and spurred his horse up the bank into the trees.

Elizabeth dismounted because her horse kept shying wildly at each blast and perhaps at the smoke smell, too. It was all she could do to keep from charging in to help oversee fighting the fire or from going after the villain in the forest herself.

She tied her horse to a tree so he wouldn't keep jerking her arm while she held the reins. It was lonely out here as darkness fell, but her anger overcame her anxiety for her own safety. Until she heard the baying of the hounds. And the nightmare of her drowning with Robin in the river came back to her.

"A pox on it!" she muttered aloud. She and Robin weren't together, and the river was frozen solid. Those foolish nightmares were the least of her troubles.

For she was sick over worry about Ned. If he died from this, she'd blame herself. And Meg would blame her, too.

Pacing to keep warm, Elizabeth counted three more rockets in the sky and heard the dogs roused again. She tried to reckon how long it would take people to come from the village or the city—or would they just think it was more of the Twelve Days celebration and merely gaze up into the sky in awe? The smoke was not drifting toward the nearby village. Would it dissipate before it brought someone from the city? The flames had not yet been visible from the roof of the east wing.

She was certain she heard hoofbeats. Too fast for Robin returning through these thick trees. No, the sound was that of studded hooves on ice, not on snow, and coming from the direction of the city.

She stepped back into the cover of the bankside trees. Though the twilight had nearly bled to night, she saw it was the Earl of Sussex, mounted and alone. But now that she was certain she knew who the killer was, she need not fear Sussex. What if he brought word of something amiss at Whitehall? She suddenly feared all this could be a diversion, and she had fallen for it. What if the Christmas killer had struck again?

"My lord Sussex!" she called out, and he drew his horse up sharply.

He looked shocked to see her, although that might be because she was in man's attire. His dismount was nearly a tumble as he came closer to stare at her.

"Your Majesty? I heard Leicester got out of his room and rode off in this direction with some men. I wanted to bring him back, could not summon my men in time, but I never thought to find you here—ah, like this."

"I remember you said we must learn to fight like those we fight, my lord," she said, coming back onto the ice. "A killer has been stalking me, so I am stalking him."

"Pray God, he doesn't disappear into the trees like the Irish into their infernal bogs and fens, but I've never seen them shoot rockets to call attention to themselves. I believe you no longer think I am to blame?" he asked, coming closer and gesturing as yet another rocket shot skyward. "Ah, those have caught something on fire at Greenwich, haven't they?" he asked, looking now at the demonic glow in the east wing. "Are you sure it's not Leicester behind this, then?"

"I am. I did think it might be you for a while, because the culprit so obviously hated Leicester." She realized then why she should have eliminated Sussex from the list of possible culprits long ago: Sussex was intelligent but not clever and had no sense of humor, perverse or otherwise, and the killer did. "But," she went on, "since you are going to vow to me now that you will not attack the Earl of Leicester anymore when we have foreign enemies we must fear, I will trust you."

"Enemies like your Catholic cousin Queen Mary?"

"And her minions who adore her. So will you vow to me as I have said?"

"Yes, Your Grace, most heartily, and, ah, pray you'll tell Leicester the same."

"I shall indeed. He's in the woods to hunt the man who has been shooting off those fireworks, and I'd like you to put aside all animosity and help him. Watch for the next rocket and try to trace its projection point. As for Greenwich, I've sent men to rouse the staff and put the fire out."

"I cannot leave you alone, Your Grace."

"Then I must help Robin myself."

"No, I'll go at once. And you have my word on, ah, peace on earth between me and Leicester." He mounted swiftly and urged his horse off the river ice to disappear between the black bars of tree trunks into the snow-laden forest.

As the night swallowed him, she heard again the distant, eerie baying of dogs from the isle across the river, like the fabled evil omen of hounds from hell. Yet they were her own animals, well fed and fit for the hunt. Perhaps she should have them loosed on the marauders in Greenwich forest. She recalled that Simon Mac-Nair had recounted the strange story of ghostly hounds when he was new to his position and in London for the first time and would have no cause to know of her kennels unless he'd been out in this very area. Or perhaps his messenger, Duncan Forbes, who was his link to Mary of Scots, had told him.

She pictured again MacNair's brilliant sleight-of-hand tricks that could pull coins from the air or make them vanish, just the way Robin's fireworks had disappeared, and her bracelet. Had the canny Scot smiled and snatched it somehow off her arm so cleverly she did not notice it was missing? Had Vicar Bane found a stack of parchment missing one day and had no notion when it had gone—as well as a red, unscented torch? Yes, she knew now whom she must capture and imprison when she returned to Whitehall.

She startled as she heard a horse—no, at least two—coming at her from the forest. Robin and Sussex returning? Jenks with Ned? She had been about to mount and ride toward Greenwich to be certain Ned was safe.

Robin's distinctive black stallion broke from the bankside trees first, with him sitting tall in the saddle. Her shoulders slumped in relief. Back already, he must have met with success, but had not another rocket just raked the treetops? Since the second horse was being pulled behind, he must be leading someone out, though not Sussex, for he'd been on a mount with white fetlocks.

"Robin!" she called, relieved. "You've brought me either Forbes or MacNair, have you not?"

"Indeed, I've brought you MacNair," the man, not Robin, said with a harsh laugh. "And dare I guess I now address the Queen of England, the one who follows her head more than her heart?"

She saw that, though the man wore Robin's hat, his shoulders were broader. MacNair! It *was* MacNair. She had guessed it earlier but far too late.

"Happy holidays, Your Grace!" he said, his voice mocking. "And for the last course at the final feast of the Twelve Days, here is your Robin, fallen off his wall with a great fall, just as you tried to dump him on Queen Mary."

Elizabeth gasped and stepped back only to bump into a tree. Robin was slumped either unconscious or dead on MacNair's horse, for the Scot shoved him and he toppled limply to the snowy riverbank.

Ned knew now that it was Jenks who had dragged him out of his smoky room. It was somewhat easier to breathe here in the corridor, but now they faced worse than smoke. Crackling red-orange flames barred their escape in the only direction they could flee. He realized he'd called for Meg and Jenks had heard. Now Jenks knew how he'd felt about Meg and that his dying thought was of her.

Yet Jenks had pulled him out.

"How'd you get through those flames?" Ned rasped.

"They weren't big then—caught the carpet."

It was the Turkey carpets of the corridor that burned, belching flames and smoke, though fire also devoured the draperies and danced toward the ceiling. It must have been a carpet jammed under his door that was set afire to suffocate him.

"About Meg—I ..." he tried to tell Jenks.

"Stow it. Let's get out of here."

Jenks thrust a piece of cloth at him, covering his face with it. For one moment, Ned thought he meant to smother him, but then he would have just left him to roast in his room. The cloth was cold and wet—melting snow packed in it, a wet cloth to breathe through, maybe to rub along skin so hot it seared the very soul.

"We'll leap through it together," Jenks told him, dragging Ned to his feet and grappling him against his side by an arm like an iron hoop. "Clear the carpet, then roll. And hold my shirt to your face, lest we're trapped by flames or smoke again."

His shirt, Ned thought. He'd tried to take Meg from him,

treated him like a dunce all these years, and he'd given him the shirt off his back to save him, maybe save him for Meg.

"Ready?" Jenks asked, coughing. "If we fall, roll!"

Ned tightened his arm weakly around Jenks's shoulder, hoping he knew it was meant as a hug.

"Now!" Jenks cried and lunged at the flames, dragging Ned off his feet with him.

"You've killed him!" Elizabeth accused and tried to break Robin's fall, though his weight took her down with him as MacNair dismounted.

"Merely hit over the head," he told her as he kicked at Robin. "My final Yuletide gift to you is his company, such as it is. Stubborn ass, he wouldn't die when I had him all trussed up, but I'll be sure of it this time."

When she was certain that Robin yet breathed, she rose slowly to her feet to face the wretch. "And all because I offered him as consort and husband to my cousin, your royal mistress, and you took offense to that?" She must stall for time. Someone would come. Sussex from the forest, Jenks from the palace, someone.

"*I* took offense at it, indeed, as do all braw, loyal Scots who know Mary Stuart is but a breath away from your throne—and that breath is yours."

"I suppose you think you've been terribly clever. But why murder innocents?"

"You've no right to a happy holiday—or happy realm, not the way you treat my dear queen," he claimed, crossing his arms over his chest and ignoring her question. "You cannot hold a candle to her."

"You said once her servants adore her. Meaning you?" Keeping Robin's prone form between them, she took a slow step out to clear the tree, though she was certain, even with the snow and ice, she'd never outrace him.

"To answer your first question," MacNair said, "your servants were eliminated to mock you and Leicester, though you owe me dearly for ridding you of Bane's Puritan presence. My poor queen is ever harassed by his like, John Knox, for one, and a host of priggish Protestant lords. Actually, Bane got in my way, preaching I should not serve a Catholic queen—popish, he called her. And then I saw how he could be part of the game."

"So once you killed Hodge Thatcher, you decided to make the most of mocking Yuletide traditions."

"Silly antics and fancied-up foodstuffs everyone fusses over," he muttered darkly, as if it were a curse. "I've always hated Christmas. In the charming chats you and I have had, I believe I forgot to tell you that my father was the master cook in King James of Scotland's kitchens at Holyrood. Like Hodge Thatcher, he thought he'd gone to heaven to work for royalty. My father ruled his kitchen realm, just as he lorded it over his family. Not a charming, warm bone in his body, not even at Christmas," he ranted on as his voice rose. "No sense of humor or tolerance of those with a clever tongue," he added and spat into the snow.

"But, somehow, under your father's tutelage," she surmised, "you became familiar with the way the royal kitchens worked."

"He insisted I follow in his steps when I found it all dirty and dull."

"But if your father served Queen Mary's father, you have followed in your sire's steps to serve her now. Do you not want to break free of his control over you by—"

"King of the kitchens, Father privily dubbed himself," he went on, as if he hadn't heard her. "I started as a wood and fire boy, then a pot scrubber. I knew nothing, he said, nothing. He wanted me to learn all he knew, but I observed things only to find a way out."

She tried another tack, uncertain whether to try to provoke or placate him. "Unless he was a trickster and murderer, you hardly followed in his steps, Sir Simon."

"I preferred magic, not daily drudgery, you see." He was speaking boldly and grandly now, as if he had a vast audience. "You liked my sleight-of-hand, I know you did. I learned that, too, at the Scots court, from a traveling magician and necromancer who slept in the kitchen. It turned my stomach to do the tricks for you which delight Queen Mary, so it was my pleasure to also abscond with other things under your people's noses."

"Bane's writing parchment?"

"And some of that stack of gold foil on your privy dresser's table. Not to mention these lovely fireworks for my special farewell display for you this evening," he gloated with a broad circular gesture toward the trees.

"And my emerald and ruby bracelet?" she prompted, desperate to keep him talking. Why didn't Sussex return? Whoever was shooting off those rockets—perhaps MacNair's man Forbes— must have accosted him too.

"And a lovely piece of jewelry, that it is," MacNair went on, his voice almost teasing now. She noted he'd let the rougher Scots burr back into his speech. The man was a chameleon in every way. No wonder he had been promoted rapidly for his fluency with languages and other talents, sadly gone wrong.

"So I can call you thief and murderer as well as magician," she said, still trying to gain his confession without vexing him over-much.

"Your bracelet will soon be en route north to Queen Mary," he explained with another laugh, "as a belated New Year's gift with another set of flagons I bought, but then, those things will pale to the other news I'll be sending her—the ultimate gift. News that the Queen of England has sadly, accidentally drowned in the river with the very whoreson she publicly suggested Mary wed and make King of Scots, so—"

She threw herself sideways and tried to dart away. Thank God she wore man's garb and not heavy skirts and a tight corset. The bank was slick, and she went down, then scrambled on hands and knees as he lunged at her. He hit hard atop her, grinding her face into the snow. He yanked her to her feet, she kicked him, and they rolled down to sprawl onto the hard ice. He seized her again, wrapping hard arms around her and bending one of her arms up behind her back. She almost blacked out from pain as he hauled her to her feet again.

Did he intend to wait until dark to take her and Robin back to the fishing hole in the ice by the palace? To drown them near the Frost Fair among her people, near the site of the boathouse he had burned, even as he or his lackey Forbes must have set the wing at Greenwich afire?

She opened her mouth to scream, but he jammed something in it.

"One of my handkerchiefs to keep coins plucked from the air in," he told her and laughed harshly. "Here I praised you for your impressive intellect and how your head commands your heart, but I have thoroughly outsmarted you, Queen of England. And so you lose the game. You forfeit your place—your throne and crown—to my Scots queen, and so ends the Yuletide entertainment."

MacNair held her in a rough embrace and dragged her out onto the frozen river; at last, to her horror, she saw what he intended. As four rockets went off quite close to them in the forest, four blasts went off on the river ice to blow a hole there nearly as big as the one at the Frost Fair.

She fought desperately as the inky, cold river water surged, then frothed wildly through the hole he shoved her toward. It was her worst nightmare, drowning with Robin in the icy water, for the hulk-shouldered Forbes had appeared and was dragging the yet unconscious Robin. With a splash, Forbes threw him into the hole.

"I told ye, mon," Forbes shouted to MacNair, "I ken how to rig the fuses just right. The wee ones went off the same time in the forest as the long ones out here, so's no one would hear the hole blasted in this bonny ice! And I smashed her other man's skull!"

Sussex! He would not be coming to save her. These demons had shot off the fireworks hoping to lure her men, perhaps her, into the forest. They had lain in wait for them. MacNair had sprung more than one trap, and he had won the game indeed.

"Don't fret, lass," MacNair said, his tone mocking, "for by the next Twelve Days of Christmas, Cecil will be serving Mary Stuart here in London, and everyone will adore her. England will be Catholic again, and your whoreson father's divorce to wed your mother and the Protestant experiment will be mere memory— more stories of the past to tell by the Yule log."

His tirade stoked her strength. Even if he snapped her arm off, she was not going in that black hole, not letting Robin drown or her kingdom go to Mary. Her nightmare flashed at her again, where she and Robin struggled only to sink as the dogs bayed at them. No! She would not allow it!

"I've never enjoyed a bonny Yuletide more," MacNair crowed to Forbes. "Ambassador Melville was wrong, for the English court was anything but wearisome this winter!"

MacNair's voice was triumphant as he slid her across the ice to the gaping maw of frothing white water as the Thames current roared under the ice. She went to her knees and managed to get one of the pitifully small gold forks out of the top of her boot. She wished she did not wear gloves, for it was delicate and she wasn't sure she had a good grip on it. Swinging the fork upward, she jabbed at MacNair's face behind her. Then she twisted her body away, jerked, and, with her back on the ice, kicked up at MacNair's crotch as hard as she could.

He shrieked and, covering his face, doubled over. Forbes came at her, but he slid past. Ripping the gag from her mouth, she began to scream, trying to dart away from him.

Cursing, bleeding, half blind, MacNair too stumbled toward her. She tried to change directions again, but Forbes snagged her hair, spilling it loose and nearly pulling it from her scalp. Robin, she had to save Robin. She had to keep from going in, but Forbes and MacNair together dragged her toward the freezing water where Robin, conscious now, flailed but kept going under.

As in her dream, she heard the dogs coming closer, closer. Was she in the water already, drowning, dying?

When the first dogs leaped at MacNair and Forbes, she knew it was no dream. The entire pack of them, yipping, snapping, twenty at least, attacked the two men, but they knew their mistress and did not harm her. Backing away from the onslaught, Mac-Nair and Forbes tried to kick the hounds away, but MacNair's face was streaming blood, and he couldn't see. Forbes tried to help him at first, then seemed to slip in MacNair's dark blood on the graying ice.

With a shout, Forbes fled toward the Greenwich forest with dogs in hot pursuit. With a massive splash, MacNair fell into the hole. At that very moment, Elizabeth saw the first of her huntsmen among the hounds.

"Oh, pardon, milady," the man cried when he saw her, "but the fireworks drove them to distraction, an' somehow they got loose. That a hole in the ice? Back, my boys, back!" he cried to the dogs, which circled it now, barking into it.

"Fetch a board or some rope!" she screamed, shoving her hair back from her face to see better. "We must get the men out of the water!"

Both huntsmen stood among their yapping charges, staring at her. "Your Majesty?" one said.

"Yes. Quickly, do as I say!"

"We'll fetch him out," the second man cried, " 'cause there's only one."

Still standing amidst the remains of the writhing pack, the queen turned and gasped. Only one man was in the water. She fell to her knees and, trembling, crawled to the edge of the ice.

Robin! Thank God, it was Robin!

"Where did he go?" she shouted, lying down flat amidst the dogs and reaching a hand to him.

"Tried to hold to m-me. I hit him of-f-f," he said, through chattering teeth. "W-w-went under."

She held on to him while the keepers of the pack fished him out with a tree limb. "Despite the darkness," she told the men, "I want you to follow the hounds on the trail of the one who fled."

"Oh, aye, Your Majesty, we'll fetch a coupla lanterns, and he'll not get far, not with a few of the lead dogs on his tail. They musta had the scent of wild animal on their persons for the dogs to act like that."

"Yes, wild animals indeed, unless the pack just came to rescue their queen," she muttered, offering silent thanks to the Lord for her deliverance. The moment Robin was out of the water, she swirled her cape around him and carefully led him toward Greenwich.

"T-that f-f-ire will f-feel good," he told her. "Look, it's almost out. But w-what h-happened?"

"MacNair and his man were behind it all." She tried to stay calm, to help him walk quickly toward the shelter of the palace. But she stopped in her snowy tracks when she saw who walked toward them from Greenwich—and the single man approaching on foot from the forest.

"Ned! Jenks!" she cried. "And my Lord Sussex!"

Her servants looked like two blackened, singed scare-the-crows as they limped toward her, arms around each other's shoulders. But she could not stop here: Robin was slowly turning into an ice man, and Sussex was shouting something about being hit over the head.

In relief and joy, Elizabeth cursed anyone who claimed she lived by intellect and not her feelings, for she burst into tears. She hugged each man in turn, the most precious Yuletide gifts she'd ever seen. And never had she been more proud to be their friend and be their queen.

Afterword

Twelfth Night Cake

In a bowl, combine ½ cup of juice of orange with 1 cup golden and 1 cup dark raisins and let stand. Cream 1 cup butter, 1 cup sugar, 2 cups wheat flour, and 4 fresh hen's eggs. Add the undrained raisin mixture and a pinch of cinnamon. Stir all together and bake until a knife inserted in center comes out clean. Do not overcook, or it can become hard as a rock. Melt 3 tablespoons of honey to glaze the cake, decorating it with ¼ cup of candied cherries. In Scotland and rural shires, they add a pea and a bean, so that the finder of the bean is king for the evening and the finder of the pea is queen. But we do seldom follow such practices in civilized London town.

TWELFTH NIGHT

JANUARY 6, 1565

"OF ALL THE YULETIDE HOLIDAYS I'VE HAD, LOVEY, THIS was the best!" Kat told Elizabeth and reached to take her hand as they sat in armchairs facing the low-burning hearth. "Why, I had to laugh at the look on Master Stout's face when you told him the extra meat pies you ordered were all to be sent to the kennels on the Isle of Dogs. Kind of you to think of your hunt packs there."

The old woman chuckled while the queen fought back tears of relief that these holidays were officially over, and that Kat had not known all her queen had been through to keep Christmas for her. After the Twelfth Night Revels in the Great Hall tonight, led by Ned Topside, since Robin had taken to his bed with a dreadful cold, the two old friends sat late in the queen's privy chamber before the hearth.

"I've asked Ned, Meg, and Jenks to come up when the corridors clear," Elizabeth said, gesturing toward the three other chairs she'd pulled up. "In all the chaos of Christmas, I failed to give them their gifts."

"I thought you were just holding back for Meg's marriage."

"I've intentionally not pressed her on that. No, I mean to give them their gifts tonight."

"I suppose I should not have spoken so fondly of these holidays with the deaths of the two Scots on top of Vicar Bane's and poor Master Hodge's sad demises," Kat went on. "Your royal Catholic cousin will say you've sent her wretched news for the coming year to have her envoy and his man fall through the ice and drown."

Elizabeth said nothing, but that is the story Cecil had written to Mary of Scots. Though MacNair had drowned under the ice and his body had not been recovered, Forbes had been caught but had hanged himself in his cell before he could be questioned. However much the queen would have liked to accuse the Scottish queen of being privy to their plot, Cecil had found nothing in MacNair's or Forbes's effects to prove such, though he had found her stolen bracelet.

"I am sending Queen Mary a gift she will like, though," Elizabeth said, more to herself than to Kat. "Lord Darnley is the messenger Cecil is sending north when the roads clear, and the stage is set for Darnley to entrance her."

"Hmph. You must have known she'd never trust Leicester, your Robin," Kat said, taking another piece of Twelfth Night Cake from the small parquet table between their chairs. Like a child, Kat always ate the candied cherries off the top first.

"Yes, I knew that well—from personal experience," she said, her voice almost a whisper.

The queen also knew the battle lines had been drawn between her and Mary, however cordial and correct they might be to each other in the future. In a single year, more than MacNair had tried to plot against Elizabeth in the Catholic queen's name, and, no doubt, more would. But she, with her friends, her true friends, would be ready for the next onslaught.

Elizabeth herself rose to answer Meg's distinctive knock on the door and let the three of them in. Meg looked as if she'd been crying; Jenks seemed glum, and Ned either exhausted or pathetic. Ned and Jenks still had bandaged hands and singed eyebrows and hair from the fire at Greenwich, which had been successfully put out after some dreadful damage to the east wing. It, like the boathouse, would need to be rebuilt this spring, along with a feigned, polite relationship with Queen Mary.

"Welcome all," Elizabeth told them as she gestured them in. "Take the chairs and warm yourselves."

To her surprise, the two men sat in the seats on the other side of Kat, while Meg took the single one by the queen. "Let me serve, Your Grace," Meg said, popping up when she saw the queen pouring ale for them, but Elizabeth pressed her back into her chair.

"I've asked you here tonight to thank each of you for all you've done for me this holiday season," she said, not mentioning specifics, for their endeavors of detection had been kept from Kat as well as from most of the court. "Also, your friendship and support these first six years of my reign have been invaluable."

"And many more years to come!" Kat chimed in.

The queen gave an ale-filled, heavily embossed silver goblet to Meg, Jenks, and Ned. "To the new year and the future," she said and lifted her drink to them.

"Oh, Your Grace, it's beautiful!" Meg cried, the first to catch on that the vessel from which she drank was her gift. "Look, such shiny silver with entwined roses around the queen's name: *From a grateful monarch, Elizabeth the Queen, to my dear Strewing Herb Mistress Meg Milligrew.*"

"Tudor roses, of course," Ned put in, coming to life at last as he perused his goblet. "Why, on this side it has my name and *Master of Queen's Revels* scripted in. Done by our St. Paul's pewterer, Your Grace?"

"He got out of his sickbed in a minute when I sent him the order for them," she said with a smile. "Meg, you see, yours has herbs as well, and Jenks's has a saddle and bridle."

"That's a good one," Kat put in, "seeing as how he's about to get bridled and saddled himself in holy matrimony with Meg."

Silence fell. Only the hearth crackled away.

"We have decided to delay that," Meg whispered.

"To delay it indirectly," Jenks added.

"Indefinitely," Ned amended. "The three of us—well, for my part, after Jenks saved my life, I just realized all I owed him, that's all."

The queen could see that was not all, but she'd question Meg about it later. Elizabeth sensed that the men, in their new-fledged friendship, had somehow decided for Meg. Not wedding because something better and grander was at stake—yes, the queen grasped that full well.

The five of them sat, staring into the settling fire in companionable silence. In that precious moment of peace, Elizabeth felt that no memories of the past could hurt her, nor did the future frighten her. With friends who were dearer than family, she could not only look forward to Christmases to come but enjoy life each day, beginning here and now. Somehow, that was the greatest gift of all.

AUTHOR'S NOTE

AMAZINGLY, MANY TUDOR RECIPES REMAIN, ALTHOUGH I WOULD NOT recommend following those I've included here, since some of them are shortened or amended, or just plain untrustworthy with unusual or vague directions. Sources for these recipes include some fascinating books such as Thomas Dawson's *The Good Huswifes Jewell*, 1580; Gervase Markham's *The English Housewife*, 1615; and anonymous, The *Good Huswifes Handmaide for the Kitchen*, 1594. Also, a book with excellent drawings about food and banquets is *All the King's Cooks*, by Peter Brears. *Food and Feast in Tudor England*, by Alison Sim, was also a great help. Thanks to Sharon Harper for her recipe for Maids of Honor.

I am also appreciative that Kirrily Robert has an excellent Web site with original old English recipes to be found at http://infotrope.net/sca/cooking.

As in all the books in the Elizabeth I Mystery Series, I take key plot points from history. On December 21, 1564, the Thames froze solid for the first time in years, and it is recorded that "the queen walked upon it." The years of 1608 and 1683 are listed as excellent freezes for Frost Fairs; 1814, the last year for such a fair, saw a catastrophe when the ice cracked and booths and people fell into the river. I have taken literary license with the fact that Lambeth Palace traditionally housed the archbishop of Canterbury rather than the bishop of London.

Under the Protestantism of Edward VI and his sister Elizabeth, some of the early raucous, pagan Yuletide practices and Catholic customs were halted, but "Elizabeth herself paid for holly and ivy to deck the palace each Christmas." As the queen could be tight with her money, this was no small concession to these holidays for her.

The queen's beloved Lady Katherine (Kat) Ashley, early governess, confidant, and the only mother figure Elizabeth Tudor had ever known, died, "greatly lamented," in 1565. It was the same year in which Mary, Queen of Scots, wed Henry Stewart, Lord Darnley, and lived to rue that day. Their child, King James VI of Scotland, later James I of England, followed Elizabeth on the throne in 1603. But in the thirty-eight years between the time of this story and the queen's death, there are many momentous events—and mysteries—to come.

I hope that those of you who have or know of book discussion groups will find the "food for thought" questions that follow useful. Although each of the Elizabeth mysteries can stand alone, this series is also an extended study of a fascinating woman and her times. The queen was a powerful historical figure but also an amazingly modern woman in many ways.

READING GROUP GUIDE

The Queene's Christmas

DISCUSSION IDEAS

1. Many amateur sleuth or detective stories are told only from the main character's first-person point of view. Why do you think the author of *The Queene's Christmas* uses multiple viewpoints?

2. In what way does the Prologue frame or foreshadow the action to come?

3. We are all partly products of our pasts. What family baggage does Elizabeth Tudor always carry with her, despite her position of power and prestige?

4. Although Elizabeth is the heroine of the tale, she is all too human. Cite examples of her honorable acts and her underhanded ones. What strengths and weaknesses does she exhibit? Do these make her sympathetic or not?

5. This book in the series and the previous one (*The Thorne Maze*) emphasize the queen's growing conflict with her cousin the Catholic Mary, Queen of Scots. How is Mary contrasted with Elizabeth, even though the reader never meets Mary? (Elizabeth never met her, either.) How do their contrasting personalities act as strengths or weaknesses in their serving as rulers?

6. How do the recipes that begin each chapter tie in with the

action and intent of the story? How do they throw light on or foreshadow events?

7. Food imagery is used throughout the story to tie in with the holiday recipes theme. Beginning with the Prologue, can you cite examples of this?

8. Comment on customs in the story that have their roots in Old England, such as drinking a toast.

9. Discuss clues laced throughout the story to hint that the villain could be any of several characters. Did you at some point suspect, like the queen, that the culprit could be Ned Topside or the Earl of Leicester? At what point were you certain who was the guilty one? Did you figure it out before the queen, with the queen, or after her?

10. Although the book is set in 1564–65, did you find some characters' thoughts of and reactions to the holidays modern? Perhaps even like your own? In what ways?

11. How is Elizabeth's relationship with her people similar to or different from that of Queen Elizabeth II or an American president? Have we lost or gained from the differences?

12. Elizabeth's longtime relationship with Robert Dudley, Earl of Leicester, was an up-and-down one. Why do you think she never wed him? Did she really wish to? (Earlier books in the series, especially *The Twylight Tower,* expand on this turbulent relationship.)

13. Many of the folk poems commonly called "nursery rhymes" hail from early England. Examples include "Ride a Cock Horse to Banbury Cross," "Sing a Song of Sixpence," and "Humpty Dumpty." If the political and personal origin of Mother Goose rhymes is of interest, you might peruse *The Annotated Mother Goose,* by William S. Baring-Gould and Ceil Baring-Gould. Note that "Mary, Mary, Quite Contrary" is supposedly a comment on Mary, Queen of Scots. Can you find other Elizabethan-era links?

14. There were remnants of pagan superstitions amid the Christian Christmas celebrations of Elizabethan England—for example, the one about holly leaves in Chapter One. Are there others you can find?

15. Last names in Tudor England (in this book, Wainwright, Thatcher, Stout, Green, etc.) obviously come from occupations, physical traits, or even dress. Do you have such an English last name, or can you think of anyone who does?

KEEP READING FOR AN EXCERPT FROM
KAREN HARPER'S NEXT MYSTERY

The Fyre Mirror

COMING SOON IN HARDCOVER FROM ST. MARTIN'S MINOTAUR

LONDON APRIL 23, 1565

"WANT TO GET YOURSELF KILLED?" SOMEONE SHOUTED.

Gilbert Sharpe threw himself out of the way of the lumbering cart and just missed being hit by another.

He knew better than to dart across the street while looking back over his shoulder, but he'd been fearful that man was following him again. Now, he hoped, it was just his imagination.

Another voice yelled, "Stand aside, you clay-brained cur!" Curses chased Gil as he silently thanked God in both English and Italian for his escape. His broken leg had never healed quite right so he couldn't run anymore. Gripping his hemp sack of sable brushes, rolled canvases, and clothes packed around his precious Venetian mirror, the seventeen-year-old pressed himself between the arches of the huge gateway and let the carts and horses supplying Whitehall Palace stream by on Kings Street.

As he scanned the passing flow of faces, Gil shook his head to clear it. Surely he was safe in the city, for he'd been certain he'd given his nameless, faceless pursuer the slip at Dover. If *Maestro* Scarletti had hired someone to silence him, would that man pursue him even into the depths of the queen's court?

He heaved a huge sigh, and surveyed the area again. On one side of the gate lay the symbol of his old life, the Ring and Crown Inn. It was there, while he and his mother tried to steal draperies years ago, they'd been caught by the queen. Instead of sending them to prison—partly because of his artistic talent—she'd taken them to the palace on the other side of the gate and into her care.

Now Gil noticed something he would never have seen when he left London three years ago: This gate which straddled the street was an awkward blend of English and Italian. Its style was like his own, he thought, and he could only pray that his beloved queen would like the *pastiche*. After all, what he'd become was partly Her Majesty's doing.

As he walked on, Gil felt utterly grateful to be back home. In Italy, his initial lack of the language, his painful yearning for England, the difficult days cleaning others' brushes and filling in their backgrounds—even his precipitous flight—would be worth it all, if his enhanced skills at portraiture could please his royal patron.

Limping markedly as he did when he was tired, Gil hurried down the street toward the towers and turrets of Whitehall Palace. He knew this massive beehive of buildings like the back of his hand holding brush to canvas, yet after studying art in the ducal court of Urbino and his visit to Venice, he saw it all with new eyes.

The rose-hued walls looked lacy with the cross-hatch pattern of the bricks. Above, opened to catch the sweet spring breeze, the thick-leaded windows of the queen's favorite London residence cast diamond designs on patches of waxy green ivy. Windows, however high, used to mean nothing to him, for he'd once scrambled through them from rooftops or trees as if they were ground floor entries.

He raised his voice over the street ruckus to call to the nearest guard at the gate, "Please send word to Her Majesty that Gilbert Sharpe, queen's painter, is returned from Italy and requests an audience."

The man guffawed in his face, belching out garlic breath. "Sure, an' I'm her Sec'tary of State, Sir William Cecil, just takin' a respite from my business runnin' the realm this fine spring day." He nudged Gil with the butt of his pike. "Be off wi' you, then," he added, squinting at the lad's disheveled state.

Years ago, Gil would have cursed the lout with hand signals, for he used to be mute, or dumb, as they called it. Then he would have scaled the back orchard wall and gotten on the grounds until Her Grace saw and summoned him, but what if these years away had changed everything? He should have gone to his mother's house to wash and change his attire, then sent word ahead to see if he was welcome here.

"Give access, give way, ho! Make way for the queen's Master Secretary!" Gil heard the shouts in the street. He saw the small party on horseback did indeed include Sir William Cecil. In his mid-forties, he looked the same to Gil, maybe thinner and grayer but still reeking royal command. The crowd stopped and gaped as they did at anyone important going in or out.

Gil summoned the last remnants of his strength. Though he was shoved back in the crush and his words were nearly drowned in the mingled huzzahs, he took the chance of calling out in Italian to catch Cecil's attention. Like the queen herself, Cecil was learned in languages. The great man had given Gil a purse of coins and a task when he left England, so Gil considered himself to be working for Cecil as well as the queen.

"*Me é, la'artista della regina,* Gilberto Sharpino!" he shouted as loudly as he could. "*Sono ritornato!*"

Cecil craned his neck and reined in, frowning, scanning the sea of faces. Hoping to be recognized, Gil snatched off his hat.

"*Sono spora qui! Qui!*" Gil shouted, waving.

Cecil's face registered surprise—as much surprise as ever crossed that long, guarded countenance Gil had sketched more than once.

"Let that lad pass to me!" Cecil said, pointing.

Gil was handed through the crowd and hustled into the courtyard where the party of six men were dismounting. Secretary Cecil handed his satchel to another and motioned Gil forward, then clasped his shoulder in greeting.

"The queen's little painter scamp Gil Sharpe has grown up, has he not?" Cecil asked as Gil swept him a half bow.

"Grown up to be Gilberto Sharpino, trained in the *Della Rovere* painter's school in *Terra del Duca Urbino* under *Maestro Giorgio Scarletti,* my lord."

"A place full of artists, no doubt, but Papists and pro-Spaniards, too, eh?"

"Oh, yes, my lord, and I have much to tell."

"Her Majesty and I want to hear it all. It's ironic you have come home now, for the Queen's Grace and I are determined to select an official portrait of her to be sanctioned, copied, and distributed in the realm. Walk with me, lad," he said, starting toward one of the guarded doors to sprawling Whitehall.

Gil's pulse pounded. He walked with the most influential man in the realm—unless Her Majesty was still smitten with Lord Robert Dudley. While yet in Italy, Gil had heard that Dudley had been named Earl of Leicester, elevated, some said, so the queen could pass her former favorite off as a possible English and Protestant husband to the Catholic Queen of Scots.

They strode past groups of courtiers, deeper into the palace toward the royal chambers. Surely, Gil thought, this was a sign that he was destined to do great things for the queen at court. Did Lord Cecil imply that he could paint the queen's official portrait?

"Two years ago," Cecil went on, not turning his head and talking out of the side of his mouth as if nothing were really being said, "the queen signed a proclamation designed to control productions of her royal likeness. Everyone was painting or drawing her, and she hated most of the results—you remember that."

"I do, my lord. Do you think that I might be allowed—"

"I know you came to speak later in life than most, lad, but have you not learned yet to listen more than you talk? The act prohibits painters, printers, and engravers from creating her picture until Her Majesty chooses a portrait of which she fully approves, which may then be copied."

Gil nodded. The standard method of punching holes in the outline and smearing the pattern with charcoal to reproduce the likeness on a surface beneath to be filled in and colored was the old way the English still used. Gil had spent back-breaking hours studying his *maestro's* identical technique. But then he'd stumbled on the carefully-guarded secret some Italian artists, including Scarletti, used to both charm and cheat their noble clients. One reason he'd clandestinely left for home was that he feared his master would discover he knew of that dark deceit.

"She's put the portrait business off of late," Cecil went on, "but has now begun to pose for selected persons."

"Oh," Gil managed as his hopes deflated. "Well-established, sanctioned artists, you mean?"

"The point is, not sanctioned yet." Cecil rounded on him, and they stopped walking. "My lad, I want a full report of Urbino politics rather than portraits later. Meanwhile, I will send you with one of my men to wash up a bit while I speak to the queen about your return. If she still favors you, perhaps you can serve her yet, though I'd say the selection of three artists for her portrait is firmly established and finally well underway." He gestured down the hall, and they began to walk again with his entourage several paces behind.

As they passed the double doorway of the privy gallery, which Gil recalled the queen often used for a council chamber, he glimpsed a makeshift artists' studio set up inside. The long table had been shifted to the wall, and the queen sat on a dais in strong window light with the easels of three artists—two men and a woman—facing her with their backs to Gil.

Though Cecil didn't notice at first, Gil stopped walking. The boy lingered as the sun cast its rippled light through the mullioned windows like flickering flames on the red hair, golden crown, and crimson costume of the queen.

Elizabeth Tudor had spring fever, yet here she sat for the initial posing which would lead to a selection of her official portrait. Though a dozen or so of her closest courtiers stood nearby, whispering and gesturing, she remained stiff and still while her thoughts raced.

The spring rains had abated of late and she yearned to leave London for the countryside or to go out in her barge—if the Thames wasn't still so unruly. Sitting ramrod straight, holding the pose she herself had chosen, perspiring in the elaborate ruff and ermine-collared mantle draped with the heavy gold chains of state, she slanted her gaze around the room.

She detested this process of trusting others to convey her presence and person to the world. She fully intended to look in a mirror as she examined each painting to be certain the art told the truth—but for a few details she might change, of course, such as her long nose and sharp chin. But her eyes were good, she assured herself, her mother's dark Boleyn eyes which offset well her father's ruddy Tudor coloring.

This was sheer agony, but she and Cecil had agreed a standard must be set. A carefully crafted image must speak of her serene power and control to friend and foe alike, especially with her Catholic cousin, Mary, Queen of Scots, spinning her webs of subtle rebellion even on England's northern borders.

Elizabeth's eyes skimmed the massive painting on the far wall, the one her father's court painter, Hans Holbein, had done of King Henry VIII in all his glory. Though he dominated the piece, it also included his third queen, Jane Seymour, and their son, Prince Edward VI, Elizabeth's long lost, dear half-brother. How she missed the boy who had died in his fifteenth year. How she wished she could see him again and comfort him from night frights and fear of their own father . . .

The queen startled and stared. As if her longing had summoned her dead brother, in the doorway stood a tall, lanky boy peering in and, with this light in her face, she could not clearly see his own.

To the obvious dismay of her artists, she rose and shaded her eyes. The lad was Edward's height but had more girth. He held some sort of sack. Oh, someone with Cecil, she thought as she saw her master secretary appear in the doorway and speak in earnest to the boy.

Her lady-in-waiting, Rosie Radcliffe, hurried to take the heavy gilt scepter and orb from her hands. "Your Grace desires a respite?"

"She desires to fly this hot cage," Elizabeth told her, stepping away from the throne and dragging her heavy train which others of her ladies hastily lifted from the floor. "Yes," the queen mused aloud, "maybe I shall go elsewhere. Send for Lord Arundel and tell him I long to take the court to his fine Nonsuch while this place is swept free of winter woes."

Cecil had entered and heard her words, for he said, "Your Grace, isn't it a bit early for a progress with possible mired roads? Besides, the Queen of Scots's envoy Maitland should be here soon with her decision on her marriage."

"*Do not* get me started on that today, my lord," she said, shrugging off her train into the arms of her women. "It's bad enough to have to sit here while my very being is copied for the likes of my enemies to possess."

"And your own people to see and cherish, Your Grace."

But she felt petulant and strolled behind the artists' easels, however much that rattled them. "Lavina," she told the woman who usually painted miniatures of court personages, "you always make me look whey-faced. It may not matter as much in a tiny, closed locket around someone's neck, but life-sized, I can't abide it."

"Hm," Elizabeth said only as she glanced at the partial portraits that Will Kendale and Henry Heatherley had done. She looked skeletal in both, but she had lost weight this winter, and they were only sketching outlines so far.

And then when the boy at the door, who had reminded her so of her brother, stood his ground, she knew who he was. Gil Sharpe! Gil had grown up and was back from Italy. He'd been gone but three years when she had assumed he'd not be back for at least five.

"Gil?" she cried and stepped around Kendale's easel so fast her skirts caught its legs and he had to lunge to save it. The boy flew through the door and knelt before her in such a blur she could hardly note how his face had matured, how he'd grown sturdier and handsomer.

"Gilberto Sharpino at your service, Your Majesty," came from a mouth muffled by the big hempen sack he toted.

"I hope you learned a thing or two on the Continent besides how to Italicize your name, Gilberto Sharpino," she replied with a little laugh. "It's hotter than the hinges of Hades in here so the court will be moving to the sweet, cool countryside, but you may come along—with my other artists, of course, and I'll pose in the sun where there's a decent breeze."

Smiling as the boy rose, she began to signal messages with her quick hands, and he silently chattered back to her in turn, just the way they used to communicate before Gil began to talk. She ignored the mutterings and murmurs of her painters and her people, for the lad seemed to bask in her presence as if she were the sun.